"Mummy, do angels live in the sky?"

I blinked, then stooped to hear you better. "Angels?"

Your small face was solemn. "Can they see us right now? If we wave?" Below, the remaining geese squawked and pecked round each other's feet. You swung my hand in yours, pulling me forward.

"No, my love," I said. "Angels aren't real like that. Not like us."

"Yes, they are." You looked cross. "I met one."

I steadied my breath, choosing my words with care.

"Gracie, do you remember when you were in the play at nursery? Angels are a lovely part of Christmas. But we don't actually meet them. Not nowadays."

You frowned, squirmed, looked at your tangled fingers.

"But I did."

I sighed. "Maybe you had a very special dream, Gracie. When you were in the car accident."

You shook your head and pushed out your lower lip. "It wasn't a dream. It was real."

Praise for

GRACIE'S SECRET

"Brilliant, thrilling, and fiendishly addictive. The author masterfully takes us on a journey, packed with twists. A book I cannot put down and one I will be thinking about for a very long time."
> —Renita D'Silva, Pushchart Prize–nominated author of *A Mother's Secret*

"It's a rare and beautiful thing to be moved to tears by a story that also makes you reflect long after the book is finished." —*Off on a Tangent*

"A gripping story full of lies and betrayal."
> —*Stardust Book Reviews*

"A breathtaking must-read!"
> —*Two Girls and a Book Obsession*

gracie's secret

ALSO BY JILL CHILDS

Jessica's Promise

gracie's secret

JILL CHILDS

FOREVER

NEW YORK BOSTON

Forever
Hachette Book Group
1290 Avenue of the Americas, New York, NY 10104
read-forever.com
twitter.com/readforeverpub

First published in 2018 by Bookouture, an imprint of StoryFire Ltd.
First Forever edition published in March 2019.

First Mass Market Edition: January 2020

Forever is an imprint of Grand Central Publishing.
The Forever name and logo are trademarks of Hachette Book Group, Inc.

The publisher is not responsible for websites (or their content) that are not owned by the publisher.

The Hachette Speakers Bureau provides a wide range of authors for speaking events. To find out more, go to www.hachettespeakersbureau.com or call (866) 376-6591.

Library of Congress Cataloging-in-Publication Data has been applied for.

ISBNs: 978-1-5387-3435-3 (mass market)

Printed in the United States of America

OPM

10 9 8 7 6 5 4 3 2 1

For Ann

gracie's
secret

CHAPTER 1

Jennifer

London, 2000

I was in the supermarket when the phone rang. The clear plastic bag was heavy with tomatoes and almost ready to tie. When I held my phone against my face, my fingers smelled of them. Ripe and pungent.

"Where are you?"

Richard.

My heart stopped. He was tense. Braced. My stomach chilled. I didn't say a word, waiting.

"Jen?"

"What is it?" It couldn't be you. It couldn't be.

"I'm at Queen Mary's. OK?" He paused and that deathly pause, that hesitation, told me everything. "You need to come."

The words hung there. The bag slipped and fell. A tomato rolled free, spilling down the display and coming to a halt against the plastic barrier. A woman pushed roughly past me to reach for spring onions and dropped them into the wire basket in the crook of her arm. Behind her, a baby, hidden inside a buggy with raised hood, started to wail.

"What?" I asked.

The woman tore a plastic bag from the roll and reached for tomatoes.

"Don't freak out, all right." Richard sounded a long way away. "Is anyone with you?"

I steadied myself against the bottom of the stand. The woman's grasping fingers plucked tomatoes and filled her bag.

Richard said: "It's going to be all right."

I couldn't breathe. "What is?"

He hesitated and that pause, his fear of telling me, told me how bad it must be.

"There's been an accident. OK? In the car." Pause. "Just come."

"Accident?" My hands tensed with rage. I wanted to throw something, to hit out.

"Call me when you get here. OK?"

"Tell me. For God's sake!"

He sighed. "Just get here."

The line went dead. I started to shake. I banged the heel of my hand into the tomatoes. Juice squirted from a split. The young woman jumped back, glared. A couple, passing behind with a trolley, stopped and turned to look, their faces hard with disapproval.

Richard's eyes were heavy. He was waiting for me at the entrance to pediatric intensive care. As I approached, my steps sharp and fast down the corridor, he looked me over, his face strained.

Inside, in the waiting area, his coat lay across a chair. A takeaway cup sat on the table in front of it, coffee stains on the lid. Behind, the wall was decorated with a giant stencil of Minnie Mouse. The tip of Minnie's left ear was peeling off.

I looked round. "Where is she?"

He pursed his lips. "Calm down, Jenny. Please."

I dug my nails into my palms as my hands closed into fists. "One night. You promised. You promised you'd look after her."

He'd begged to have you that weekend. I should never have let you go. My voice was strangled as I struggled not to shout at him.

"Tell me right now. *Everything*."

He sat down and gestured to the chair beside him. I was so brittle I could barely bend my legs.

"A car hit them. Head-on. It was going the other way and skidded and . . ." He hung his head, spoke into his solid brown lace-ups.

"Hit them?" He'd said *them*, not *us*. I leaned closer, struggling to understand and caught the old, familiar scent of his skin. "Weren't you there?"

He didn't answer. The heaviness in his cheeks made him suddenly old. My legs, my feet flat on the hard hospital floor, started to judder.

"The airbag went off. Ella's OK. Bruised but OK." He broke off. "They sent her home. But the other driver . . ." He bit down on his lip and looked away.

"What about Gracie?" I pulled away, angry. "Where is she?"

Richard's eyes found mine. They were red-rimmed. I saw the fear there before they slid back to the floor. He swallowed.

"She's in a coma. They're not sure—"

A sharp pain in my stomach made me lean suddenly forward, doubled over. I opened my mouth, tried to speak, closed it again. My hands pressed against my belt, holding back the pain.

A pause. Behind us, heels clicked down the corridor, turned a corner, faded.

Richard said: "Keep calm. Please. Everyone's doing their best. OK?"

I struggled to steady myself, lifted my head. I looked past him to the double doors that led farther into the ward.

"I need to see her. Now."

He nodded and got wearily to his feet. At the doors, he made a performance of pressing the flap for a blob of hand sanitizer and rubbing it over his knuckles, his palms, pointing me to do the same. He tugged out blue wads from a plastic dispenser and handed one to me. I stared at it, then watched him unfold the other one into a mask, slip two elastic loops round his ears, and open the flap across his mouth and nose. My stomach contracted. The pain again. *My God. My dear God.*

He gave me a sharp look. "She may be able to hear." His voice through the mask was muffled. "Be careful what you say."

You don't look like you. You're so pale and fragile, your face still, your eyes closed. Your fringe is brushed back from your forehead and there's a clear plastic mask fastened across your nose and mouth. Your arms are arranged outside the sheet as if you've already been laid out for death to take, and a needle, stuck sideways into the soft skin of your forearm, feeds pale liquid from a bag on a stand. Machines on both sides whirr and click, and, through it all, your breathing makes a soft steady suck in the mask.

I stand and stare. My arms shake at my sides. I fight the urge to leap forward and tear out all their damn wires and tubes and scoop you up in my arms and hold you, run with you, take you home.

A nurse fiddles with the drip. When she turns away from it, she doesn't look me in the eye. Her face is hard and too carefully neutral as if she really wants to say: *So you're the mother, are you? Really? And you let this happen? Where were you, exactly?*

Richard pulls a chair from the bottom of the bed and sets it by your side and I sit down, reach through the metal side bars that form your cage, take your hand and encase it in my own, squeeze it, stroke your small fingers and start to sing to you, my voice so low that only you and I can hear, the songs we sing together in the night, when you're feverish or just can't sleep and need a cuddle, the songs we've sung together ever since you were born and the midwife first put you in my arms, wrapped round in a snowy white towel, all red and scrunched and beautiful. Such a perfect baby...I thought the other parents on the maternity ward must be mad with jealousy.

My breath makes the inside of the mask hot and moist. I don't know how long we sit there, you and I, joined at the hand, singing together. You can hear me, I know it, you know I'm there, reaching for you, willing you to come back to me.

CHAPTER 2

The doctor wasn't old enough. She looked barely out of medical school and her manner was officious. She spoke to us in a bare consulting room off the corridor. It had squares of rough beige matting on the floor, a cheap settee, and several matching armchairs with wooden arms and lightly padded seats. An insipid picture of a vase of flowers hung on one wall. On the other was the stencil of a gawky cartoon dog and cat, grinning.

"We are grateful, Doctor." Richard sounded lost. He always tried to ingratiate himself with important people in the hope it made a difference. "Everyone's been so kind."

We were sitting side by side on the settee. It was low and our knees rose awkwardly. I reached across and squeezed his hand. His fingers were cool and firm and familiar in mine. He pulled away, giving me an absent-minded pat in the process. We made you, this man and I. We were happy once, before our small family broke apart.

"The brain bleed is extensive." The doctor spoke with exaggerated care, as if we were half-wits. "That bleeding puts a lot of pressure on brain tissue. It's still unclear how much damage it has caused."

She sat forward on the edge of her chair with her hands neat in her lap. She gave the impression she didn't plan to stay long.

"Why?" My voice was abrupt. "She was in a child seat, wasn't she?"

Richard cut in at once. "She was. I've already—"

I nodded, carrying on. "That's the point of it, surely? It protects her."

The doctor hesitated. "The seat probably saved her life." She lifted her forearm and demonstrated a rippling motion with her hand. "But even strapped in, the force of the impact still causes internal trauma to the brain. We call it a coup injury. The soft tissue is thrown forward against the inside of the skull, you see. That causes blood vessels to tear and bleed and the blood has nowhere to go. So it can invade brain tissue and cause damage."

Richard blinked. "So what"—he paused, groping for the words—"what does that mean?"

The doctor looked at a spot on the wall behind us. She had no softness in her face, just awkwardness.

"The prognosis isn't clear. If there's no change, we'll keep her comatose for as long as twenty-four hours and then review the bleed." She drew her eyes from the wall and glanced at me, at Richard. "The coma supports recovery by reducing cranial pressure." She took a deep breath. "Her body has been through a significant trauma. You do realize she was resuscitated? She's done well to get this far." She hesitated. "There's also the possibility of a contra-coup injury. Bleeding caused by a secondary impact at the rear of the skull. But so far, there's no evidence of that."

Shouting outside. Voices far below, called from another universe. My car was in the car park, waiting. A space where your seat should be. The footwell strewn with toys and biscuit wrappers and empty juice cartons.

"She's a fighter," I said. "She'll be OK."

The doctor cleared her throat. "In my experience, in cases like this—"

"How many exactly?"

She paused, gave me a questioning look.

"How many cases have you had? Like this?"

"Jennifer!" Richard, embarrassed.

The doctor's face was impassive. "In my experience, stability at this stage is crucial. It's the body's best chance of recovery. I suggest you go home and get some rest tonight. We'll call you at once if there's any change."

"No." I shook my head. "No. I'm staying."

Richard frowned. "Maybe the doctor's right. If she—"

"I'm not leaving her. I'm her mother."

He shook his head at the doctor, as if to apologize for me.

I didn't care. All I wanted was to scoop you up into my arms and leave this desperate, sterile place and take you home and draw the curtains and settle in the lumpy armchair in the corner of your bedroom and rock you and hold you close and never let you go.

The doctor rose to her feet. At the door, she turned back and looked at me.

"I can assure you, she's getting the best possible care."

They didn't let me see you often. In the early afternoon and in the early evening, I was allowed to sit beside you for a short time, to hold your hand in mine and press it to my lips, to stroke your cool, smooth forehead and sing to you. You seemed so far away, my love. Flown from me to an unknown place.

I strained forward to check the slow, steady flutter of your breathing, proving to myself that you were still with me, still in this world. The machines by your bed whirred and pulsed and numbers on monitors climbed and fell and sometimes flashed and on another screen, a line rose and fell in an eternally undulating wave.

A television screen on a mechanical arm was tucked up high against the ceiling. A white enamel sink stood against the far wall with surgeon's taps beside shiny metal dispensers of liquid soap and paper towels and, underneath these, a white metal pedal bin labeled Offensive Material.

No clock in sight. This was a room outside time, where day and night, morning and evening were the same sterile nothingness and the only rhythm was the suck and puff of your breath inside the mask. And I sat there, watching you, aching for you, dreading the footsteps that would come to make me leave.

The hours away from you were heavy. The waiting area was largely deserted. I tried to imagine Richard and Ella at home. She would be resting and he would be fussing over her, awkward and slightly inept but gentle. I wondered how much of him was there with her, and how much was here with us and how anyone could split themselves in two like that.

The ward stilled and quietened. I stood on a side table and pressed Minnie's peeling ear back into place against the wall. I watched the nurse behind her desk, shuffling papers and chatting in a low voice to the young woman who came to relieve her. Resting the side of my head against my hand, I stared at the large clock on the wall behind her as it slowly turned toward night. The light above me emitted a low buzz. The floor shimmered with shifting, cloudy patterns. My mind was numb.

They were wrong. You wouldn't leave me. You were a fighter. I sensed you there, reaching out for me, battling to survive. I closed my eyes, hunched my shoulders, and strained to send you all the strength I had, to tell you I was here, willing you well.

"There's a café down the corridor."

The nurse, a youngster with freckled cheeks, was bending over me. She made an attempt at a smile, pointed to the right, out of the ward doors.

"It's not much but it's better than nothing. You haven't eaten, have you?"

I shook my head. I felt sick.

"It'll close soon. I'll come and get you if anything happens." She gave my shoulder a pat. "Go while you can."

I tensed, ready to fight, then tilted and saw her face. Her eyes were kind. I heaved myself to my feet, swayed, and she took my elbow to steady me.

"Try to have something. You've got to keep your strength up." She paused, considering. "You might be here all night."

The café wasn't much, she was right. A sprinkling of a dozen plastic-topped tables with hard chairs and a counter selling tea and coffee, sandwiches and panini, bars of chocolate and crisps. The tables were deserted and the whole place felt forlorn, as desolate as a motorway service station at three in the morning.

I bought a bottle of fizzy water and settled in a corner, rested my head against the cold, whitewashed wall, and closed my eyes.

"Are you Gracie's mum?"

A gentle male voice. I opened my eyes, sat up at once.
"What's happened?"

He smiled, put out a hand to calm me. "Nothing. I'm
sorry. I didn't mean to startle you."

He was tall with floppy dark hair and wore a gray cashmere coat. He was carrying a coffee in a takeaway cup
and had a newspaper tucked under his arm. The *Daily
Telegraph*.

"May I?" He nodded to the chair opposite mine.

I shrugged. What did it matter? What did anything
matter apart from you?

"Matthew Aster. I'm in pediatrics. Just coming off shift."

I looked more closely. He looked about forty-five, perhaps a little older. His skin had a lined, lived-in look as
if his life had been more interesting than easy. His eyes
were intelligent and thoughtful and they were searching
mine, waiting.

"You're a doctor? Are you treating Gracie?"

"Not exactly, but we're a small team here. We talk. I
saw you in IC earlier." He shuffled his feet. They stuck
out from under the table. Black lace-ups, neatly polished.
"I'm sorry. Not an easy time."

He set the newspaper down on the table. There was a
picture of the Royals on the front page, a smiling Charles
and Camilla on their travels. I'd seen it on the newsstand
as I went into the supermarket all that time ago. An image
from another lifetime.

He gestured to the water. "Is that all you're having?
Can I buy you something?"

I shook my head. "I'm fine. Really."

He pulled a Kit Kat out of his pocket, snapped it in
two, set one stick in front of me, and unwrapped the other,
then ate it, sipping his coffee after each bite.

I peeled off the silver paper and nibbled the chocolate. The sweetness was cloying. I put it down. "Will she be all right?"

He narrowed his eyes. I wondered what the officious young doctor had told him about me. *The mother's difficult. Rude. No wonder the husband strayed.*

"It's too early to know," he said carefully. "But she's doing well. No sign of complications, so far. That's very positive." He hesitated. "One step at a time."

I sipped my water and looked past him into the drab hospital corridor. A stout woman was shuffling down toward the toilets on a walking frame, her head craning forward, her legs swollen.

"This can't be happening." I spoke almost to myself. "She's only three. I just want to take her home."

He reached forward and briefly covered my hand. His fingers were strong and warm with curling black hair above the knuckles. I thought of the way Richard had pulled his hand from mine and how comforting it felt to be touched, even for a moment.

I swallowed, trying not to cry. "She's everything to me. Gracie. I'd do anything. If she needs, you know, organs, she can have mine."

He nodded. "I know. I'm afraid it's not that simple."

The woman at the counter started to pack away the crisps and chocolate into cardboard boxes. He crossed to her, took one of the few remaining sandwiches from the fridge, and bought it, then came back to me and set it on the table.

"Just in case. It might be a long night." He reached into his coat pocket and took out a pen, scrawled "Matt" on the top of the newspaper, along with a mobile phone number, and tore it off. "If you have any questions. Or if you just need to talk. Anytime."

He picked up his newspaper, nodded to me as if something unspoken had been agreed between us, and turned away with a swish of his coat. He had a long, confident stride and a broad back. I stared after him down the corridor long after he had disappeared from sight.

CHAPTER 3

Ella

My body aches. The bed is soft and warm and I long to rest but I'm too afraid to close my eyes. Every time I do, I see her face. Hanging there, a second before the bang. Her eyes are wide, staring into mine. Her eyebrows two neat wedges. Her mouth, the lips painted deep red, parted.

Then the almighty crash, the crack of the airbag exploding in my face, thumping me in the chest, my own limpness, thrown back and forth, as helpless as one of those stuffed crash dummies catapulted to and fro in slow motion.

A moment later, utter silence. Life was suspended. Traffic stopped. A high-pitched screeching inside my ears blotted out the living world. The dead world too.

I asked one of the paramedics, "Is she all right?" My voice was a croak.

"Don't worry, flower. She's fine."

Their hands were thick and strong and worked briskly over my body, checking, assessing, easing me out, laying me flat on a stretcher. Above, the arc of a streetlight against a low cloud as I was carried away from the wreckage. I wondered at it. A perfect curve. So graceful. The bending arm of a dancer.

They thought I was asking about Gracie, still ominously silent in the back. They lied, of course. She was anything but fine. That horror was still to come. But at that moment, in the madness of the accident, when the world was still spinning and I barely knew who I was, where I was, I actually meant *her*, that girl whose face was lodged in my head, that complete stranger.

Later, Richard told me.

"It was instant," he said. "That's what the doctors said. She didn't suffer."

What did they know? They didn't see her eyes. The horror in them.

"Don't think about her."

How could I do anything else? I couldn't help it. I had to keep asking. All the time the doctor was examining me. How old was she? What was her name? I needed a name.

"Don't, Ella." Richard looked desolate. "Stop it. There's nothing you can do."

He was finally forced to tell me about Gracie when he put me in the taxi outside the hospital. He was all apologies, flustered as he handed the driver a bundle of notes to get me safely home. Sorry he couldn't come with me. So sorry. He ought to be looking after me. He knew that. But Gracie—well, it wasn't looking good. They weren't sure she'd make it. His eyes were red.

He bent low to kiss me before he closed the taxi door.

"You'll be all right?"

I didn't answer. I felt sick. Little Gracie. What if she died? Dear God, what if?

"It's not your fault, Ella." He read the wretchedness on my face. "You do know that?"

Wasn't it?

There's a tree outside the bedroom window. Its bare branches are sharp and scrawny, a scribble of black lines on white sky. A few more months and the buds will come again, leaves will clothe it. Sunshine and nests and greenery and she, that girl—they say her name was Vanessa—she won't see any of it. All the plans she made, whatever they were, will never happen now.

Downstairs, the bang of the front door. I lie very still and listen. He goes into the kitchen and the fridge opens with a soft suck. The click and fizz of a can opening. Beer, probably. Or Coke. I wait.

His tread is steady on the stairs. When he comes in, I close my eyes and pretend to be asleep. Why? I want so much for him to hold me. I want to cry on him and tell him it's me, it's all my fault, if Gracie dies, it's because of me. I want to let it out and be comforted but I can't. Instead, I build a wall. It's what I do.

He stops moving and, in the silence, I feel him watching me from the doorway, wondering if I'm awake, unsure what to do. I hold my breath. Inside, I'm screaming: *come to me, hold me, my love, please*. The silence stretches, taut as skin.

Then it tears and he turns away, retreating, and it was my own doing; I'm pushing him away, and I shake, lonely for him. Why shouldn't I hurt? What right have I to be safe and whole when Gracie struggles for life and that girl, Vanessa, is already cold?

Later, much later, the mattress shifts as he lies beside me. A warm arm threads itself round my waist and I shudder and sigh. He kisses the skin between my shoulder blades. Not a sexual kiss, just tender. Just kind. *I don't blame you*, the kiss says. *It's not your fault.*

Gradually, his muscles relax and become heavy and I wonder how he can sleep, after all that's happened, knowing Gracie may not be alive in the morning.

He has come home to me but she will be there in the hospital, that dreadful woman. Sitting at her daughter's bedside. White-faced and frantic and making a martyr of herself. She will blame me. I feel it already. It's just one more reason to hate me. To wish I were the one who died.

I lie very still. My neck throbs. Richard breathes steadily against my skin, warming it. I am afraid to sleep and I keep myself awake for a long time, reading the shapes in the shadows. I don't understand. How is it possible that, just this morning, a girl called Vanessa was alive and now she is not?

It terrifies me. Not the dying itself but the darkness, the oblivion that waits for us all. After all that's happened, after all I've suffered, how could it not?

Was she afraid of it too? Did she have any premonition that death was stalking her? When she put on her lipstick, slid into the seat of her car, and switched on the engine, did she have the slightest sense that she was starting an endless drive headlong into nothingness?

CHAPTER 4

Jennifer

That night, I half sat, half sprawled across the chairs in the waiting area, opposite the peeling Minnie Mouse, close to the nurses' station. Time shimmered and blurred.

When I closed my eyes, strange images swam in and out. You, my love, lying so small and still in the hospital bed, surrounded by machines. Richard's drawn face and the fear in it. The supermarket with its bright, hard music as my hand reached in my pocket for the ringing phone.

I lost track of time. The only sounds were the slap of plastic doors and the soft hum of the overhead lights. Occasionally, shoes squeaked to and fro between rooms. The nurse, sitting over a book in a cone of artificial light, cleared her throat or shuffled her feet. The ward was infused with the smells of disinfectant. It brought back a sudden memory of my father when I was a child, of his lab coat, strange with the scent of the hospital where he'd worked.

I closed my eyes and leaned my head back against the wall.

The nurse shook me. I must have dozed. I was slumped against the hard arm of the chair and my back ached, my head throbbed as I struggled to sit up quickly. My mouth was dry and tasted sour. The nurse handed me a cup of milky coffee.

"I thought you might want this."

I stared at her blankly. There was movement behind her. Life was returning to the ward as cleaners and nurses pushed trolleys at the start of a fresh shift, a new day. The wall clock read five to six.

"How is she?"

"Doing well. A doctor will come and see you in a while." She paused, watching me. She seemed to be deciding how much to say. "He'll explain. But Gracie's doing well. You should have a wash. Drink that first. You look done in."

In the cramped toilets, I splashed cold water on my face and dried it with a rough paper towel. My eyes were bloodshot, my hair straggly. As I watched, my eyes filled with tears and I blinked, rubbing them away. *Please God. Please. Make her well. I'll do whatever you want. Anything.*

I sat stiffly by the nurses' station, waiting for the doctor, jumping at every fresh footstep. Seven o'clock came. The kind overnight nurse said goodbye and good luck and went home. She was replaced by another, younger but brisker. At seven twenty, I got to my feet and went to the nurses' station.

"I'm waiting to see the doctor."

The nurse had her back to me. She spoke over her shoulder. "If you'd just take a seat."

I leaned forward over the desk. "I've waited all night. It's my daughter, Gracie. They said there might be news."

"I've told you." She turned round, impatient. "He'll be with you as soon as he can."

At eight o'clock, the doors to the ward swung open. A man's tread. I twisted to look. He had his back to me as he negotiated the doors, his arms burdened, but the shock of dark hair, the smart coat, and the shining shoes were familiar.

I jumped to my feet as he approached me.

"Is it you? The doctor?"

He gave a rueful smile. "Not exactly. I'm in pediatrics, not IC."

My shoulders sagged.

"I just came by to see if you were still here." He set down a takeaway cup of tea and a paper bag. "Thought you might need breakfast." He opened the paper bag to show a croissant inside.

"Thank you." I didn't move to touch it. "The nurse said she was doing well. I'm waiting to see a doctor."

He looked so compassionate that I bit my cheek to stop myself from bursting into tears.

"A nurse wouldn't say that unless it were true. Look, I know it's hard, but it won't be much longer." He checked his watch. "The day shift's just coming in."

My legs buckled and I sat down with a bump.

He watched me, his face concerned. "Try to eat something."

He disappeared down the ward. I hunched forward, looked at the croissant but didn't move to touch it.

A moment later, he came back, his step brisk, and he leaned over me. The nurse watched us with a frown.

"I've had a word." He kept his voice low. "As soon as they're briefed, they'll be out to see you. OK? It won't be long."

I nodded. I wanted so much to thank him but my mouth wouldn't work.

He looked at his watch. I imagined his own ward, his own patients, waiting.

"I've got to go but I'll try to look in again later, OK? And please, try to eat."

He turned abruptly and left the ward again. The croissant was warm. I broke off an end, scattering flakes of pastry.

At eight forty, a new doctor introduced himself and led me along the corridor to another small side-room. He had an American accent. He pointed me to a low chair with wooden arms, then perched on the edge of the desk in front of me, one ankle crossed over the other. His short white coat hung open and a stethoscope dangled from his neck. He looked barely forty.

"I'm cautiously optimistic," he said. "We're not out of the woods yet, but a few hours ago, Gracie showed signs of renewed brain activity in the frontal lobes. Where she had the bleed."

"Is that good?"

He scratched his nose. "It's early days. The overnight team reduced the medication. If she responds well, we may be able to start bringing her out of the coma by the end of the day."

I stared, trying to follow. "And?"

"So far all the indications are good." He studied his bitten nails. "I've just spoken to your, er, to Gracie's father. He's on his way. But if you'd like to see her?"

I was on my feet at once.

"Don't expect too much. She's still unconscious. We won't know the extent of the tissue damage for some time."

He may have said more. I can't remember. All I heard was that you were making progress and I could see you and that was all that mattered.

The blinds in your room are drawn. The only signs of morning are the sharp lines of light along the edges. You seem so small beside the banks of machinery, so very vulnerable. Pale and silent.

The nurse leaves us alone together and I slip off my shoes and climb up onto the hard hospital bed alongside you, deep into your metal cage, thread my arms through the spaghetti tubes from your face, your arm, the pads taped to your temples, and lift your shoulders gently from the pillow until you're lying to one side with your head resting on the pad of my shoulder and I pull that stupid damp mask off my face so I can put my lips to your cool skin and whisper to you: "Gracie, my love. It's Mummy. Mummy's here."

I start to sing "You Are My Sunshine" very softly—it's one of our favorites—and as I sing, I see you twirling in the sitting room with your arms outstretched, your eyes widening as you spin and become dizzy, saying in your high voice as you start to wobble: "That's lovely dancing, Gracie," to prompt me to say it myself.

Time stops as I lie there with you and stroke your cheek and the only sounds in the world are the low whirrs and clicks of the machines and your soft breathing and it's all that exists, all that matters, you and me, little Gracie, you and me together, keeping each other safe, hidden away from the rest of the world.

CHAPTER 5

Richard looked terrible. His chin was dark with stubble and his eyes were bloodshot. He came hurrying in through the slapping doors and stopped, adjusted to the stillness, the quietness on the ward. He shrugged off his coat to show a baggy sweater and jeans and sat heavily beside me.

"Have you seen her?"

I nodded. I didn't trust myself to speak.

His knees bounced with jumpiness. "They phoned me earlier. Doctor Anderson."

I shrugged.

"He sounded very positive. She's responding well, he said."

He leaned in, looked at me more closely.

"You all right?"

My mouth twisted and I sat forward, hiding my face in my hands, and crumpled into tears. I hadn't expected to...hadn't wanted to; he couldn't cope with crying.

"I'm sorry." I sobbed like a child, snotty and hot. "It's just—I keep thinking..."

His arm reached round my shoulders and he drew me to him, clumsily patted my hair. His body was tense but I didn't care, I just folded into him, collapsed, wet-faced, into his chest.

"I know. I know."

You don't, I thought. *You have no idea.* He loves you, Gracie, he does. But not the way I do. He was never overwhelmed by it. He didn't suffer with love for you. That was one of our many differences.

And he left us both, left us for her. Don't forget that. He isn't the one putting you to bed alone every night, then sitting in a silent house with a glass of wine for company, worrying about money and childcare and wondering where it all went wrong.

"It's going to be all right." He let me cry on until the front of his jumper was damp, then pulled a huge handkerchief from his trouser pocket. He shook it open and handed it to me. It smelled of fresh ironing. "It's going to be OK."

How many times had he said that to me, over the years? I blew my nose, pulled away from him, and dabbed at his jumper. All the promises he made to me, to us, he broke. How could I trust him now?

I pulled away from him and he took his arm back from my shoulders and fixed his eyes on the opposite wall while I recovered and we settled there, side by side, exhausted, watching the wall and waiting, waiting, waiting.

I was young when I met your father. Too young. I'd just moved down to London after university and everything felt unsettled. I was on a graduate scheme with a telecoms company and already deciding I was more interested in HR than the accounts department I'd joined. I had a small room in a flat, sharing with two other girls. They were nice enough but older and both had steady boyfriends and I found myself staying out as much as possible, keeping out of the way.

It was a barbecue. A friend of someone from work. I didn't know many people and I wandered out of the kitchen to the garden, a drink in my hands, and there he was, a lean young man in a chef's apron, bent low, blowing on smoky coals.

"I'm guessing it's going to be a while."

He didn't turn to look at me straightaway but I saw his smile.

"One of the ten rules of life. Always eat before a barbecue."

I thought about that. "What are the other nine?"

He twisted at last to look me in the eye. He was thin-faced and handsome in those days, and you know that smile.

"I refer you to rule number one," he said. "Never reveal the other nine." Then he clapped his hand to his face in mock dismay. "D'oh! Now you know two."

He was just shy. I know that now. That was why he was standing all alone in the garden, pretending to be busy. That was why he spoke in riddles. But at the time, I was intrigued. He was three years older than me and had his own car and was training to be a solicitor and he seemed mature and safe.

I became his helper, carrying out raw burgers and sausages and pepper and mushroom kebabs from the kitchen, and watching as he sprayed oil and turned them. The irony is, that was probably the first and only time he cooked for me in all those years.

At the end of the evening, he gave me a lift home and

listened, and I found myself telling him about work and my boss and the girls in the flat and how strange it was to get up at seven o'clock every morning and go to work on the Tube after all that time studying and how I missed it, sometimes—the freedom to lie about all day and read and think, but of course I was grateful too; I was lucky, I knew that, to have a job at all.

When I finished, it went very quiet in the car. He focused on the road and it gave me the chance to look at him. He had a strong profile. A straight nose.

"I'm going to the South Bank tomorrow," he said. "To see what's on at the Festival Hall. You could come, if you like?"

And that's how it started.

CHAPTER 6

Ella

She thinks she can use this against me, their shared anguish about Gracie. A new weapon. She knows so little about me.

She's a fool, and from the start she got me all wrong. I was never the enemy. Not in the way she thought. And especially not now. For once, we're actually on the same side. She could use me.

If I had the strength, I'd be there in the hospital at Richard's side, making myself unpopular with the doctors and nurses by demanding everything on earth for Gracie, anything to give her the best possible chance. Like me or hate me, I don't give a damn. I'm beyond caring.

But I can't. I can barely lift my head from the pillow. Every nerve in my neck, in my shoulders is pinched and throbbing. My brain is a big, black ache.

So I lie here, sick with misery, thinking about Gracie and about *her* and remembering how it once was.

I wanted Richard as soon as I saw him. It was just one of those things.

We were at a gallery launch and he was the most awkward person there, wearing an old-fashioned suit, standing with his back to the smart crowd and staring for too
long at each picture as if he were counting to a hundred
before moving on. Knowing him now, perhaps he was.

There was an old-fashioned kindness about him. But
he was also unhappy. I smell that on people. Misery is
musty like mold.

He looked dazed when I appeared at his side and stood
closer to him than necessary.

"Let me guess now." I looked at the pencil drawing of
a fox's head in front of us. "Either you have a thing about
foxes. Or you've found yourself trapped in the wrong
party and don't know how to escape."

He smiled, rueful. "Is it that obvious?"

"Yes, my friend."

His suit was a sober navy but his socks were sky-blue.
I liked that. He struck me as a man who needed rescuing
from his life, at least for an evening.

"Are you here with anyone?"

He shook his head. I drank off my glass of Prosecco,
then took his from his hand and drank that too.

"Follow me."

He wasn't the first strange man I'd taken home. People
react to hurt in all sorts of ways. I'd reacted by hurling
myself back into the world and pretending to be tougher
than I was. But even then, at the beginning, I think
I sensed, deep down, that he was different. Something
about Richard's quiet sadness made me want to take him
in my arms and hold him close and never let go.

I told myself that it didn't matter if I took him home
because it clearly wouldn't go anywhere. He had "married" written all over him. Worse than that, he wasn't

even duplicitous enough to take off his wedding ring. And besides, I was far too damaged to fall in love again. It was the last thing I needed. A real, caring relationship? Never again.

He was uneasy in my flat. I fed him drinks and pretended to be drunker than I was and watched him out of the corner of my eye. He couldn't sit still. He kept a distance from me, which in that flat wasn't easy, and scrutinized every picture, every photograph, every ornament, batting back my questions as if engaging me in conversation was itself an act of infidelity. I couldn't help but like him.

Richard. Married for three years but they'd been together for ten. He shrugged when he talked about it and I noted the heaviness in his voice. He had nearly backed out, when they were engaged, but it was too late. He couldn't do that to her. The invitations had been sent and the hotel was booked and everything.

"It's never too late."

He turned, gave me a sharp look. "Jen's lovely. I'd never hurt her."

I raised an eyebrow. "So where's the lovely Jen tonight?"

He blushed, looked down into his whiskey glass. "She's not well."

I sat back and waited. "What sort of not well?"

He opened his mouth to speak, then looked cross. "Are you always like this?"

"Always," I shot back at once. "Are you?"

He took a seat wearily in a chair on the far side of the room. I was playing a part, acting the femme fatale who took married men home for no-strings sex and forgot them in the morning. It was an act, of course. When I think back to that time, I taste loneliness. He wasn't the only one going round smelling like mold.

And he hadn't come for sex, anyway. He'd come for companionship. Which is a much more dangerous act of infidelity.

"So what sort of not well?" I said again. "Depressed?"

"No, nothing like that." He answered too quickly. That was yes, then. "She's pregnant. She's . . . I mean, we're expecting our first child."

He said it as if he still didn't quite believe it.

"Ah." Complicated. "So now you're thinking: holy shit, it really is too late."

He drank off his whiskey, put his glass down with a bang.

"Look, I never said that. I'm sorry. I shouldn't be here."

"Of course you shouldn't." I leaned forward, poured him another whiskey. "But you are, aren't you?"

He was the sort of man who made love, rather than had sex. Afterward, he tried to cuddle and I had to fend him off and protect myself from all that tenderness, all that potential to get hurt.

"You haven't done this before, have you?"

"Had sex?" He smiled.

"Cheated on the lovely Jen."

His face clouded. He looked past me to the clock. Still only ten past nine. He could still make it home and pretend nothing had happened. He could rub this out and start again.

"Out you go."

He looked surprised. He didn't know me yet. I liked to stay a step ahead.

At the door, I did my best to act nonchalant.

"Well, Mr. Richard. You know where I live. Same time next week?"

It wasn't a good idea to see him again. I tried to pretend it was all a joke but we weren't the type for games, neither of us. Not really.

I found myself staying in the following Tuesday night, against my better judgment, and bought a fresh bottle of whiskey. Just in case. I had a long shower and, when the bell rang, I went to the door in my underwear and a silky dressing gown.

He stared. Nervous. Clutching a bunch of flowers and a shop-bought cheesecake.

"I didn't think you'd come."

He swallowed. "Neither did I."

But I think we were both lying. We both knew.

CHAPTER 7

Jennifer

Richard went home that evening, leaving me to spend a second night at the hospital. I knew there was nothing I could do. I just needed to be as close to you as possible.

The late-shift nurse handed me a packet of wet wipes when she came on duty and I wondered if I was starting to smell. She pulled a wooly hat off and her coat was damp across the shoulders. She made some remark about the rain as she hung it up in the cupboard behind the desk and I realized I had no idea what was happening in the outside world and I didn't really care.

The hospital settled into sleep. I was learning its rhythms. The bustle of early morning with its rumbling trolley wheels. The coming and going during the day. Red-eyed parents, clutching hands. Endless coffees. Waiting. I recognized the look. Dazed and disbelieving. None of us expected to find ourselves here.

They let me see you, just for ten minutes, to say good night.

I put my head on the pillow, my cheek against yours. You

had a special ritual for settling your toys—your children, you called them. Kitty cat, the glove puppet, on one end. Then puppy, wrapped round in a piece of white cloth. Then the battered rabbit you'd had since you were a baby. Finally, your bear. We kissed each of their noses before I kissed yours.

You weren't allowed to have them in hospital, for fear of infection. But I talked you through the ritual just the same and pretended they were there and finally kissed the tip of your nose.

"I love you, little Gracie. Good night. Mummy's right here."

Your eyes were closed. The drip, feeding liquid into your hand, clicked and whirred.

When my time was up, I trailed down to the café and sat in the same seat with a dreary sandwich and a cup of tea. The corridor was quiet. Another hour and the café would close. I picked at the ham in the sandwich and stared at the tabletop, thinking about you and wondering how long it would be until I could take you home.

"Is that all you're having?"

I looked up. Matt, smiling as he strode toward me, his coat unbuttoned.

"Hi."

"I thought I might find you here."

I shook myself. "How was your day?"

He shrugged. "Long. How about you? How's Gracie?"

"I'm not sure." I paused. "They keep saying there's progress. But she doesn't look any different."

He nodded. "It's a slow process." He hesitated, looking again at my dry sandwich. "Look, there's an Indian round the corner. I'm going for a curry before I head home. Come and eat some proper food."

I shook my head. "That's nice of you but—"

"Come on." He reached for the sandwich and pushed it back into the packet. "Keep this for later. They'll call you if there's any change."

I frowned. I didn't like the idea of leaving you. Just coming off the ward felt hard. And I certainly wasn't interested in being sociable. But I was exhausted and frightened and very alone and he seemed kind.

"It's only a few doors down."

I'd imagined something cheap and cheerful but the Indian was a proper restaurant with linen tablecloths and low lighting. Matt had an easy manner with the waiter, ordering us a bottle of wine and a few dishes.

I unfolded my napkin on my knee and stared at the candle on the table. It struck me how unreal this all felt, having dinner with this doctor, a stranger, while you, my love, fought for life in a nearby hospital bed.

"You're doing so well." His voice was gentle. "You must be shattered."

I bit my lip. "She means the world to me. Gracie."

"Of course she does." He hesitated. I felt his eyes on my face as I focused on the tiny flame. "Is there anyone you can call? Who can stay with you?"

The flame bent and flailed as I sighed. There wasn't anyone. No brothers or sisters. My father had died when I was a teenager. My mother was frail now and increasingly forgetful. I hadn't even told her about the accident. I hoped I wouldn't have to. She was still angry with Richard for leaving us.

"Not really." I didn't want to talk about it. "Her father, Richard, was here earlier. It was his partner, Ella, who was driving."

I lifted my eyes to look at him, wondering how much he knew about us. How much doctors talked.

"Keep positive. Gracie's doing well. And at this age, they can rally very quickly. You'd be surprised."

I didn't answer. The waiter brought the wine and poured us both a glass. A strong red. The taste of it was overwhelming. Matt reached forward and steadied my hand, guiding the glass back to the table.

"Eat first. You're running on empty."

When the food arrived, he took my plate and served me, as if I were a child. I let him. It was a long time since anyone had taken care of me and, God knows, I needed it. My shoulders sagged. Just lifting my knife and fork seemed a monumental effort of will.

While we ate, he chatted lightly about the film he'd seen at the weekend, the thriller he'd just finished reading. I was grateful for the distraction. His voice was low and thoughtful and as the wine slowly spread its warmth, my body started to relax, just a little, and my eyes to close.

He insisted on paying, waving the waiter away with his credit card before I could protest. He walked me back to the hospital's broad revolving doors.

"There's a chapel, you know. On the third floor. If you want somewhere quiet."

I looked at my feet. "I'm not really, I mean, I haven't been to church for—"

He lifted his hand. "Sure. I just meant, a safe space, that's all. Somewhere a bit more private where you can sit and think." He paused. "It's usually empty."

I don't know how it happened but I turned away to go back inside, then turned back and stepped wordlessly into his arms and he enveloped me in a strong, warm hug and for a few moments I felt safe and protected, for the first time in a long time.

                              *   *   *

The chapel was hidden away down a long corridor. It was
a modern room, hushed and carpeted, with two high,
round windows decorated with shards of stained glass.
Printed notices at the back declared it a place of sanctuary
for those of all faiths and those of none. Laminated prayer
cards were piled beside copies of the Bible and the Quran.

A plain wooden cross stood on a table at the front,
which was covered with a freshly laundered cream cloth.
An aisle led the way toward it, between rows of soft-
seated chairs.

I sat at the front and focused my eyes on the cross and
tried to calm down. My thoughts ran everywhere. To the
church I'd attended with my mother as a child, a drafty
stone building that had smelled of damp. The priest had
been elderly and given endless, rambling sermons. I'd
stopped going as soon as I could.

I bent my head forward over clasped hands and tried to
remember how to pray.

"Please, God. Please don't take her. She's too young. I
need her."

My knuckles whitened. I didn't know whether to beg
God or to rail against Him for putting you through this.
What was He thinking, letting this happen to a three-
year-old?

My chest heaved as I started to sob.

"Please don't take her. She's all I've got now. You know
that."

My voice sounded hysterical. I barely knew what I was
saying.

"Don't take Gracie. Don't. I'll do anything."

I sobbed for a long time, desolate, trying to strike a
bargain with a God I wasn't even sure I believed in.

Finally, I wiped off my face, went miserably back to the ward, and slumped there, facing the wall, keeping watch as best I could until morning came.

At some time in the small hours, I must have fallen asleep. I woke with a start just after seven, aware of the ward once again stirring into life.

A warm coffee in a takeaway cup and a croissant sat in front of me on the table. "Try to eat" was scrawled across the paper bag.

The day nurse was already on duty.

"Any news?"

"They'll tell you if there's any change." She looked at me pitifully. Her hair was neatly pinned and she smelled of soap. I felt the contrast with my own wrecked, crumpled self and wondered how much longer I could keep this up.

I rubbed a wet wipe over my face and sipped the coffee.

At eight o'clock, they let me see you. I lie beside you on the bed, one arm across your chest, the other slipped under your head, resting it on my shoulder.

"Good morning, my love."

Your cheek is smooth and cool. The early morning sun filters in through the blinds and paints stripes across the floor. I think of the chapel with its round stained-glass windows and the colored light that must be streaming there.

"I love you, Gracie. Mummy's here."

I keep my voice low and whisper into your ear, willing you to hear me.

"It's the start of another day, sweetheart. And you know what day it is today? It's the day you're going to start to get better. Much better."

I sigh and my breath stirs strands of your hair. I lie quietly, utterly exhausted, feeling your small body in my arms, staring at the blank wall beyond the bed. As I look, scenes from the last four years play there in that small, sterile room, running in slow motion on the painted wall like a soundless black-and-white cine film from decades ago.

Your blotchy scrunched-up face the day we carried you home from hospital, holding you as fearfully as if you were glass. Richard, sitting on the settee and cradling you, your tiny head resting in the crook of his arm, gazing at you with so much tenderness that it stopped my breath. Your first wobbly steps in the garden, pushing a toy buggy piled with furry bears and rabbits.

A wall of such sadness rises up and knocks the breath from my body that I start to shake, my legs juddering on the bed.

I whisper to you, trying not to cry: "Don't leave me, Gracie. Please. Stay with me. You're my whole world, my love. Please. Don't you know how much I love you?"

Then I see it. Your eyelids flutter and the tip of your tongue pokes out between your lips and a flicker of life, real life, comes back into your face. I pull away from you, jumping off the bed, and lean on the red emergency button and, at the same moment, the machine on the far side of the bed starts to bleep.

Footsteps slap hurriedly down the corridor and voices come with them and a tall, dark-haired nurse runs in, one I haven't seen before. She takes one look at you and calls back over her shoulder to someone else and rushes to the bed, snatching up the clipboard from its base and scribbling some readings from the screens. Even as she does so, another nurse appears with the American doctor and

someone else takes me forcefully by the shoulders and
moves me back, away from the bed, to give them all room.

Not long afterward, Richard appears in the doorway, his
face tense. A nurse, understanding nothing about us, propels
me toward him and he opens his arms and holds me, looking
over my shoulder at you as you lie motionless in bed, and
at the frantically working, rushing medics suddenly filling
the room with their movements, their short, sharp, urgent
exchanges.

I'm crying now, weeping into your father's collar,
bathing in the old familiar smell of his skin. I press my
face into his neck and the crying veers in and out of wild
laughter and he pats my back awkwardly and murmurs:
"Hush, Jen. Calm down."

I don't care. I know what's happened. The doctors do
their best but they only know so much. You were lost in a
place where even they couldn't reach you and somehow,
even there, you felt me and heard me and came back to
me, back to this troubled world just to be with me. I don't
know how that's possible but it is. It really is.

CHAPTER 8

You progressed rapidly after that, moving first out of intensive care and soon, in a matter of days, there was talk of your coming home. All the tests came back clear. The bleed dispersed, the swelling subsided, and your brain function was normal. The doctors spoke, some more robustly than others, of a full recovery.

I agreed, at last, to leave you for a few hours each day and for much of the night to go home to shower and change my clothes and sleep. It was during one of those brief returns to the house that a pair of police officers turned up and began asking questions about the accident.

"So the driver, Ella Hicks, I understand she's your ex-husband's partner? Did she often have sole charge of your daughter?"

The police officer speaking was middle-aged, her torso further thickened by body armor and an arsenal of equipment. Something in her manner made me anxious.

"Not often." I shook my head, vehement. "If I'd known she'd take Gracie out on her own, I wouldn't have agreed. I thought she'd be with her father all weekend."

The police officer narrowed her eyes. "Why wouldn't you have agreed?"

"Well, she has no business. I mean, Gracie's not hers."

They both scrutinized me. A young Asian policeman sitting beside me, his hat on the carpet at our feet and his leather gloves inside it, made a note. He kept quiet, the more junior of the two.

"I understand that." The policewoman leaned forward, probing. "But why would you have objected to her looking after your daughter? Was there anything about her driving specifically that gave rise to concern?"

I searched my mind, trying to think of something.

"Not really." I thought of Ella, confident behind the wheel, risking your life. "But I don't trust her."

"You don't trust her?"

"No. And I'm right not to. She nearly killed Gracie."

The policewoman's eyes bore into me, appraising.

"You seem to blame Ms. Hicks for the collision. I wonder why?"

I felt myself flush. *Because I don't like Ms. Hicks. Because she broke up my marriage and stole my husband. Because she'd do anything she could to hurt me.*

I shrugged. "She was the one driving."

Her eyes stayed on my face. Beside her, the Asian police officer was alert, his pen poised.

I reached for the mug of tea on the coffee table in front of me and drank a little. My hands shook and the china juddered against my teeth. I used both hands to put it down again.

"There'll be a coroner's inquest, of course. But it should be straightforward."

"An inquest?" I shook my head. "Does that mean she'll face charges?"

"It's standard procedure, ma'am. When there's a fatality. We need to establish the cause of the accident."

The young Asian flipped his notebook closed and reached for his gloves, his hat.

"I'm sorry. I know it's a difficult time." The senior officer put a business card on the table beside my mug as she heaved herself to her feet.

"Who was she?" I asked. "The other driver."

"Vanessa Parkes. Twenty years old."

"Twenty?" It shocked me. She was so young. "A student?"

"An estate agent."

I couldn't answer. I thought of her mother. Of the call from the police, breaking the news.

"We'll see ourselves out."

I sat very still, following the creak of the floorboards in the hall, the heavy sound of their footsteps, the squeeze of the latch as they closed the door behind them and went down the path to merge with the early evening darkness gathering there.

At once, the house was too silent. I sat on the settee, my legs trembling, unable to move. Neither of them had touched their tea and I wondered why they'd asked for it, if there was some hidden trickery in keeping me busy in the kitchen while they lingered, unobserved, in here.

Finally, I forced my legs to take me upstairs to wash and change before I headed back to the hospital. Your room was hollow with emptiness. I sat for a while in the battered old armchair in the corner and simply looked. Then I made up your bed with clean sheets and arranged the mess of soft toys at the bottom of your bed—kitty cat, puppy, rabbit, bear—all waiting for you to bring them back to life.

CHAPTER 9

You came home but life stayed far from normal.

For some time, although I was exhausted, I struggled to sleep. My world became a dull blur of night and day. Footsteps in the street woke me, night after night, and I stood at the window, drawing the edge of the curtain round my body, looking out at the dark road and the soft stripes of lamplight along the pavement. Sometimes I thought I saw a figure there in the shadows, looking across the street to our house, and I imagined it was Richard, coming home again too, coming back to us.

When I went back to bed, my body shook as if the mattress were vibrating beneath me. The hard outlines of the wardrobe, the chest of drawers, the bedside table, melted and swayed as I watched.

During the day, I tried to stay calm, for your sake. I delivered you to nursery each morning, collected you each lunchtime, took you to soft play and to the library and to parties. But wherever I went, a shadow hung behind me, just out of sight. I never saw it. I felt it. A feeling or a phantom? I didn't know. All I knew was that when I turned to catch it, to look it in the eye, there was nothing but empty air.

Inside, I felt as if the physical laws of the universe, which all my life had formed the solid edges of my world, warped and gave way around me. When I think back to that time, my memories are a swirling snowstorm of static with occasional moments of horrible clarity.

Richard sensed something. He was the one who urged me to see a doctor. That in itself gave me hope that he still cared about me, at least a little. In the early days, when we first met, he made me feel so cherished. A beautiful word. He still cherishes you, Gracie. You must believe that. He carried on loving you long after his love for me died.

Do you remember the days before he left us for that awful woman? You slept so badly as a baby and he sat with you in his arms for hours on end, stroking the soft line of your back with tenderness. I'd wake with a start and reach for him across the bed only to find a rumpled absence and then pad through, bleary-eyed, to your room to find him in the armchair, a dark shape in the half-light, patiently caressing you back into sleep.

The doctor said I was experiencing post-traumatic shock. She prescribed tablets to help my nerves, as she put it. I don't know what was in them but I did take them each night for a while, mostly to please Richard, and gradually the wardrobe and chest of drawers settled back into place and let me sleep a little.

On the surface, we began to return to our old life, you and I, but it was a lie. We had both changed.

All I wanted now was to be with you. The bank agreed to let me take a leave of absence. Unpaid, of course, but I calculated that, if I was careful, we could manage on savings and the money from Richard. It would only be short-term, just until September when you'd start school and pull away from me, into your own world.

So in the afternoons, when you came out of nursery, we spent time together, living simply, just enjoying ourselves. You so nearly left me, my love, and suddenly nothing seemed more precious than being with you. I thought of the last few years and the hours I'd spent in offices, chairing meetings, running training programs, and suddenly I didn't want to miss another minute of your life.

We read stories and crayoned and, if it was dry enough, we wrapped up warmly and went to the park, with its bouncy animals and seesaws and roundabouts and a brightly colored train with an engine and carriages to sit inside, where we shouted "Tickets, please!" and "All aboard for Toyland!" and imagined chuffing off on adventures.

Life seemed simpler. I realized, for the first time, that most things didn't matter. If you wouldn't put your coat on and wanted another story instead, why not? If you threw your spaghetti Bolognese on the floor or smeared finger paint on your clothes, who cared about the mess? You were alive and well and I was so grateful I sometimes felt I couldn't breathe.

You were different too. It took me a while to realize. I assumed at first that you were quieter because you were still convalescing but it was more than that.

Your drawings changed. You always loved to crayon—well, scribble in multicolors the way small children do—announcing, if I asked what you were drawing: "I'm not drawing, Mummy, I'm *writing*."

When you first started, at the age of about two and a half, you only used black. Whole pages of princesses and rabbits and fairies were devastated by thick dark lines, etched with deep concentration by a small scrunched fist. That wasn't long after Richard had finally packed his bags and, after more than a year of rows and threats and time apart and struggles to reconcile, he'd left for good. I remember worrying that you were prematurely traumatized, that you were becoming the world's first toddler Goth.

Now, though, you went to the other extreme. You wore the yellow crayon to a blunt stump. You drew with the tip of your tongue sticking out between your lips, lost in your work as deeply as any Michelangelo. I sat at the table with you, coloring neatly and evenly inside the lines by way of example, and watched your passion as you made strong strokes of brightness across the paper, then sat back to consider them, then dipped again back into work.

"That's lovely, Gracie." I pointed at the streaks across the paper. "Look at all that yellow. It's like sunshine..."

You barely acknowledged me. You were too intent, too serious. You were nearly four years old and you knew your own mind. When a picture was done, ended as abruptly as it began, you pushed it away from you, dropped your crayon, and slipped from the chair, running through to the sitting room with the same intense focus with which you did everything, to find something else to do.

And then you started to make extraordinary claims, saying you'd seen things so bizarre I didn't know what to make of them.

CHAPTER 10

The first time, it was a cool, bright day and we'd spent the afternoon in the park on the far side of the river. I had more time to spend with you but little money—at least, until I went back to work again—and we often hung about in the park, one of our many sources of free entertainment.

You played on the swings for a while, then rode your scooter up and down the paths, looking like an astronaut in your bulky pink helmet. Finally, we stood together on the embankment and threw bread down to the ducks that waddled far below on the stony shore revealed by low tide.

We had just hurled the last crust and shaken a final rain of crumbs out from the corners of our plastic bag. The mallards and large Canadian geese turned and waddled back toward the water and, one by one, launched themselves into the current, starting to disperse. I reached for you with one hand and, with the other, stuffed the empty bag in my coat pocket.

You tilted your face to the low, white cloud over the river, thoughtful.

"Mummy, do angels live in the sky?"

I blinked, then stooped to hear you better. "Angels?"

Your face was solemn. "Can they see us right now? If we wave?"

Below, the remaining geese squawked and pecked round each other's feet. You swung my hand in yours, pulling me forward.

"No, my love," I said. "Angels aren't real like that. Not like us."

"Yes, they are." You looked cross. "I met one."

I steadied my breath. You had been known to tell tall stories. You didn't mean to lie. You were still working out the difference between what was real and what was imagined. I remember finding a page torn out of a book and saying sternly: "Did you do this, Gracie?" and you looked me right in the eye and said: "No, Mummy, Bear did."

But this seemed different. I steered you to one of the wrought-iron benches on the other side of the path and sat you down beside me.

"What do you mean, Gracie?"

"You made him laugh." You looked thoughtful, remembering. "In the hospital. Sticking the mouse's ear back on the wall."

My breath stopped in my throat. "In the hospital?"

You smiled, gave an emphatic, exaggerated nod. "Typical Mummy. That's what he said. Always trying to put things right."

The lorries and double-decker buses made dark silhouettes against the sky as they followed the rounded arc of the bridge. I thought of the peeling picture of Minnie Mouse and the way I'd stood on the table to press it back.

How did you know? Did someone else see and tell you? That was the only way I could explain it.

I slowed myself down, choosing my words with care.

"Gracie, do you remember when you were in the play at nursery? Angels are a lovely part of Christmas. But we don't actually meet them. Not nowadays."

You frowned, squirmed, looked at your tangled fingers.

"But I did."

I sighed. "Maybe you had a very special dream, Gracie. When you were in the car."

You shook your head and pushed out your lower lip. "It wasn't a dream. It was real."

You looked away from me, out over the water where seagulls were swooping.

I steadied myself, trying not to get cross. "Sometimes I have dreams that feel very real."

"No!" You screwed up your mouth.

I reached out and put my hand on your back and stroked you between your hunched shoulders. You shrugged me off, annoyed.

"OK. Tell me about it then."

You glanced at me, judging whether it was worth saying more. A young woman in a tracksuit jogged past, listening to music. A moment later, a dog nosed round our feet, sniffing, and you drew up your legs, frightened of being licked.

When the dog's owner passed, calling the dog after him, I tried again.

"So where did you see him?"

You hesitated. "Remember when we had the accident?"

"Of course."

You paused, searching for the words. "Well, in the car, I had a funny feeling in my head."

"A funny feeling?"

"In here." You pointed to your forehead, then hesitated. "I was all floaty and I could see myself in the car seat and the car was all crumpled like paper and there were big men shouting and using knives to cut off the doors and get in."

"You remember that?"

You nodded, your eyes clear. "They put something round my neck like a dog and put me on a bed and we went in the ambulance. One of the men called me petal but that's silly, I'm not a flower. And suddenly I left them all behind and started to fly."

"To fly?"

"One minute, I was looking down on them, rushing, rushing, and the next I went whoosh through a dark tunnel and there was a bright, bright light at the other end and he was standing there with his arms open, stretched really wide like this, waiting for me."

You looked sideways to see how I was taking this. I tried to keep my face impassive.

"What makes you think he was an angel?"

"He was tall and he had light shining."

I hesitated, thinking about the pictures of angels we'd colored at Christmas, complete with wings and halos.

"He gave me a big cuddle and he was so happy to see me and I was happy too and he took my hand and started to lead me away." You smiled. "It was amazing."

I bit my lip. You seemed lost in the memory.

"Then what happened?"

"We talked for a bit and then he asked me if I wanted to go with him or if I wanted to go back. When I looked round, I saw Daddy outside the hospital and when they lifted me out of the ambulance, he came running, shouting, and he was crying." She paused. "I've never seen Daddy cry before."

"He cried the day you were born," I said. "But that was because he was happy."

"Then I saw myself on a trolley and they put a needle in my arm and a mask on my face and pushed the trolley into a big lift and a nurse pressed the button with a four on it. When we were in there, the ambulance man put his hands on my chest like this and leaned on me and Daddy was shouting."

I didn't know what to say. I just kept quiet and let you talk.

"Daddy was sad and I knew you would be too so I told the man: I think I'll go back please. And then I was there again, in my body on the trolley, and my head hurt and I felt sick and my ears were full of noises and when I opened my eyes, lights in the ceiling were rushing past me and I thought they were hardly lights at all, compared to the light I'd just seen, but Daddy's face hung over me and the doctor's and that man said 'Stay with us, petal, stay with us,' and then I fell asleep."

You seemed tired when you finished and I reached an arm round you and hugged you to me, stroking hair from your forehead.

"Do you believe me, Mummy?"

I didn't want to tell you that I didn't believe you—it seemed to feel true to you and it is a terrible thing not to be believed by people you love. So I just said: "I'm very glad you came back, Gracie. You don't know how glad. I love you very much."

A chill wind blew along the river and clouds thickened overhead. You were starting to get cold. I stood up and you jumped to your feet and we walked back toward the bridge, hand in hand. I clutched you very tightly. I wanted to be normal with you but my head throbbed with the effort of understanding the implications of what you'd said.

"Please will you tell me," I said, trying to sound matter of fact, "if you remember anything else?"

"OK." Your voice was chirpy.

A moment later, you let my hand fall and started to skip, jumping sideways on and off the edge of the path, your hair flying as if you'd forgotten about the whole thing.

That evening, after we'd read a story and I sang you to sleep, I sat on in your room, gazing down at your face in the shadows. Just you and me, in the silence.

You were sleeping on your knees, hunched forward over your bear, one arm flung out, your head lolling to one side, hair splayed across the sheet. You were so still that I kneeled down beside you and lowered my face to yours to catch the soft, barely audible suck of your breathing. You didn't stir when I put my lips to your cheek and stroked the hair from your eyes. Your skin smelled of lemons.

You stirred and I retreated at once and settled in the lumpy armchair and sat, my legs curled under me, my cheek against the rough fabric, thinking about you and how blessed I was to have you back again, here, alive. And thinking about that poor young woman, Vanessa, the estate agent, and her desperate mother, somewhere out in the darkness, who had lost her daughter forever.

CHAPTER 11

The following morning, you went to nursery and, as I shopped and cooked and did the laundry, I thought constantly about the strange story you'd told. All I could imagine was that you were experiencing your own form of post-traumatic shock, processing in some way all that had happened and reliving it in the only form you knew: a story.

By the time I collected you from nursery, I'd decided to take you with me to do something that had been in my mind for a while. To go and see the scene of the accident for myself. Perhaps, I thought, it would help us both.

I bought flowers. It was an overpriced winter bouquet and as I paid for them, I hesitated, wondering what on earth I was doing, busting my budget for someone I'd never even met. I seemed to hear my beloved father's voice, always the pragmatist. He laughed in my ear. *Nineteen ninety-nine? Really? And you're going to tie them to a lamppost and leave them there? Oh please, Jen, please.*

You clung tightly to my hand as we jumped off the big

step of the bus onto the pavement and I looked round, trying to make out the landmarks. A dry cleaner's. A chem-
ist's. A convenience store. A coffee shop.

I looked warily at the surface of the road. No dark
patches that might be the remnants of spilled blood. No
shattered glass. Nothing at all. Just the endless rumble of
fast-moving cars and buses and lorries and a hard, damp
chill in the air.

You helped me to find the end of the roll of brown tape
and pick it free. We wrapped it round and round the flowers and the lamppost behind. The stems stood upright, the
heads leaning forward. I thought of witches, tied to the
stake, waiting to be burned. I blinked, stuck the card on
the front in its plastic sleeve. For Vanessa.

I drew you in front of me and stood there for a moment,
my hands gripping your shoulders. A religious person
would say a prayer. We were not religious people. You
twisted round, expectant, trying to look at me.

"Did you know her?" A stout woman, full in the door
of the coffee shop. Her hands were across her bosom,
holding thickly padded upper arms, warding off the cold.

"Not really. I mean, no. I know the woman driving the
other car."

"Oh." Her hand flew to her mouth. "Is she . . . ?"

"She's fine. Barely a scratch."

"I saw it happen. I was stood right here." She nodded
at the doorway that framed her. "That poor girl's car went
out of control, swerved right across the road. Bang. Head
on."

I nodded. I wanted her to say more, to tell me what
I knew in my heart, that whatever the other woman did
wrong, the accident was partly Ella's fault too. Despite
what the police said.

"And that poor kiddie in the back."

My eyes traveled down to you and hers followed.

"Hello, darling. What's your name?"

You didn't answer, twisted back to me for guidance.

"Gracie," I said. "She's three. Well, nearly four."

"Nearly four! What a big girl!" Her eyes rose again to mine and read my expression. "Was it her, then, in the back?"

I nodded.

She looked you over. "Come into the warm. You like marshmallows, Gracie?"

The coffee shop was almost deserted. We slid into chairs in the window and I ordered drinks and a toasted sandwich. You faced the interior and watched with round eyes as the woman worked behind the counter.

I looked out at the street. The table juddered each time a heavy lorry rumbled past. The flowers hung unhappily on the lamppost. They blurred as rain spattered the glass. It was a sad offering, already desolate.

"I didn't know what else to do."

"Of course you didn't." She seemed to understand at once. She was bustling now, hissing steam and pulling levers as she made you a hot chocolate and stuffed the tiny cup with pink and white marshmallows, then made me a cappuccino and shook chocolate shavings over the foam. "It's a lovely gesture. Two plates with the toastie?"

She waved me away when I reached for my wallet and came to sit beside me, facing the window. She jerked her head toward you and mouthed: "Is she all right?"

I nodded. She considered us both, then pulled herself back onto her feet and returned with a tin of worn crayons and a printed coloring sheet and put them in front of you.

"Could you tell me a bit more, please?" I kept my voice

low, watching you pick out a crayon and start to scribble, hoping you were too absorbed in your coloring to listen. "What happened, exactly?"

She blew out her cheeks. "I was stood right here. It was quiet, you see. I like to get some air." She made a discreet smoking gesture over your head. "See what's going on."

You scribbled hard, the tip of your tongue sticking out between your lips as you concentrated. Yellow. Every now and then, your small fingers reached for a marshmallow and you bit into it, your brow tight as you chewed.

"Who was she talking to?" the woman asked. "Do you know?"

I shook my head. "Who?"

"Your friend. Didn't she say?" She nodded. "On her mobile." She put her splayed fingers to her cheek to demonstrate. "Shouting. Right old ding-dong. Don't know what she said but I heard her through the window, just before, you know. That's what made me look up. And then, bang." She made the sign of the cross on her breast.

I set down my cup, spilling coffee in the saucer and out across the plastic tabletop. For a moment, my chest was so tight that I could barely breathe. I was right. I knew it from the start. Ella was to blame. She was shouting down the phone, distracted, when the accident happened. Not paying proper attention. With you, my love, in her care. You could have died.

The woman looked embarrassed. "I'm sorry. I didn't mean—"

I swallowed hard, pressed the flat of my wrists to my eyes to stop myself crying. She filled the silence by reaching for a serviette and mopping at the splashes of coffee.

"And to think, that little one in the back. And she's all right, you say? Well."

I couldn't speak. My hands, at my face, shook.

She looked away. You, oblivious, crayoned furiously.

"They took forever getting her out. Put one of those things on, round her neck. Poor little mite." She raised her eyes to check on me. "And she was your friend?"

My *friend*? Ella? I didn't reply.

Something seemed to occur to her and she got to her feet, dropped the sodden serviettes in the bin, and went behind the counter, rummaging there. You lifted your head and watched. When she came back, she carried something small inside a folded carrier bag.

"I was going to take it to the police, you know, but I didn't know where to go. There used to be a police station just down there, along Flyfield Road, but they closed it. Turned it into a kebab shop. And I didn't want to get her into bother. Anyway, take it. You can give it to her now, can't you?"

I opened up the bag. A phone in a red leather case.

She pointed toward the listing flowers. "It was just there, in the gutter. I thought I'd better pick it up before someone nicked it."

You looked too. "Is that Auntie Ella's?"

The woman gave you an indulgent smile. "Well, aren't you the cat with nine lives? Bet you gave your mummy a scare, didn't you?" She looked back at me and lowered her voice again. "I tell you, I didn't think she'd made it. When I saw her out there in this bad light, I thought for a minute I'd seen a ghost."

CHAPTER 12

A day or two later, as we walked home from nursery, I had the sense that we were being watched. You chatted away about a story the teacher had read but I only half listened. I stopped, there in the bustle of the high street, and feigned interest in a powder-blue dress and jacket in a shop window. Beside me, you flattened the tip of your nose and your lips against the glass. A tall figure, a man in a cashmere coat, his hair neat, grew in the reflection as he came toward us. His shoes shone with polish.

I turned to greet Matt as he reached us.

"Jen!" He smiled down at me and, although I felt awkward, I found myself smiling back. "How are you?" He crouched down to your level. "And this is Gracie? Wow! High five!"

He held up his hand and you slapped it.

"I'm a doctor, Gracie. At the hospital. Do you remember when you were there? You were such a brave girl. I've got a present for you, if that's OK with Mummy. To say well done."

He opened his shoulder bag and pulled out a small chocolate bear, wrapped in gold foil.

"A bear!" You danced with excitement. I was conscious of living off my savings, so treats were rare.

He raised his eyes to me. "Is that OK?"

You looked from him to me, waiting for my decision. I nodded. What else could I do? You took it and ripped off the foil at once, stuffed it into your mouth.

"What do you say?"

"Thank you."

"You're welcome."

"That's very kind. Really."

"I always have a bear or two about my person." His eyes were bright and amused. "I'm so glad I caught you. I thought I saw you back there"—he pointed vaguely back toward the river—"at the traffic lights. But I wasn't certain."

You tugged at my hand, feet still dancing. "I want to go home now."

"So how are things?" His look, intense and concerned, reminded me of those wretched days in the hospital. Of his kindness. Of the food he bought me, the coffees and croissants, the curry.

"I meant to call you. I'm sorry. To say thank you."

"No need." He broke into a grin. "I mean, no need for thanks. Not no need to call me."

A woman with a double buggy powered past, filling the pavement and forcing us against the side of the shop.

"Mummy!" You began to fret at my side, pulling me. "Let's go home."

"I should probably . . ." I hesitated.

He must have sensed that you were restless but he didn't take the cue to leave.

"Do you live round here? I go to the dentist off the high street." He pointed. "Not exactly convenient but a friend of the family." He paused. "I was just going to get a coffee, actually. Don't suppose—"

"Mum-my!" You twisted and tugged, getting cross now, pulling me away.

He looked at you, then back to me. "Don't worry. Another time."

"Look, we only live round the corner." I didn't really want to invite him but he looked so disappointed that it just came out. "Come for a coffee at our place, if you like?"

"Really?" His eyes lit up. "Well, only if you're sure. I'm on lates today."

I led the way across the high street and turned into our road. You ran ahead, racing to be first. By the time we got there, you were swinging backward and forward on the rusty gate.

I warmed some milk for you and left you to play, then went to put the kettle on. Matt leaned back against the cupboards, large and solid in our small kitchen. He looked very much at ease, his expensive coat already draped over the back of a kitchen chair.

"Nice place."

"Thanks." I turned my back to him and began to put the shopping away.

He peered through the connecting door to the sitting room where you were busy rummaging through your toys. "Been here a long time?"

"Six or seven years. Richard chose it. He wanted a bit of garden." I shrugged, remembering. "And now, of course, it's just Gracie and me."

Matt broke into a grin. "I'm so pleased to see you. I've thought a lot about you, Jen. Wondered how you were."

I didn't answer. I turned my back to him, hiding my face, suddenly awkward. A mechanical tune rang out from the sitting room as you pressed buttons on a toy laptop. I concentrated on unpacking the shopping, wondering how long he planned to stay, whether I'd need to offer him lunch. He moved to the fridge and studied your drawings and paintings displayed there, bunched together with magnets.

"Does she like drawing?" He considered one closely. "She's good."

Your bear sat squarely in the middle of the kitchen table, propped against the fruit bowl from where he'd watched us eat breakfast. I moved him to the sideboard alongside placemats and coloring books and old shoeboxes of felt-tip pens, paintbrushes, and crayons.

"Have a seat."

His physical presence dominated the space. He pulled out a chair and sat a little away from the edge of the table, his long legs crossed. He was wearing black jeans, a smart pair, with a jacket and tie. They suited him. When Richard wore jeans, he always looked as if he were trying too hard.

I finished tidying and reached for mugs. His eyes followed me as I moved.

"It's only instant coffee, I'm afraid. Or builder's tea. Milk? Sugar?"

I made him a mug of tea and sat on the far side of the table, conscious of toast crumbs and traces of jam on the surface.

I had a clear view through to the sitting room, where you'd settled on the settee with a book on your lap, your lips moving as you told yourself the story. I recognized the book from here. *Beauty and the Beast*. You couldn't read; you just had it by heart.

"So you're doing OK?" His voice was gentle.

His fingers, wrapped round one of Richard's old mugs, were long and delicate. His chest was broad. He smelled fresh, a pungent scent of apples. It was so odd to see him sitting here, at the kitchen table. I didn't really see friends nowadays, not since Richard left. It was just you and me. And in the evenings, just me.

"Yep, think so." I nodded. "I've taken some time off work. They've been very good. Just until Gracie starts school in September."

"The days are long but the years are short." He smiled. "So what sort of work aren't you doing?"

"I run a training and development unit at a German investment bank. Not corporate training but personal development, one-on-one mostly."

Richard always zoned out when I talked about work. I stopped bothering long ago. But Matt's eyes stayed attentive.

"It's all about helping people work toward what they really want to do. It's very rewarding. Well, most of the time."

He considered. "Do people know what they want?"

"That's half the battle. Helping them find out. Then we break it down into steps and work out how to get there." I paused. I didn't know why I was telling him all this. I didn't really know why he was here at all. "It can mean leaving banking, for some people. And that's OK too."

I lifted my eyes, looked through to the sitting room. Your head was bent low over the story. I watched you for a moment and the sight of you, so engrossed, made me smile. I realized he was looking at me and turned. His eyes, on my face, were kind.

"Gracie's doing so well. I was frightened to death. You can imagine." I stopped. I still found it difficult to talk about without crying. "But she's completely fine. Just as bright and lively as she always was." I nodded toward the open door. "Well, see for yourself."

He kept his eyes on me. "And what about you?"

"What about me?"

"You've really been through it, haven't you?"

I shrugged, then bit my lip.

"I thought you were amazing." He lowered his voice. "What you did for her. The way you stayed there night and day. I was worried about you."

I shifted my weight, feeling awkward.

"Well, all over now. Thank God." I hesitated. I wasn't used to sympathy. "Thanks."

He changed the subject and started chatting about the book he was reading, a novel set in Peru or Bolivia or somewhere. I only half listened. I studied my hands, thinking how engaged he seemed with the world and how isolated I'd become and wondering what he made of me. How had I turned into such a hermit—such a sad and lonely recluse that it felt like a major event to have someone round for a cup of tea?

Later, he said: "You and Gracie seem so close." He paused. "How long has it been just the two of you?"

I considered. "She wasn't quite two when Richard left. Now she's nearly four."

"What a fool."

He said it with such quiet intensity that he caught me off guard. I lifted my tea and the rim of the cup juddered against my teeth.

"That's what I said." I tried to force a laugh. "Well, it's one of many things I called him."

He didn't smile. He sipped his tea and the silence stretched.

"Maybe I was the fool," I said at last. "I didn't have a clue, you see. Turned out he'd been seeing this woman— the one who was driving that day. He'd been seeing her for years."

It felt easier, somehow, to discuss it with a stranger. As if I were talking about something that happened to someone else. I'd spoken about it so little, in the last two years. There was no one really to tell. My mother wasn't well enough to understand. Friends were busy with their own lives. Besides, there was only so much they wanted to hear.

He didn't flinch, just said quietly: "Even before Gracie came along?"

"Seems so." I swallowed, still feeling stupid. "I had no idea."

I never had made sense of it. Not really. How could anyone not know their husband was having an affair? But it's amazing what you don't see. Richard often worked late. Always had. And besides, I trusted him.

"I'm sorry." Simple but the most sensible thing anyone had said about the whole sad mess.

I shrugged. "Gracie wasn't an easy baby. I was shattered all the time. I focused on her. He must have wondered what the hell he was hanging around for. I see that now."

"What did he expect? It's hard, being a new parent. You just have to get on with it, don't you?"

I thought about that for a moment. "Do you have children?"

He twisted to look out through the window, at the flagstones, rimmed with weeds and set round by overgrown bushes. Richard was the gardener, not me.

"A daughter." He shrugged. "Her mother and I . . . well,

let's just say it's a similar story. She moved on. Only in my case, she took our daughter with her."

For a moment, he looked so hurt that I nearly reached out to touch his hand, the way he'd touched mine in the hospital. I turned and looked through to you, your head bent over your book, and tried to imagine Ella taking you away from me, after taking Richard. I'm not sure I'd survive that.

"What's your daughter's name?"

"Katy." He looked up at me again and smiled and I found myself smiling back.

"Great name. Solid as a rock."

"It was my grandmother's." He hesitated, his face suddenly shy. "Jenny's lovely too."

I studied my hands for a moment, then pushed back my chair and went to the sink to wash up my mug.

He got to his feet at once. "I'm intruding." He reached for his coat. "I'm sorry."

"Not at all."

On the doorstep, he hesitated and turned back to me.

"You're doing so well," he said, and nodded. It was a professional voice now, the doctor in him. It confused me, as if we'd just slipped seamlessly from friends to a home visit.

When I closed the door, I leaned against it for a moment and stood there in the quietness, trying to make sense of him and wondering what had just happened.

I went through to the kitchen, put bread in the toaster, and rummaged in the fridge for lunch. As I stirred the pan of baked beans, you wandered through. You climbed onto a chair, reached for your bear, and sat with it in your arms, watching me.

"You hungry?"

You didn't answer. I broke off a breadstick and gave it to you to eat while you waited.

"Did you like that man? He's a doctor. One of the doctors in the hospital who made you better."

You munched the breadstick, spraying crumbs. Your eyes were thoughtful.

I thought you'd moved on but when I ladled the beans onto your plate and added the warmed-up sausages and set it in front of you with your miniature colored knife and fork, you said: "It was a lady doctor, in the hospital."

I sat beside you with my own plate.

"There was a lady, that's right. But there were men doctors too."

You shrugged, looked down without enthusiasm at your lunch.

I pointed. "Do you want me to cut the sausages?"

You shook your head. "It's hot," you said. "I'm waiting for it to warm down."

I looked out at the overgrown patch of garden and had a sudden vision of Matt, stripped to the waist, wielding a pair of shears. A man, a kind, capable man, bringing companionship. Making me feel less alone. I blinked it away.

"Good idea, Gracie." I reached over and moved your hair out of your face, tucked it behind your ear. "Good girl."

CHAPTER 13

The next day, I came back from nursery to find a card on the mat. Hand-delivered. Firm, ragged handwriting in black ink. I stood there in my coat, looking at the envelope, reluctant to open it and be disappointed. It could be anything.

I carried it through to the kitchen and put it on the counter while I unpacked the shopping, put the kettle on. I forced myself to wait until I'd made a cup of tea and settled at the kitchen table before I opened it. There was a plain, cream-colored card inside. Thick card. And just a few simple lines scrawled across the center.

"Hi Jenny, I wondered if you were free for dinner one evening? Give me a call. Matt." His mobile phone number was written underneath, just to make quite sure I had it. I sat very still and listened to the blood in my ears, to my heart. I was acting like a schoolgirl. All needy and excited. Just for a moment, I pretended to myself that I might not call him. I looked out at the messy kitchen, at the toys littered across the sitting room floor, waiting to be tidied away. I'd thought it was just you and me from now on. Just silence in the evenings and early nights. Maybe that was best, after all.

I remembered the warmth of his chest when I pressed myself suddenly against him, there at the hospital. His gentleness and kindness. The wounded look on his face when he talked about his daughter, Katy, and his ex-wife. My heart raced. Because I knew that I would say yes, that we would have dinner and that perhaps, just perhaps, it might lead somewhere.

I rushed to get my phone.

That evening, I was settling you down in bed after our story, arranging kitty cat and puppy and rabbit and bear in a little nest for you, the way my father did for me when I was your age, when you said:

"Mummy, are you going to die?"

I reached out and pulled you toward me, kissing your mess of soft, sweet-smelling hair. "Everyone has to die someday, my love. But I'm planning to stay around for a very long time."

Your forehead tightened. "I don't want you to die."

I hesitated. I didn't want to die either. Death never seemed real until it nearly took you away from me. Now it did. And when it came, however old I was, I knew I wouldn't want to leave you. I tried to remember what my own mother used to say when I was a child.

"By the time I die, you'll be grown up, Gracie. You'll be married. You'll probably have your own children."

Your lips quivered. "But I don't want you to die."

"Well, when people get very old, they get tired and they just want to go to sleep and rest. That's what happens. Dying is just like a very long sleep."

You bowed your head and I couldn't see your face. After a few moments, you quietly asked, "Was that lady very old?"

"Which lady?"

"The lady in the car. She died, didn't she, Mummy?"

I sighed. "Yes, my love. I'm afraid she did. And you're right, she wasn't very old."

You looked confused. "So why did she die?"

"I don't know, my love. There are some things even mummies don't know. It's just what happened. It was very, very unusual." I bent down and stroked your cheek with my finger. "Now cuddle up to that bear and go to sleep."

When you finally settled, I felt weighed down by an overwhelming exhaustion. I didn't have the energy to cook myself something to eat. I just sank into an armchair and sat alone in the quiet of the sitting room.

Outside, the rain had become heavy. Passing cars slushed on the wet road. Their headlights threw shifting shadows across the far wall. I imagined the noises rising in the high street, just a few minutes' walk away. They were the sounds of the old life before you came along, of bars and restaurants, cinemas and theater, youngsters in huddles in doorways and bursts of raucous chat as heavy doors opened and closed.

During the day, I didn't let myself stop and think very much. You kept me moving. You lived so lightly, so intensely in the present. Now, without you here, the sitting room seemed dull and heavy. I sat very still, listening to the clock ticking on the mantelpiece, the low hum of the lights, and the muffled splashes of the world outside.

You nearly died, my love. I nearly lost you. And she, that woman who took your father from us, she nearly took you too—shouting on the phone when she should have been watching the road. And no one seemed to realize, to blame her, except me. My hands came to my face and I rocked, hurting, trying to hold myself together.

Finally, restless, I got to my feet and stood at the mantelpiece, looking at the items there as if they belonged to a stranger. A framed photograph of you and me, one of the few Richard had taken. You were just a few weeks old, your eyes tightly closed. I looked haggard with tiredness but happy, really happy. I picked it up and studied it. It seemed a long time ago.

Farther along, a pile of cards and postcards and old photos, stuffed behind the clock. I pulled them out and looked them over. A few postcards from last summer from friends in Cannes and Dubai, a photo-card from Disneyland of a friend's child hugging Mickey Mouse, a Mother's Day card you'd made at nursery, your green crayon scribbled inside over an adult's steady writing: *I love you, Mummy, from Gracie.*

I sat in the chair with your card in my hand, thinking about you. Why were you so determined you'd flown down a tunnel of light and seen a man? Was it your brain playing tricks on you while you were in the coma? But why call him an angel? We never went to church, you and I. We never talked about God or Heaven and the only angels in your life so far had been the ones wearing wire-framed wings in the Christmas play and the plastic one on top of the tree. It made no sense. I looked at the card in my hands, traced the scribble with my eyes.

I shook my head. You'd described the accident so vividly. All that detail about the neck brace and the man calling you petal and Richard running to meet you at the hospital. And how had you known about Minnie Mouse and that ear peeling off the wall? Did someone see me do that?

I looked through to the empty, shadowy kitchen, to the table, outlined against the conservatory doors, where you and I liked to sit, side by side, eating cereal and toast. I narrowed my eyes, trying to understand and finding nothing but the quiet of my own loneliness.

Finally, I pulled myself to my feet and went through to the kitchen to get the phone and call Richard. We hadn't spoken for a while. His manner toward me had changed since those first days after the accident when he'd seemed so solicitous. Now he was back to off-hand, even brusque. Her influence.

"Jennifer." He only called me that when he was annoyed. "This isn't a great time, actually."

"Can I just ask you something?"

He tutted. That would be for her benefit. He was making the point that he was the unwilling victim of my phone call, not a collaborator. I could almost see the pained look on his face. He used to do the same with me years ago when his mother phoned just as I was putting our dinner out and I rolled my eyes, gestured to him to hang up, call back later. He never did. He was too polite.

Anyway, it was after eight. Surely they'd eaten by now.

"It won't take a minute. It's important."

A sigh. "What?"

"What happened when Gracie arrived at the hospital? Do you remember?"

He spluttered. "What happened? What do you think? She was unconscious. They rushed her straight to intensive care. I phoned you as soon as I could, as soon as they got her stable."

Now he sounded defensive.

"I know. It's not that." I paced up and down the kitchen with the phone. "But what exactly happened? I mean. Were you actually there when they lifted her out of the ambulance?"

"Yes. Right there." He reverted to that new tone of voice that had emerged recently in our few conversations, patient and long-suffering, as if he were dealing with a madwoman who might also be dangerous. "OK?"

"Did you shout?"

"Of course I bloody shouted. What do you think?" He paused, started again. "Yes, I shouted. I don't know: 'Oh my God' probably, and 'That's my daughter.' Something along those lines. OK? Can I go now?"

"You know how they said that she needed resuscitating?"

He hesitated. "Yes . . ."

"Who did it? A doctor?"

"The ambulance guy." I could hear him struggling to remember. "Honeyman. Chris Honeyman. Looked about twelve. Maybe you didn't meet him. Anyway, he did CPR and she gave a sort of gulp and by the time we reached the ward, her breathing had settled again."

"Where was it?"

He made an elaborate show of calling to Ella, like a ham actor calling offstage. "Coming! On my way." Then to me: "Look, I've got to go."

"Was it in the lift?" I raised my voice. "Did Honeyballs give CPR in the lift?"

"Honey*man*." He sounded cold. "It might have been in the sodding lift. Maybe it was in the corridor. What does it matter, Jennifer? It's past. It's history. Don't you get it? I don't want to talk about it. OK?"

The phone went down. *Now he's feeling guilty*, I

thought. He always did that. He'd try so hard to be patient and then he'd snap and blow it and feel bad about it for hours. *I've become his mother*, I thought. *And Ella has become me.* How strange life is.

I put the phone back and opened the fridge to search for something to eat. I had forgotten to ask him if he'd cried. I'd meant to. But the rest of it, the rest checked out.

I found an old yogurt, a week past its sell-by date, on the bottom shelf. It had separated and I stirred it back to life with a teaspoon, took it through to the sitting room. You must have been conscious. It was the only explanation. At some level, you must have been aware of what was happening.

I settled on the settee, switched on the television, and watched, blankly, some program about a couple looking for their ideal home.

I wanted so much to believe you. To believe you went flying off to meet your angel and found him peaceful and smiling. However irrational, it would be a comfort. I shook my head.

The program stuttered on. I scraped out the yogurt pot without tasting it, letting my eyes glaze as I stared, barely seeing, at the television. However much I pushed it away, the thought wouldn't leave me: What if you were right? You seemed so matter-of-fact in discussing it, so sure about what you'd seen. What if it were possible, for you, with all your innocence, if not for me? What if, in some way I couldn't yet fathom, something of us survived death and lived on?

I opened a bottle of wine, sank back into the cushions, and let the chatter from the television wash over me. Finally, I found the will to rouse myself and start the weekly ritual of tidying up, sorting out toys and dropping them into plastic tubs and boxes. Next, I started on the pile of junk that always collected on the dining room table.

Underneath the old newspapers lay a crumpled carrier bag. I remembered it at once. It was the one the woman in the café had handed me, with Ella's phone inside. I went to find a charger and plugged it in, then poured myself another glass of wine and watched the screen flash as it came back to life. I clicked into her text messages and started to scroll through them, looking for Richard's name. My hands shook as I read her texts to him:

See you in 5.

On my way.

Running late—see you at the restaurant. Love u. x

Somehow the fact they were so boring made it worse. It showed how intimate they were. I recovered and carried on reading, picking through the rest of her messages. I don't know what I was looking for. Some sign of an affair, perhaps, that I could brandish in Richard's face. But there was nothing incriminating at all.

I sat in silence for some moments, looking at the screen, thinking about Ella's life. I had a piece of her right here in my hand and I should have been triumphant but all I felt was emptiness.

I remembered what the woman at the café said about Ella being distracted by an angry phone call just before the crash, clicked out of messages, and went to look at the call log. The last call she'd received was at three eighteen in the afternoon, on the day of the accident. I narrowed my eyes. It could fit. That must have been roughly the same time. I bit my lip. It came from an unlisted number: No Caller ID.

CHAPTER 14

Ella

She has no idea how lucky she is.

I am sorry she and Richard weren't right together. Heaven knows, he tried. It was painful to watch. He contorted every bone in his body in the effort to change shape and fit into that marriage and be happy with her and he just couldn't do it.

And I never tried to prize him away. She needs to think that. I understand. But it's simply not true. I lost count of the number of times we made ourselves miserable by breaking up. We could never stay apart for long. He adores Gracie but suffocating in an unhappy marriage was never going to work. He's a better father for being happy with me.

She has Gracie. That's the point. She's the mother of a gorgeous, funny, bright, kind little girl. And if that isn't enough, heaven help her. However much I love Richard, and I do, I'd swap places in a heartbeat.

Hurt isn't clean. It's putrid. It makes strangers out of everyone you ever thought loved you. Once it touches you, you're on your own.

All that stuff about emotional damage bringing people together? Forget it. Hurt surrounds you with such a powerful force field of misery that no one else can enter. I know. I've been there.

All those so-called friends? Nowhere. They came the first time with their solemn faces and shuffled on their seats, trying not to look at the clock, while I cried. They didn't come back. And I don't blame them. Who would?

I've been there too. It took a while but I got it into my thick skull in the end. No one else was going to help me. No one else wanted to know. So I learned to shut up and paint a face on and say I was fine and where's the party? Stupid loud music. Stupid loud clothes. Stupid loud men. And pretty soon, rooms stopped falling silent when I walked into them. People stopped ducking into shops to avoid me on the street. *Thank God*, they thought. *She's over it.*

You don't get over it. If you're doing well, you get used to it. You save it for silence. For darkness. For three o'clock in the morning. For the nights you're alone.

So that's the state I was in when I met Richard, with all his gentleness and kindness and decency. I lay next to him in bed as he slept, his arms wrapped round me, his breath warm and steady on my skin, and absorbed love from him like a dried-up sponge sucking in water.

I couldn't talk to him about what had happened to me. I didn't know how to put it into words. And I was frightened to try. In the early days, when I first realized I was falling in love with him, I was scared of spoiling it, of contaminating what we had and driving him away. He was sad enough. He didn't need more pain in his life.

And then the moment passed. It started to feel too late. So I just walled it off and lied when I had to and, right or wrong, it seemed best.

It's my hurt. Maybe it's better it stays secret, even from him.

CHAPTER 15

Jennifer

We were coming back from the shops that afternoon when you pulled free from me and ran.

"Gracie!"

You caught me by surprise. You never ran off. You were an obedient child but also you had more sense than most children your age about traffic and waiting for the green man and the danger of getting lost in crowds.

"Gracie! Stop!"

You weaved through the shoppers like a weasel. I felt a lumbering fool, chasing after you, laden with carrier bags. My handbag, strapped over my chest, banged on my ribs. You were wearing your mauve padded anorak, a hand-me-down from the family across the road, and by the time I got clear of a broad elderly woman with a shopping trolley on wheels and round the front of an oncoming buggy, it was rapidly disappearing round the corner, turning off the high street and down a small side road.

I ran after you, cursing under my breath. The side road was less crowded and I saw you clearly as you made a sharp left and disappeared just past the music shop. It was a road that was only ten minutes from home but one I had no reason, in normal circumstances, to go down.

There was a pub across the road with a hedged garden. You couldn't have gone that far, I'd have seen you cross the road. A car park attached to a housing block. On this side, a café with chairs and tables outside, an overpriced delicatessen, and the dingy music shop that had been there for as long as I could remember. I scanned both as I ran by. No sign of you.

I pressed on. *Here*, I thought, *just here. This must be where you'd disappeared.* I found myself at the entrance to a small parish church. I must have passed it a hundred times over the years and never really noticed.

It was a Victorian building, set back from the road. The metal gate and railings looked as if they'd seen better days. The front lawn was in the building's shadow and the bushes planted round its edge needed a trim. A notice-board read: *Parish Church of St. Michael, Anglican. All Welcome.* Underneath, a modern printed notice said: *Café* and listed the opening hours.

"Gracie!" I stood at the gate, heavy with bags, and looked in. No sign of you. Standing still, away from the distant rumble of traffic on the high street, all I could hear was the thump of blood in my ears. Panic made me shake. The gate stood open. I set off down the path and ran round the side of the church, looking for the entrance.

The plot extended much farther than it looked from the road. It opened out into a narrow graveyard, set about with mature trees and bounded by a stone wall. We were so close to the modern rush of the high street and yet here I felt at once the sense of timelessness, of the passing of ages, of the unknown dead lying under the feet of the living.

"Gracie!"

Sunlight straggled through the foliage and made shifting patterns on the grass and its unkempt path and it stirred a memory of early childhood in me, someday when I must have played in such a place, in and out of shadows. I scanned the graveyard. No sign of you. Had you taken a different turning after all? My stomach clenched.

A modern, glass-walled annex rose along the far end of the church, invisible from the road. Inside, I could see the café and, through it, the entrance to the church. A movement drew my eye. A small figure in mauve, disappearing into the interior. I broke into a run again, frightened in case I was wrong, in case I was chasing a different child, pushed open the glass door with my shoulder, and fell into the café.

Faces looked up. A cluster of elderly women, drinking tea together at a wooden table. A smartly dressed young man, sitting alone with a plate of bacon and eggs, his laptop open at one side. A care-worn couple, retired perhaps, sitting in silence, shoulders slumped. A young woman with swept-back hair stood behind a counter with a magazine open in front of her and, to her side, a display cabinet full of cakes and puddings and pots of salad.

I ran across. "Did a little girl just come running in? She's three."

My voice was loud and breathless in the quietness. Unlike every other café in town, there seemed to be no background music to hide behind. A display of cheaply printed leaflets about the history of the church, postcards, and a stack of video cassettes in cellophane stood on the counter by the cash register.

The young woman lifted her eyes reluctantly from the magazine. She pointed toward the large wooden doors of the church, opened up to the public.

"She ran in there."

I rushed after you into the dim interior of the church.

"Gracie!"

You were standing at the side of the altar, gazing up at the stained-glass windows. A matter of feet away, several votive candles burned on a metal stand. The building had the hushed dim mustiness of thick stone walls, high-leaded windows, and centuries of prayer. The pews were solid wood and worn smooth by generations of worshippers. I crossed to you, conscious of the click of my heels on the stone flags and the rustle of the shopping bags against my legs.

"What on earth—"

You looked up, smiling, pleased with yourself. I wanted to grab you by the arm and give you a lecture about the perils of running off but the silence of the building pressed in on me and its sense of holiness too and, besides, you seemed so delighted with what you'd found and I was weak with relief. *Sanctuary*, I thought. You'd picked the right place to hide.

You pointed up at the windows, craning your neck back to see.

"You know what this is?" I said. "It's a church. It's a quiet place where people come to think. And it's very, very old."

"I think that's him."

"Who?"

I looked up at the section of stained glass. It gleamed red, blue, and yellow with sunshine. The picture, high above us, showed a man with a beard and flowing white robes. His foot was on the head of a writhing serpent and he held a staff high above his head as he prepared to strike. He had large, bird-like wings and a halo. Straight out of an Old Testament picture book.

"That man." You looked at me with joy. "In the funny clothes."

"What man?"

"When I was in the accident." Your face was radiant, expectant, as if you'd proved your point. "That must be why I wanted to come here. To find him again."

I took a deep breath. "It was just a dream, Gracie."

Your face clouded. "You don't believe me, do you, Mummy?"

I hesitated. "I believe you think you saw him, my love. But that doesn't make it real. You see? You were asleep."

You looked wounded. I set down my shopping bags and opened my arms to you but you turned away. I had disappointed you and it was unbearable but what else could I say?

"That isn't a real man." I spoke in a whisper. "Angels are"—I hesitated—"they're an idea. A lovely idea about goodness and the fact kind people are always more powerful than bad ones."

You frowned. "But I saw him."

"I know." It was cowardly of me but this wasn't the time. You were starting to get upset. "I know you did."

"You don't believe me."

"I do."

You gave me a skeptical look, clearly not convinced, and ran away into the deep shadows along the wall, touching your face and hands to the cool stone. I lowered myself onto a pew and sat too, shopping around my feet. It was a peaceful place. A place of prayer.

I sat quietly, thinking. The pews were worn and I imagined the grief, the despair, the loneliness people must have brought here over the years. It gave me a strange sense of connection, not with God but with all those other unknown women who had been before. Mothers who had lost daughters. Daughters who had lost mothers. I sighed. Even the stone flags under my feet were monuments to the dead, and I turned my head to read the engraving nearest me.

Anne Elizabeth McIntyre, Beloved wife and mother, Gone to Join Our Lord, May 12, 1831. Aged 54. Death thou art but another birth.

"There are several McIntyres. Anne's daughters, Beatrice and Mary, are both buried in the churchyard. And there's a memorial stone over there to her son, James. He was lost at sea."

I jumped. A woman of perhaps sixty had appeared beside me. She wore low-heeled soft shoes, shapeless black trousers, and a baggy black top with a clerical collar. A large wooden cross hung round her neck. She smiled.

"Sorry, did I startle you?"

I reached toward my bags. Vicars make me nervous. I had refused point blank to go to church as soon as I became a teenager. I don't see the point in discussing religion, especially with people who think they have all the answers, answers to unanswerable questions. It's never an honest conversation. All they want to do is prove that they're right and you, if you dare to disagree, are wrong.

She was still smiling. "I've disturbed you."

"Not at all. I just came in to get my daughter." I looked over to see what you were doing. You had settled quietly on the end of a pew, your legs swinging, humming to yourself. The vicar lifted her eyes to watch you for a moment, her face serene.

I pointed up at the multicolored angel. "May I ask you something? Who is that?"

She lowered herself heavily into the pew beside me. It

creaked under her weight. "That's St. Michael, the arch-angel."

I hesitated. I wanted to ask more but I didn't want to look ignorant.

"Is he slaying a snake?"

"The Devil himself." She smiled. "The Victorians were very literal. They liked drama. A different age."

"And what are we now?"

"Now? Ah." She looked thoughtful. "Skeptical, certainly. And very metaphorical. Not many people nowadays believe in a Devil with a forked tail and horns. Do you?"

I shook my head.

"Exactly. Neither do I. We're generally a more"—she paused—"conceptual age." She pointed back to the window. "The striking part is the raised lance, isn't it? The eye is drawn to it. But look at his other hand. See what he's holding?"

I narrowed my eyes. She was right; I hadn't noticed his left hand before. Old-fashioned weighing scales on chains hung from it.

"For weighing sin?"

"Good and evil. A symbol of justice. It's the other side of power. Something we're still apt to forget even today, I fear."

I smiled. Her manner put me at ease.

She held out her hand. "Angela Barker."

"Jennifer." Her grasp was firm. "And that's Gracie. My daughter."

"Ah. God's favor."

"Indeed." I'd read up on your name once we finally chose it, although Richard seemed more inspired by Grace Kelly than by anything spiritual.

You came running over and stood beside me, looking into the vicar's face with open interest.

"This is Angela," I said. "She works here, in this church."

You considered her. "I like the windows."

"They're special, aren't they?" Angela spoke to you evenly, as if to an equal. "They're very old."

"What's that?" You pointed to the cross round the vicar's neck.

"It's a cross. I always wear it."

"Why?"

"Come on now, Gracie." I reached for the shopping, embarrassed. "Let's go home."

Angela raised her hand. "That's OK." She leaned forward to you and spoke quietly. "It reminds me of something important that happened many years ago, before any of us were born. Of a very special man with amazing powers."

Your eyes gleamed. "The angel?" You twisted round and pointed back at St. Michael. "I've met him. When I had my accident."

"That's enough, Gracie." My voice was sharp, eager to get you out of there. "Come on." I held out my hand for you to take and said to Angela: "I am sorry. We'd better head home."

She looked intrigued, her eyes on your face as I steered you away. She heaved herself to her feet and walked with us to the great stone archway separating the entrance to the church from the modern café beyond.

"Lovely to meet you, Gracie. God bless you." She raised her eyes to me. "Come and see us again soon."

In the café, the young man was powering down his laptop and reaching for his coat. I crossed to the counter and picked up one of the leaflets about the church.

"How much are these?"

The young woman shrugged. "They're free."

I dug in my pocket, found a pound coin, and dropped it into the tip pot.

As we left, the elderly ladies lifted their heads again and their eyes followed you out. I suspected you were the liveliest person to visit St. Michael's for some time.

CHAPTER 16

"Do you know what we're going to do now, Gracie?"

I settled you down at the kitchen table with felt-tip pens and paper and a packet of multicolored tissue paper.

"You remember those colored windows you saw in the church? Let's make our own."

You set about working with me, watching as I drew a simple flower for you. I planned to cut the petals out of the paper and stick pieces of tissue paper across the holes. I'd done something similar one Christmas, years ago, when I was at primary school. It wasn't hard.

You crayoned with care the center of the flower, the leaves and the stem, your brow puckered and the end of your tongue sticking out between your lips.

I opened the leaflet up on the table. "That's the window, isn't it?"

You paused to look, considered. "He has a beard. But it still looks like him. My angel."

"He's called St. Michael." I tried to remember what I'd learned from my halting search on the Internet while you were eating your snack. "People have been drawing pictures of him for hundreds of years. He was probably based on a real man but he lived so long ago, no one really knows what's true and what's just made up, just stories."

You were crayoning again. "I know. He's my friend."

I didn't answer. I was trying hard to be patient but it was a growing struggle. I didn't know why the idea of an angel was tangled up in your head with the trauma you'd suffered. You were an intelligent child. Perhaps you'd heard people talking about your death and were trying, in your own way, to get the measure of that?

But St. Michael? A gaunt, bearded man in ancient robes, slaying the Devil? He had no place in your subconscious. None at all.

I looked at your head, bent forward over your picture. I was cutting green and red and blue tissue paper into petal shapes for you to stick on, once the coloring was finished. It was easier to talk when your hands were busy. That's why Richard and I had some of our most difficult conversations in the car when he was driving and neither of us could escape.

"It's not your fault, you know, Gracie. The accident. You do understand that, don't you?"

Red tissue paper, snip, snip. Out of the corner of my eye, I saw you look up, guarded, then turn back to your crayoning.

"Daddy and I were so worried about you, when you were in hospital."

The crayoning slowed. A pause. "Is that why Daddy cried?"

I took a deep breath. "Of course."

I picked up a sheet of blue tissue paper and started to

cut that. You sounded worried but your face was low over your drawing and I couldn't see your expression.

"That's looking lovely, Gracie." I couldn't even see, I just wanted to soothe you. "That yellow is so cheerful."

You didn't lift your head. I reached forward and scooped a clump of falling hair, tucked it behind your ear. Such soft, fine hair. Hairclips never stayed in place for long.

"I'll get some glue. When you've finished coloring, we'll cut out together and I'll show you how to stick tissue paper on the back so light shines through."

I knew you. You would talk if you wanted to. You never responded well to questions. I rummaged in the back of the kitchen drawer through blunt scissors and scattered paper clips and an unfolding ball of string until I found the glue.

You sat, eyes on my fingers, as I carefully cut out the paper panels and we started to stick on the tissue paper.

The window was almost finished when you suddenly said, in that way you had of launching a sudden remark from nowhere: "Was the accident Auntie Ella's fault?"

The breath caught in my throat. "Auntie Ella?"

You nodded. "She was very cross, Mummy."

My fingers fumbled the piece of tissue paper, stuck it crookedly.

"What makes you say that?"

Your eyes stayed on the petals.

"No, not red. Blue." Your voice had a tremor as you pointed to the next petal, ready to fight me. I gave in at once. You could do it any way you wanted; what did I care? All I wanted was to keep you talking.

Once we'd glued the blue one into place, you said: "She kept talking on the phone. She shouted. Screamy shouting. I heard."

I stopped, looked at you. That's what the woman in the café said, that she'd been arguing on the phone. I hadn't considered that you must have heard too.

"Gracie. This is important. When did she shout?"

You looked petulant, annoyed by my sudden change of mood, by the fact I was interrupting you at a crucial creative moment.

"In the car."

"But when?" My fingers trembled. "Before the accident?"

You nodded.

"Auntie Ella shouted on the phone?"

"Yes, Mummy. I already said."

I stared at you, imagining it. If she held the phone in one hand, she only had one hand on the wheel.

"You're spoiling it."

You pointed at the tissue paper, crushed between my fingers. I set the picture on the table and you fell to smearing glue along the edges, ready for the final panel. A prick of sweat ran along my hairline as I watched you.

"Gracie, what did Auntie Ella say, do you remember?"

You didn't answer at first. Your face was tight with concentration. You held up the yellow tissue paper for me to cut.

"She said: 'Go away. Stop it. Leave me alone.' Like that." You finally tore your eyes from the picture and looked up. Your eyes were mischievous. "That's not very polite, is it? She should have said please."

"Yes, she should have said please." My head spun. "Even silly grown-ups forget sometimes, when they get cross."

"Silly sausage." You smiled to yourself. "Silly banana."

I wrapped my arms round your small body and

squeezed you tightly, even as you struggled to pull away. I whispered into your neck. "I love you, Gracie."

You battled to extract yourself from me, brushed fallen hair from your cheeks, smoothed out the crumpled tissue paper and handed it to me. The sight of your sweet face, so serious, so intent, made my eyes swim. I blinked. I thought about what might have happened, about what so nearly did.

"I love you so much. You have no idea."

If you heard, you gave no sign of it. You were here, fully focused on the present.

I left you to squeeze the glue on your own, getting it everywhere. I just couldn't help. My hands shook in my lap. I sat, trembling, watching you and thinking about the accident, wondering who had made Ella shout down the phone that day. I knew now with absolute certainty that Ella was every bit as responsible for that crash as that poor girl.

CHAPTER 17

That night, you cried out in your sleep. I stumbled through to you. Your eyes were screwed closed but your face was contorted, your arms flailing.

I sat on the floor by your bed and stroked the hair from your hot face, whispered: "It's all right, Gracie. Mummy's here."

Wherever you were, lost in some dream, I couldn't reach you there. What business did a girl have with nightmares when she wasn't yet four years old? After a few minutes, when you still didn't settle, I sat you up. You reached out, still half-asleep, arms wide, to be lifted and I carried you through, your bear pressed between our chests, to my room. You lay in the middle of the bed, your compact body kicking and elbowing me as you made the space your own.

You opened your eyes, looked round at the shadows, and smiled, pleased.

"Mummy and Daddy's bed."

Just Mummy's bed now. I stroked your hair and you

curled yourself round your bear, your head on his back, and dropped again into sleep.

I looped an arm round your firm body and put my face against your neck. Your hair was soft and fine and smelled fresh. You should always sleep here with me. Why did you have your own bed now, anyway? What did it matter? I lay quietly in the darkness, listening to your slow, soft breathing beside me, feeling your warmth.

We argued about this too, Richard and I, when you were a baby. One of many arguments. I never thought, when I was pregnant with you, so full of joy, of hope, hands protective on my swollen stomach, relishing the sight of it, everything an expectant mother is supposed to be, that he'd have so many dogmatic opinions about childcare. I thought he'd leave all that to me; wasn't that what men were supposed to do? But he was a passionate father, determined to do everything right and someone else filled him with ideas, I was sure of it. Ella, perhaps. She was in the background all along; I know that now.

I reached out and stroked your cheek with my fingertips, wondering if you could sense me, even through sleep. He was fiercely opposed to "co-sleeping," as he called it. He said it was dangerous; we might smother you. We needed to set boundaries.

He wasn't the one breastfeeding every few hours. After you fed, you fell asleep against me, cuddled in the crook of my arm, your face against my warm skin, listening to my heartbeat. What could be more natural? It was the comfort and warmth all animals needed.

He ended up sleeping in the spare bedroom and moved his clothes into the wardrobe there so he could creep out to work early without disturbing us. I was glad. It put an end to the argument. There was no one to sigh and raise himself on an elbow and grimace when I brought you into bed to feed and kept you there. Was that very wrong? I went over and over it afterward, once it was all too late and he'd left and news broke of the wonderful Ella, glamourous, amazing Ella with her pert breasts and tight stomach, who wanted him in her bed all night, every night.

You were my daughter. Of course I was besotted with you. Of course you were my life. I thought he'd understand that. I thought he'd feel the same.

I was clasping you too tightly. You twisted and bucked in your sleep and kicked away from me to settle again in the empty ocean of the bed. I shifted my weight to move a little closer to you again. I didn't want to let you go. I wanted to feel the heat rising from your body through the Dalmatian pajamas you loved so much.

I lifted a finger and ran it gently over your hair. Ella, you said, screaming down the phone, just when she most needed her mind on the road. The thought of it, of your anxiety as you listened from the back seat, made me physically sick. *I should have been there. I should have protected you.*

I closed my eyes. An image swam up of your tiny pale body, stretched out on the hospital bed, pierced by tubes and needles. I sat up, shook it out of my head, and looked down at you now, sleeping beside me, your eyelids flickering as you dreamed.

CHAPTER 18

My mental image of the inside of police stations came from watching television dramas. Old-fashioned ones, mostly, full of dingy corridors leading to dark offices with shields mounted on the walls and heavy wooden desks with swivel chairs. And in some bright communal area, a large incident board, pinned with photographs of suspects, linked by pins and string and dotted with yellow sticky notes.

Our local police station wasn't like that. I'd walked past it a thousand times and never really noticed it until now. A 1980s multi-story office building with tall glass doors, all chrome and concrete. The young man on the ground floor reception desk looked dubiously at the business card.

"Is she expecting you?"

I stood my ground. "She told me to get in touch. Is she in?"

He narrowed his eyes, then hit a button on the phone box. His headset bobbed round his cheek.

He lowered his voice as he spoke into it. "There's a Jennifer Walker, ma'am. Yes, ma'am. Right away."

The police officer stood there in the lift lobby, waiting, as I emerged on the fourth floor.

"Mrs. Walker. How's Gracie?"

"Fully recovered. Thank goodness." I laughed nervously.

Her handshake was hard and her pace brisk as she led me past broad windows that showed an open-plan office beyond, two banks of desks crammed with people. It looked as soulless as a call center.

She ushered me into a small, bare room with a plastic-topped table and four metal-framed chairs and gestured to me to sit. The walls were beige and the only object on them was a metallic clock with black numerals. Five past eleven.

She pulled a second chair up to mine and sat, her feet flat on the ground and her legs apart. She was no taller than me but her brusque manner and her uniform made her thick-set and masculine and, although she made an attempt at a smile, the overall effect was intimidating.

"So, how can I help you?"

The window behind her faced down the high street. Everything looked different from this angle. The three-story rows of shops were low and poky. The red roof of a double-decker bus slid to a halt as the lights directly below changed to red and the small figures of pedestrians, two mothers pushing buggies, a stout middle-aged man, a willowy youth, an old lady walking with a stick, pressed forward from the edge of the pavement. It was the ragtag, anonymous public of which I was part, which she was here to protect.

"It's about the accident." I hesitated, feeling my way. "I've got new information. I thought you ought to know."

"OK." She nodded, her expression non-committal. "What's the information?"

I took out Ella's mobile phone and handed it to her. She looked it over, then raised her eyes, waited for me to say more.

"It's hers. See? Ella's."

I couldn't tell what she was thinking, but it was clear she didn't understand how significant this was. "It's Ms. Hicks's phone? Had she lost it?"

"Yes," I stuttered. She made me nervous. "I mean, she probably didn't tell you, did she? That she'd lost it?"

She shook her head. "No, I don't believe she did. Should she have?" She seemed at a loss. "Was it stolen?"

"No!" My words were thick with emotion as I struggled to make her understand. "It was at the scene of the accident."

She gave a slight sigh. "I'm sorry, Mrs. Walker. I'm not sure I understand."

I leaned forward, earnest. "It's evidence. Of what happened. I just thought, if there's an investigation, you might need it. It's evidence *against Ella*."

My voice sounded thin and insubstantial in the echoing acoustic of the small room.

Her eyes never left my face. "Evidence of what, exactly?"

"Of what really happened." I sat forward, my voice rising with my frustration. "It was left at the scene of the accident. A woman picked it up. She saw everything and she gave it to me."

"Why didn't she bring it to us, if she thought it was evidence?"

"I don't know." I looked down at my hands, clasped in my lap. "I don't think she realized how important it is. It shows, you see, that Ella was on the phone at the time of the crash. The call's logged." I pointed to the phone, willing her to take me seriously and to look for herself. "That proves it."

She didn't even blink. "Proves what?"

"That she was responsible too. For the accident. Yes, OK, that poor young woman veered across the road. But why didn't Ella react? Swerve to avoid her? Because she was on the phone. She was preoccupied. That's dangerous driving, right there."

Below, in the street, the lights changed a second time and the traffic slowed, stopped. A ragged line of pedestrians hurried across.

"Is that why you've come to see me?"

"Ella was shouting at someone. Angry. Telling them to leave her alone. Clearly she wasn't watching the road properly. The accident—that girl's death—Ella is to blame too."

She didn't answer. She just waited.

"That woman heard her. She's a witness. And so did Gracie, my daughter. She was right there. She saw everything."

She got to her feet. "I'm afraid I've got a lot of work to do."

I jumped up. "But you need to do something. If she was distracted—"

The police officer raised a hand to silence me. "These are very serious allegations. You should be careful."

"Me?" I blew out my cheeks. "She's the one who—"

"Mrs. Walker. The coroner has already given a verdict. Accidental death. The case is closed." She handed the phone back to me. "You might want to return this to Ms. Hicks as soon as possible, if it's her property."

I shook my head. "But two people heard—"

"Listen. First, even if this were a continuing investigation—which it is not—testimony from a traumatized three-year-old would not be reliable. Second, even if the timing of the call had matched the exact time of the accident, no coroner would have found Ms. Hicks responsible." She leaned in closer to me. "The post-mortem found that Ms. Parkes had excessive levels of alcohol in her blood at the time of the collision. She had a history of similar offenses."

I stared at her, my cheeks hot. "So you're not going to do anything?"

Her face was hard. "Such as?"

"I don't know. You're the police officer, not me. Prosecute her for dangerous driving. If Ella hadn't been distracted that young woman might still be alive today. Think of her family."

She turned away from me toward the window and her shoulders rose and fell as she breathed deeply. I waited, my legs juddering. When she turned back to me, her features were stony.

"Mrs. Walker, I understand you've been through a lot."

"She had my daughter in the back. She nearly died too. What if I'd lost her? Then what?"

"That's enough, Mrs. Walker." Her tone was icy.

"She wasn't watching the road. She was on the phone, shouting. How's it not her fault, at least—"

The police officer raised her hand and the look on her face silenced me. She shook her head, crossed the room, and opened the door for me to leave.

At the lift, she said: "I'm very sorry. But as far as the police are concerned, this is now over. Take my advice. Leave Ms. Hicks alone. Leave everyone alone. You have a lovely daughter. Go home and look after her."

The lift doors opened and I stepped inside. She reached in to press the button for the ground floor. By the time the doors slid shut, she had already turned back toward the soulless office.

Downstairs, I walked straight out into the street and stood at the crossing, waiting for the lights to change, wondering which unseen people might be watching me from above and trying hard not to cry.

CHAPTER 19

Ella

It's early evening and the drone of a male voice, leaking through from the sitting room, tells me Richard is watching the evening news while I cook pasta. My neck and shoulders still hurt from the accident and I move round the kitchen with stiff robot arms, laboriously turning my whole upper body to reach for things, instead of bending naturally.

Then the doorbell rings. I go. I assume it's that young offender who keeps trying to sell me tea towels and oven gloves or one of those charity workers who come door-to-door just when we're about to eat and opens with cheesy lines like: "Do you care about sick children?" If Richard goes, we'll never sit down to dinner.

So I open the door with a scowl on my face, to find two police officers standing there, the same pair who interviewed me in hospital.

"Ms. Hicks?" The female officer. Hatchet-faced. "May we come in?"

I hesitate for just a moment, wondering if I have a choice.

I decide that, as Richard would say, non-compliance might not be in the best interests of the client.

They loom large in the sitting room, looking round, taking it all in. Richard jumps up to switch off the television and straightens the newspapers into a pile as if untidiness might be used in evidence.

"Good evening." He goes into solicitor mode, all eager to please. "How can we help?"

The female officer sits down without being asked and turns to me. Her sidekick, the young Asian man, takes out a notebook and pencil.

"Ms. Hicks, we wondered if we could ask you a few more questions?"

I incline my head. In the kitchen, the pasta is no doubt turning to mulch but no isn't really an option. "About the accident?"

"Yes." She gives nothing away. "At the time of the accident, were you having a conversation on your mobile phone?"

No beating about the bush, just straight out with it.

I stall, feigning surprise: "Mobile phone?"

She isn't fooled. "We've interviewed a witness who says she heard you. She says you sounded angry."

"Ah." I make a big show of remembering. "I was cross with Gracie. That must be it. She was being a monkey in the back and I told her off."

The young man writes furiously in his notebook.

Her eyes are on mine. They narrow. "Just to clarify, you're saying you didn't take a phone call? Are you quite certain of that?"

I bite my lip a bit and try to look thoughtful. "I may have had a call earlier. Work stuff. But not then." I pause. "I'd have remembered."

I'm a damn good liar. There are two vital ingredients.

Consistency. In other words, stick to your story. And keep your cool.

Her eyes bore right through me and I see in an instant that we understand each other perfectly. She knows I'm lying and she knows I know she knows. The question is: What's she going to do about it?

"It's a very serious matter, Ms. Hicks." Her tone is dry. "A young woman is dead."

I look pained. "I know. Awful. I can't stop thinking about her."

Richard, always a soft touch, reaches for my hand and squeezes it.

The police officer's eyes are still on mine.

"If necessary, would you testify to that effect?" she says. "Under oath."

I nod. "Of course. Anything."

Richard shows them out. When he comes back, he puts his arm round me.

"All right?"

I don't answer.

"Thank God you weren't on the phone," he says. "That could've been really serious. Imagine."

The next day, Richard makes some calls and finds out that the inquest has already taken place. A verdict of accidental death. He seems puzzled. Why would the police come round and talk about testifying when the inquest is already over? I see at once. I know a warning when I see one. *We know exactly what happened, Ms. Hicks. Too late this time but watch your step.*

So that's it. I'm safe, after all. It wasn't fear of punishment that kept me awake at night. It was fear that, if all this came out, Richard would discover who it was who called me. And why.

CHAPTER 20

Jennifer

I opened the door to the babysitter and went upstairs to say goodbye to you. You smelled the guilt as soon as I walked in. I never went anywhere in the evenings. I hated leaving you with anyone else, now more than ever.

"Mummy!" You sat up in bed, your arms round your bear. Kitty and puppy and the rest of the menagerie were lined along the wall. A storybook lay open across your knees. You pointed. "Read this."

"Sweetheart, I've got to go. Dianne's here. Remember?"

You looked cross. "Why?"

"Because I'm going out for dinner."

"Why?"

"Because mummies have play dates too, sometimes."

You narrowed your eyes. "But I don't want you to."

I wavered for a moment, seeing you there, then thought how ridiculous I would sound if I tried to explain to Dianne, now settling herself in the sitting room, that I didn't have the willpower to leave you for a few hours.

"I'll ask Dianne if she'll come up and read you a story. Would you like that?"

No answer.

I kissed each of your toys and then you. "I love you, little Gracie. See you later."

You wrinkled your nose. "I'm not little."

As I reached the door, you added: "I don't like Dianne."

I sighed. "Gracie."

"What if she touches my railway?"

"I'll make sure she doesn't."

"Or my books?"

"Or your books."

"But you won't be here."

"Go to sleep." I inched out of the bedroom door. "Tell that bear all the things you did today."

I brushed my hair, pulled on a dress, and sprayed a little perfume. My hands trembled as I closed the front door, and my stomach churned. I wasn't sure if the nerves were about leaving you or meeting Matt.

As I got off the Tube and walked from the station to the restaurant, I started to feel sick. I tried to remember what I really knew about Matt. Not much. I hadn't had a date since Richard left. I just hadn't been interested, hadn't met anyone. My evenings were all TV dinners and early nights.

I hesitated in the street, scared of the bustle around me, of the women in high heels and short skirts who looked so fashionable and confident. My own dress, years old, seemed dowdy. I clutched my handbag and breathed heavily, in and out. After all this time, the rules must have changed. Maybe he'd expect sex if he bought me dinner. I wasn't ready for all that.

I stopped. It wasn't too late. I'd call him and make an excuse. Say you weren't well.

"Jenny!"

Matt, emerging from the restaurant a few doors down, had spotted me. He was wearing a well-cut blazer, his shirt open at the collar. That flop of fringe was pushed to one side. His eyes were amused.

"Are you OK?" He reached me, took my arm, led me forward into the tapas bar, which was teeming with music, with chatter. "It's a bit noisy down here." He leaned close to make himself heard and his aftershave came too. "I've got a table upstairs. Come on."

As I walked ahead of him, his hand hovered at the small of my back, guiding me through the crowd. Warm and strong.

He had chosen well. A corner table tucked into the broad windows, which gave onto the street below. A bottle of claret sat open beside wineglasses the size of goldfish bowls. Richard hated glasses like that. He said they were designed to make people drink too much. Up here, the clamor of the bar below was muted.

"I kept popping down to look for you," he said. "It's not the easiest place to find."

"You've been here before?" I was fishing, of course, angling for little pieces of his life so I could fit them together and understand him better. Always, with Matt, it felt as if there were pieces missing.

"It's my local." He smiled. "My flat's down the road, near the Tube. Small but central."

He poured us both wine and we clinked glasses. I tried to cross my legs, then uncrossed them, shuffled on my chair. I took a sip of wine, then another.

The claret was full-bodied and spread itself through my chest, down into my stomach, my legs. I let my shoulders fall an inch. The lights were low and a candle burned steadily in a glass holder. All around us, people chattered, ate, laughed. This was it then, being out. I had the sense of setting down a heavy burden, of emerging, lighter, from a cocoon. I was having dinner with a man who wasn't Richard. A man called Matt.

"So," he said, leaning across the table, "tell me something about yourself. Something about Jenny the person, not Jenny the mum."

I hesitated, trying to remember. It had been a long time since anyone asked about her.

Matt was a good listener and when I finally faltered, he picked up the conversation with ease, chatting about a film he'd seen at the weekend and the writers he enjoyed. We ordered half a dozen types of tapas to share but the restaurant seemed overwhelmed. The waitress brought us all sorts of things in a complete muddle, some we'd ordered and some we hadn't.

As time passed and the claret flowed, we gave up trying to sort it out with her and ate whatever arrived, making a game of guessing what it was. He made me laugh. I noticed too the way the waitress flirted with him as he teased her about the chaos and thought how attractive he was, how charming, and wondered why on earth he was bothering with me.

Later, as we waited for coffee, the conversation slowed. My head was thick with wine and my fingers clumsy. Downstairs, the bar was still raucous but the upstairs diners were more subdued.

"How's Gracie doing?"

I considered, pleating my napkin absently in my lap. "She's different."

"What do you mean? Tired? Clingy? She's probably still healing, even if it doesn't show."

"Not that." I paused. "She's said some bizarre things."

He looked surprised. "Like what?"

"Technically, Gracie died in the accident. I mean, they had to revive her." I steadied myself, struggling to explain. "Well, she says she went on a journey and there was a man waiting for her. An angel."

Matt didn't move a muscle; he just looked at me.

"I know it's weird." I swallowed. "The thing is, Gracie's adamant. I've tried talking to her about the fact angels don't really exist and she just gets upset."

Matt didn't reply. His eyes slid away from me, down to his hands.

"What?"

"What do you think?" he asked carefully.

I shrugged. "I'm not sure." I hesitated. "I think she really believes it's true. That it really happened and there are angels with halos and wings in the sky."

Matt looked out at the darkness. His reflection hung in the glass.

Finally he said: "It might be chemical."

"Chemical?"

He turned to face me. "Her body was in shock. The brain bleed was extensive. It may have caused a vivid hallucination." He paused, trying to gauge my reaction. "It's just a theory."

I considered. His voice was matter-of-fact and made it sound so plausible.

"It seems very real to her." I thought of your happiness when you saw the stained-glass window. "She talks about the angel as if he's her friend."

Matt pursed his lips. "Damage to brain tissue is complex. And it takes time to repair. It's possible, that when she's in a state of deep relaxation and her brain is processing information"—he shrugged—"well, it's perfectly possible she might have a secondary reaction."

"Really?" I shook my head.

A faint shadow of embarrassment crossed his face. "I mean, do you mind my asking, are you religious? Because I didn't mean to—"

"Not really." I said it too quickly. "I mean, I was christened, so I suppose if I was filling in a form, I might put Church of England, you know, but I haven't been to church for a long time. A very long time." I gave a quick nervous laugh. "And I never took it literally, Heaven up there and eternal hellfire down below and all that."

The coffee arrived and we sat in silence while the waitress set out our cups and milk and the cafetière. She tried to catch Matt's eye but he didn't notice her and she withdrew.

Matt poured the coffee and stirred in milk. I did the same. I was preoccupied, uncertain what I did believe.

"They're not uncommon, you know," he said.

"What aren't?"

"Out-of-body experiences. I've heard of them before from patients who've been clinically dead and then resuscitated."

I blinked. "What do they say?"

"There's a classic pattern. Tunnels, bright lights, a sense of detachment, then hurtling back into a rush of sensory experience, of bodily pain."

I stared. "That's what she said. She flew down a tunnel and the angel was there at the other end, waiting for her. In bright light."

He nodded. "There you are then."

I narrowed my eyes. My senses were befuddled with the wine and rich food. "So what are you saying, that people imagine it?"

"Not imagine it, exactly. I'm not saying they make it up. They may experience those sensations, those images, as brain function is compromised." He pulled a face. "I'm just saying, Gracie's far from the first to describe something like that."

I tutted. "I take it you're not religious."

"I'm a doctor. I treat the body." He hesitated. "But I try to respect what other people believe. When someone dies on the ward, a lot of nurses like to open the window so the soul can depart. Some of the doctors stop them. I don't."

I stared. "They think the soul flies out of the window?"

"Something like that." He shrugged. "People deal with death in their own way. There's no right or wrong about it. They do what they need to do."

I twisted in my chair to look out at the lights in the street below. The beams of brightness from passing cars. The pools spilling out from shop windows and bars. The dark mass of people, shuffling and jostling, shouting and laughing, down the crowded pavement. I lifted my eyes and had a fleeting image of Gracie's soul flying in a streak of light through the night sky.

"What are you thinking?"

His voice drew me back into the warmth.

"I don't know. I've been thinking about it such a lot. About why Gracie would say that if it isn't true. Where do people go when they die? My father. He died years ago. I don't believe in Heaven, in pearly gates. It makes no sense. But if I try to imagine him as dust, as not being, not existing, well, that doesn't make sense either. He was such a strong personality. He knew so much." I paused. "I don't understand where he went."

He reached out and put his hand over mine. It was kind and comforting and I stroked his long fingers.

"Were you very close to your father?"

No one had asked me about him for years. I opened my handbag and pulled out my wallet, opened it. There were two clear plastic pockets inside for photographs. On one side was a picture of you, my love, all bunches and a beaming smile. On the other there was a washed-out old Polaroid from decades ago. I'd found it in Mum's house when I was sorting through papers.

I looked about your age, three or four. We were posing by the Royal Pavilion at Brighton. I was in a cotton summer dress and strappy sandals. Mum and Dad stood together behind me, their hands protective on my shoulders. Their faces looked impossibly happy. Mum must have been barely thirty then, younger than I was now.

"He worked in a hospital too. Not a doctor though. A technician."

"He looks kind." He nodded, smiled. "And that's your mum?"

"She's still around." I paused. "Well, just about. Dementia."

He shook his head. "I'm sorry," he said simply.

Afterward, we set off together for the Tube, threading our way through the groups cascading onto the pavement from pubs and bars. He took my hand. I felt awkward at first, then relaxed into the warmth of his fingers, their firmness. It felt safe.

I had an acute sense of his body, now loosely attached to mine, of his breathing, of the muscles in his arms, his shoulders. I sensed the tension in my own body as it imagined being touched.

My mind raced ahead. He'd said his flat was close by. If he asked to come home with me, I'd say no. I rehearsed the words in my head: *I've had a wonderful evening,*

Matt, but it's a bit soon. I don't think I'm ready. And Gracie—

"There's something I wanted to say, Jenny." He slowed his steps and I kept pace with him, my eyes on our moving feet. "Look, I can see things haven't been easy. What with Gracie being ill. And Richard and everything."

My cheeks grew hot. My hand felt heavy in his.

"I really like you. This isn't just about Gracie. I want to get to know you properly, you know? If you like."

He seemed bashful. A different man from the confident doctor who strode down hospital corridors and swept me off for curry that night. I smiled in the darkness.

"It's been a while." I hesitated. "I nearly bottled out tonight, you know."

"I know." He looked round and we grinned at each other like fools for no good reason. "If I hadn't grabbed hold of you, you'd have run screaming the other way."

We'd almost reached the Tube. A bright cone of light flooded out into the street from the concourse. We both slowed our pace as we approached it.

"So where's the flat?" I paused to look.

On the far side of the road, just beyond the Tube station, a large square stretched into the darkness, bordered by railings. The trees rose tall and black against the night sky. It was surrounded by grand Georgian mansions.

He pointed down a much narrower street beyond the square. "Just down there. Second block on the left. Flat twenty-two."

"Handy."

"Not bad, as long as you don't want to swing any cats."

I wanted to see it. You learned a lot about someone from their home. But it also felt too much, too intimate, to suggest.

"Well," he said.

I opened my mouth, ready to give my prepared speech about not wanting to rush things, to take my time. I didn't need it.

"Thanks, Jenny. It's been a lovely evening."

"Thank you." I tried to sound casual. "It has."

He smiled down at me. "I bet we've both got an early start in the morning. Can I call you?"

I nodded. A moment later, he drew me to one side, out of the flow of passengers and into the shadows, cupped my chin with his hand, and touched his lips to mine, so softly I felt almost cheated. His cashmere coat brushed against my legs as he moved to walk away.

It was only then that I remembered something I'd meant to ask him.

"Matt!"

He turned back.

"Intensive care at Queen Mary's. What floor is it on?"

He looked surprised. "Pediatric ICU, where Gracie was? Five. Why?"

"Five." I nodded. "Thanks. I just couldn't remember."

He hesitated, considering, then added: "But Pediatric A&E is on four. She'd have gone there first."

He disappeared into the crowd. I went through the turnstiles and started down the escalator to the platform.

Four. That's exactly what you'd said.

CHAPTER 21

"Gracie! Stop it!"

You pulled at my hand like a dog straining on a lead.

"Please, Mummy."

We were coming back from the park and I was laden with shopping. My feet ached. I wanted to go home and have a cup of tea but you persisted, trying to drag me sideways off the high street toward the church.

"Please, Mummy. I want to see Mr. Michael."

"St. Michael." I wished I'd never told you his name. "He's not a real person, Gracie. You know that. He's pretend."

You understood the difference between real and pretend. Heaven knows, your small life was already filled with animals in books and cartoons who talked and rode bicycles and went to multi-species playgroups, with dolls who had tea parties and a stuffed bear who was your best friend. You believed in them but you also knew, at a different level, that it was play.

But now you frowned. "He isn't pretend."

I sighed. I knew you. You were tired and if I tried to force you home, you might just tantrum.

"Quickly then. Just for a minute."

You dashed off joyfully at once, darting ahead of me down to the railings and through the gate into the church-yard. I shook my head and plodded after you. It was a church. You were three. Whatever the reason for it, surely this fascination wouldn't last long?

The church was heady with the smell of flowers. Arrangements of lilies and roses bloomed alongside the altar and at the back of the church. The afterglow of a wedding, perhaps.

You went running to the front, the lights on the heels of your shoes flashing as they hit the stone flags. You stood for a moment beside the metal stand of votary candles, mesmerized by the three burning flames. Then you tipped back your head and looked up at the stained glass, at the robed man from another time and the vanquished serpent at his feet.

"Hello, Mr. Michael." Your voice was high and chirpy and full of warmth. I slipped into a pew close to the front where I could watch you.

When I was your age, it was Sunday school every week. Nothing too heavy. Pictures of angels with wings and God in Glory on clouds and the usual Bible stories in which Noah's Ark and the Good Samaritan dominated every year and there was a lot of coloring and sticking to fill in time before Communion when we could rejoin our parents.

I resented the older girls from school who were allowed to stay with the adults during the service. They lorded it over the rest of us because they were invited to take the bread and wine while we just lowered our heads for a blessing.

One by one, girls ahead of me got their white confirmation dresses and floated around in them, showing off the frills. At the altar, they placed their palms together in prayer, a far-away holiness in their eyes, glorying in their big moment. Later, the dresses were dyed red and worn to the school disco.

I didn't stay long enough to earn mine. I kicked up such a fuss about Sunday school that our family attendance dropped to a trickle, then finally stopped.

Now, I got to my feet and wandered through the empty church to the Lady Chapel off to the side. It was more intimate than the main body of the church, a miniature space with two short rows of pews and a simple crucifix on the altar. Vases of white lilies stood on either side. I sat for a moment and thought about your angel. He was there in the hospital, you said, watching. He saw me sticking back Minnie Mouse's ear. Trying to put things right.

I closed my eyes and tried to sense him. The chapel smelled of polish and I wondered who cleaned it. My mother used to rub down the woodwork at home every Saturday morning with a yellow duster and white wine vinegar. I used to make fun of her, said the house smelled like a fish and chip shop.

I thought of my father, how gentle he was. And humorous. Spending all day in a hospital lab looking at germs. My mother starched his long white lab coats every Saturday and ironed them on Sundays with my school blouses, hanging them all in a row along the back of the kitchen door. I was only thirteen when he went to work one morning, no sign of a weak heart, and never came home again.

I ran into the house from school that day, bursting with excitement because I'd been picked for the hockey team and stopped short in the kitchen, stunned by the sight of my mother, slumped at the kitchen table, her face red and swollen, a wet handkerchief balled in her hand.

A neighbor, Mrs. Tebbit, sat next to her. The teapot was on the table and they were using the wrong mugs.

"Now, Jennifer," Mrs. Tebbit said. "Mummy needs you to be a very brave girl."

"Why?" my mother said, and I felt she was asking me. "He was in a hospital. Why didn't they save him?"

Now, in the stillness of the church, a door banged. The door to the café, perhaps. I looked round to check on you. You were crouched on a flagstone, tracing the engraved letters with your finger and murmuring to yourself.

A prayer board hung at the back of the chapel and I stopped to read the cards. Poorly written, most of them, with spelling mistakes. *Thank you for many blessings. Please guide Gregory at this difficult time. God give Harry strength in his ill health. Prayers for Amy and Keith and family for God's help to bear their loss.* A child's loopy writing: *Please get Daddy a new job.*

On impulse, I took a card from the pile and wrote in neat block letters: *Please look after my dad.* I looked at what I'd written, felt ridiculous, crushed the card, and pushed it into my pocket. If he could see, he'd be laughing his head off.

I was just about to round you up and leave when the vicar, Angela, came into the church. She padded soundlessly on low, soft shoes.

"Hello again."

I nodded to her. You were sitting on a pew, swinging your legs and looking through a sheaf of notices. You seemed in a world of your own.

She pointed me to a pew and sat beside me, looking

forward but talking sideways. Her voice was low, not quite a whisper but never loud enough to disturb the dusty silence of the building.

"How are you?"

For a moment, I wondered if she mistook me for someone else.

"Very well, thank you."

A silence. "Have you lost someone?"

I started and she gave me a sudden quick look.

"That's what brings most people here. Loss of one sort or another. You looked so deep in thought."

"Did I?" I felt myself flush. "Well, my father, a long time ago. I was thinking about him."

"I'm so sorry." The big feet in their soft black shoes shuffled a little on the stone. "Shall we say a prayer?"

I could hardly say no. I was, after all, in her church. I couldn't explain that you'd dragged me there against my better judgment.

"What's your father's name?"

I hesitated. Again, I sensed that if he were watching—which I doubted—he would be scoffing. *Honestly, Jen. Look at yourself.*

"John."

I put my hands together in my lap and bowed my head and willed her to get it over with. I hardly listened as she murmured a short prayer. I was too busy wondering if you'd noticed what was happening, if you could hear, and how to explain it to you afterward.

"Were you very close?"

"I don't know." Images of my father crowded into my mind. Coming home in his lab coat, smelling of chemicals. Pottering at weekends in leather slippers. The back of his neck as he drove, towering over my mother at his side. His ruddy arms, sleeves rolled up, as he gardened. "I think so. He died when I was a child."

I expected her to come out with some comforting Bible verse or some chat about God working in mysterious ways. She didn't. She just sat quietly. The low hum of lorry and bus engines rose and fell between us.

"I keep thinking about him," I said. "Gracie had an accident, you see. She was in hospital. It's brought it all back." I swallowed. "I miss him."

"When my grandpa died," Angela said, "I tried to phone him in Heaven. Not from home. I thought it would cost too much. I saved up my pocket money and went to the phone box at the end of the street and dialed a random number. I thought God would guide my finger and put me through."

I turned to look at her, trying to imagine her as a child. "What happened?"

She smiled. "A man answered and I put the money in and of course it wasn't Grandpa at all; it was a complete stranger and he was very kind but I was so disappointed. I didn't forgive God for a long time."

You jumped down from the pew, glanced over at us, then wandered to the edge of the altar and plopped down onto a stray hassock there.

She too turned to look at you. "How's Gracie now?"

"OK." I hesitated. "She worries about dying. I mean, she asks me impossible questions, like whether I'll die. I don't know what to say."

"That's a tricky one." She turned to face me. "What do you tell her?"

I considered. "I flannel. I mean, of course I'll die. I can't say I won't. But I don't want to frighten her either."

"Ah."

In the café, someone called goodbye and a door slapped shut.

"I never lie to children," she said. "Sometimes it's surprising how much they understand."

I paused. "So what do you tell them?"

In Sunday school, they used to talk about God in white robes, sitting on a throne in Heaven with angels at His side. *Think of the most wonderful place you've ever been*, they used to say, *and it's even better than that, all the time.*

"I try not to be specific." She paused. "They need space to work it out for themselves. It's like explaining how big God is or how He can be everywhere at once."

I hadn't meant to talk so much, but she was such a good listener and the church felt a safe place and the words just came.

"My daughter was in a car crash. The other driver died. A young woman. Gracie nearly died too. Well, technically she did for a while. She's fine now. But she's convinced that she saw an angel after she died and"—I hesitated, looking up at the stained-glass window and the stiff, medieval figure of the saint with glowing halo, doing battle with a serpent—"and she thinks he looked like St. Michael. That's why she keeps wanting to come back here."

Angela sat very still at my side. "And what do you think?"

I exhaled, blowing breath noisily out of my cheeks. "My friend says it's chemical. Something to do with the way the brain heals."

She didn't reply.

"But one or two things she said...I don't know. Little things. Odd things. Things she couldn't have known."

It was a relief to talk, to talk to a stranger, to admit how confused I felt.

"I've never thought much about Heaven." I gave her a quick look. Her face was calm. "But it's bothering me, the way she talks about what happened. I don't understand it."

"Maybe you don't have to understand." She sounded thoughtful. "Maybe that's OK."

I lifted my head. "Really?"

"We only find answers when we're ready to hear them."

You jumped on and off the low altar step, glancing across at us from time to time. When I got to my feet, you came running over.

You climbed onto the pew and knelt next to Angela, looking her directly in the face.

"Hello."

"Hello, Gracie."

The two of you shared a smile. I sensed how comfortable she made you feel and felt a pang of exclusion.

"Come on, my love." I gathered together my bags. "Time to go."

I expected Angela to get up too, to make room for me to leave. She didn't.

"We have a small group here once a month." She hesitated, reading my face. "Older people mostly, but some younger ones too. Tea and cake and a chat. A lot of them have lost someone. You should come along."

"Oh, I couldn't, I mean, I don't think—" I stuttered, trying to not show how horrified I felt.

"It's very informal." She reached out a hand to pat my arm. "Do pop in. Even if you don't stay. It's eleven o'clock on Friday, in the café. The next one's on the eighteenth." Her expression suggested we'd somehow reached an agreement.

I blinked, feeling wrong-footed.

"Bless you, Jennifer. You won't regret it." She smiled. "For one thing, it's jolly good cake."

She pulled herself to her feet at last and moved sideways into the aisle to let me out.

As I moved on, she said: "See you on the eighteenth. Don't forget, will you?" Then, as we drew away from her, your hand now grasping mine, she said: "God sent you both here for a reason, Jennifer. I know He did."

I didn't answer. I just wanted to get the two of us out of there as quickly as possible.

CHAPTER 22

You were crayoning. Another one of your shining drawings, all yellow swirls. Your concentration was so fierce
that you didn't look up when I came to sit beside you at
the kitchen table.

"That's very bright." I pointed to the tiny stick figure in
the middle of the sun-storm. "Who's that?"

You frowned. "I can't do it."

I patted your shoulder. "Of course you can. You can do
anything."

"I can't." Your voice rose in a wail. You grabbed the
paper and screwed it into a ball, threw it across the table.

"That's a shame." I picked it up, smoothed it out on the
tabletop. "I like it. It has a lot of energy."

"No!" You were annoyed now. "I can't get it. The crayons aren't right."

I hesitated, not understanding. "Can't get what?"

"That place." You were beside yourself. "Where Mr.
Michael lives. I *told you*."

I didn't know what to say. All those drawings, the

worn-down yellow crayon, suddenly swam into focus. "That's what you're trying to draw?"

You gave me a look of contempt and climbed down from your chair, ran out into the sitting room. A moment later, a furious banging as you hit your toy bin with a stick. I sat quietly, looking at the scrunched drawing on the table and the deep scores in the paper from your furious strokes, your attempt to reproduce an atomic burst of light.

I left you for a while and waited until the banging subsided. Then I came through with a plastic pot of raisins and a beaker of milk and sat on the carpet with them. You came over to join me. Your movements were weary. You looked miserable.

You sat on my lap and I stroked your hair from your face. I handed you the milk and you drank without enthusiasm, painting a thin white mustache on your upper lip, then reached for the pot of raisins.

"Are you sad, sweetheart?" I sat with my arms round yours as you steadily munched. "Because of the accident?"

I hesitated, wondering if I was reading you correctly. You seemed restless and distressed, as if your emotions were too powerful for you to handle.

"It's OK, if you are. It was sad, what happened."

You were quiet for a little while. You were facing forward, away from me, and when you did finally speak, I didn't catch the words.

I leaned forward. "What was that?"

"Can we go to Venice?"

Your voice was a mumble and I strained to hear.

"Venice?"

"Is it a long way?"

You were making no sense. "Why do you want to go to Venice?"

You raised your head, your chin defiant. "Mr. Michael told me. That's where Catherine came from."

I shook my head. "Catherine?" I searched my mind for a girl called Catherine at nursery, in a story, in a television program.

You twisted round to look up at me, your eyes solemn. "Auntie Ella's little girl." You hesitated as if you were working something out. "Why don't she and Daddy ask me for sleepovers anymore? Are they cross with me?"

I tightened my arms round you. "Oh no, Gracie. You mustn't think that. Daddy does want you to have sleepovers." I hesitated, thinking of Richard. "He wants that very much. It's just that I love having you here with me."

You reached the end of the raisins and spent a moment using the tip of your finger to hook the last one from a corner of the pot. I sat quietly, puzzled, wondering where this story about Catherine had come from. Ella couldn't have children. Richard had made a point of explaining that to me when he first broke the news that he was leaving. He seemed to expect me to feel sorry for her, as if it were only fair that if I had you, she should be allowed to take him.

"She really liked me, Mummy. I cuddled her." You made a cradle with your arms. "Like this. She's teeny-weeny."

My mind raced. I thought of the neat stick figure, set in an explosion of light.

"And Auntie Ella's her mummy?"

You nodded. "So we're sort of sisters, aren't we?"

"But Auntie Ella hasn't got any children, Gracie. You know that."

You shrugged. "Mr. Michael says Ella sent her to him to look after because... because something bad happened so she couldn't stay with her mummy. He looks after lots of children."

I turned you round on my lap to face me, your legs astride mine, and held your arms, trying to force you to look at me.

"Gracie, my love, do you think this was another dream?"

"Stop it." You squirmed and lashed out at me, struggling to get free. "I met her! I did."

I tried to think of books with girls called Catherine that might have given you the idea. "What did she look like?"

You twisted away. "Red hair and a nice face." You considered this. "I said I wanted to take her home with me but Mr. Michael said I couldn't. But he said maybe I could see her in Venice. So can we go? Please?"

You looked relieved once you'd finished speaking, as if you'd transferred a weight from your shoulders to mine. You ran across to your books and began to pull them out and pore over them, picking through the pages.

I went through to the kitchen to make myself a cup of tea. I stood, dazed, leaning against the counter as the kettle boiled, watching you through the doorway. Catherine? I didn't know a child with that name. Neither did you. And why Venice?

Wherever this strange story had come from, you seemed instantly happier now you'd shared it. By the time I poured the tea, you were sitting by the toy bin, rifling through an assortment of hand puppets and a threadbare wooly sheep, chatting to yourself, lost already in your own world.

CHAPTER 23

"Daddy!"

You bounced on the bed, eyes shining, giddy with excitement.

Richard fell to his hands and knees on the carpet and crept over to you, starting your old game together. He'd called the following day, asking to come round after work and you were as pleased to see him as I was. You ran to jump on his back, clung on as he bucked and twisted and neighed.

The towel I was folding, still damp from your bath, hung limp in my hands as I watched. The two of you rolled about on the floor, Richard's shirt rising, showing the rounded flesh of his stomach above the waistband. Your eyes were joyful as you wrestled, as he swung you, ending with a bear hug.

You wriggled out of his arms.

"Take them off, Daddy!" You pointed at his shoes. "Take them off!"

"You sure about that?" Richard looked amused as

he pried them off, brandished his feet. "Stinky smelly socks."

I knew what you were thinking. Shoes meant he was about to leave. You wanted him to stay.

Richard read the bedtime story. The two of you cuddled up in the lumpy armchair, his broad, strong body curled round your smaller one. You rested your head against his arm, drowsy but safe. This was how it was meant to be, the three of us, cozy here in this home we bought together, made together. Richard looked happy as he held you, giving his all to the story. The strain eased from his face. He was never a handsome man. Not to other people. But he was kind and loving. And loyal, I'd thought.

Afterward, once we'd settled you with your bear and kitty cat and rabbit and the rest of the menagerie, his mood stayed thoughtful and a little sad. I watched as he kissed you good night, stroked your hair from your face. Maybe he did miss us. Maybe the accident had forced him to think how much he loved you and what he'd lost. Maybe visits like this reminded him of how happy we once were.

He followed me through to the kitchen, chewing the corner of his lips. He pulled on his jacket and I reached out and put a hand on the top of his arm, smiled.

"She's thrilled to see you."

He turned away, embarrassed.

"She loves you, Richard."

I had the sudden urge to say much more. To open up to him all over again. To say: *When I see you with her, I feel as if I still love you too, you do know that? Maybe it's not too late, after all. If you've realized what a mistake you've made. If you want to ask my forgiveness and ask if we can start again* . . .

He mumbled: "I love her too."

I turned to the bottle of red wine, open on the counter from the previous night, and poured two glasses, handed him one. He came through to the sitting room with me, his wine in one hand and his shoes bunched in the other, and perched on the edge of the settee.

"So." His eyes strayed to the vase of roses on the mantelpiece. Matt had sent them, to say thank you for our date. I'd made sure they were prominently displayed; I couldn't help it. "How are things?"

I shrugged, settled into an armchair across from him. "OK. You know."

"Not missing work?"

"Not really." I bent down to pick up a stray piece of Lego on the carpet. I wasn't going to admit to him that I worried about money. I'd be earning again soon enough. "Gracie keeps me busy. She seemed to need me more now. Since the accident."

He bent over and started to loosen his shoelaces, push on his heavy shoes. "She'll be off to school soon."

"She will." The house would be so quiet all day without her. So tidy. "I'll miss her terribly."

He finished with his shoes and sat stiffly, sipping his wine. His awkwardness was all the sadder because he was once so at ease here.

"Has she ever talked to you about Venice?"

He didn't look as if he were listening.

"She says she wants to go. I just wondered where it came from."

Richard shrugged. "A story?"

"We've never read a story about Venice. Don't you think it's odd?" I went to the table at the far end of the room where clutter gathered and picked up one of your pictures to show him.

"Look." I held it out. It was one of your yellow light drawings, small dark figures set in a landscape of brilliance. "She keeps drawing these. She says it's where she went when she had the accident."

Richard glanced at it. "She's always liked coloring."

"It's more than that." I paused. "It's weird. She seems to... know things. And she keeps talking about death and what happens when people die. Maybe she ought to see someone. Like a child psychologist."

He looked tired. His cheeks were soft pouches and the flesh below his chin was slack round the bone. When we first met, he was a lean young man, hungry in every sense, keen to make his mark on the world. That was a long time ago.

I put the picture down. "I just thought you'd be interested."

Richard leaned forward, cradling his glass. "I think she's fine, Jen. Really. Let her be."

"*Let her be*?" I looked up, stung.

He shook his head. "I just mean—" He looked as if he wished he hadn't spoken. "Maybe she needs her own space. Don't overanalyze everything."

We sat awkwardly for a few moments, Richard staring into his wine.

"What's that supposed to mean?"

He sighed. "Forget it, Jen. Really."

He got to his feet, set down the glass. For a moment, he looked about to leave, then he crossed to stand at the window, looking out into the darkness. His reflection in the glass was ghostly.

"I want to see Gracie more often."

His tone was suddenly formal. I steadied myself.

"Not just here. Not just a story at bedtime and the odd

day out." He paused. "I want to take her properly again. For weekends. Maybe on holiday."

He turned to face me. He spoke quickly but gently, as if he'd already practiced the words, as if he was relieved to get them out.

"I know you've been through a lot. We all have. You've wanted to cling to Gracie since, you know, the accident. But she's my daughter too. You need to let go a bit, Jen."

My pulse quickened. "It's her, isn't it? Ella."

"What is?" He sounded cross. "Why I want access to my own daughter? It's nothing to do with her."

It was everything to do with her. I didn't trust her. I took a deep breath.

"The accident was partly her fault too, you know. Ella was on the phone when the car swerved. Did you know that? Shouting. She was distracted."

He made a guttural sound. "God help me."

"It's true. Gracie told me."

"You should hear yourself."

He moved away from me, toward the door.

"Gracie's your daughter. You can see her." I got to my feet, grabbed at his arm. "But not *her.*"

"That's ridiculous." He shook his head. "She adores Gracie. And Gracie loves her. You should see them together. Honestly—"

"Oh please." I bit my lip, steadied myself. "I don't want her anywhere near Gracie. I don't like her. I don't trust her."

"She told me not to come." He pried my fingers off his jacket. Our faces were close and for a second, I thought he was going to kiss me. Then he pulled away.

"I'm filing for divorce, Jen. I'm sorry. Ella and I want to get married. You understand?" He paused, reading my face. "She's going to be part of Gracie's life from now on. Whether you like it or not."

He disappeared into the hall. I wanted to follow him but I couldn't move. The sitting room seemed suddenly very cold. I found the edge of the armchair and sat on the arm with a bump.

Richard strode back in, buttoning his coat. His face was tight.

"I'm trying to do this the nice way, Jen. But if you make this difficult, I'll go to court. I'll have no choice. Don't make me."

I couldn't answer.

A moment later, the front door banged as he let himself out. I sat quietly, perched there on the edge of the chair, my feet juddering on the carpet, listening to his footsteps fade in the street. I reached for my glass, drank off a gulp of wine.

It was over. He was going to marry her. She was taking Richard from me and she wanted you too. My stomach tightened. I bent over, one arm clutching my front. A dribble of wine slipped out from the bowl of the tilted glass and ran down my leg. The smell rose at once, rich and lush. I shook my head, thinking of you asleep upstairs. I'd nearly lost you once, my love. I wasn't going to lose you again.

CHAPTER 24

Ella

There's something about me that Richard struggles to understand. I'm not even sure I understand it myself.

He's kind, you see. And fundamentally, he's happy. And I'm not sure that I ever can be.

I'm in love with him. That's not an issue. Before I met him, I didn't think this battered old heart of mine was capable of it, but it's proved me wrong. But it's precisely *because* I love him so much that I'm afraid of being with him. That's the part he can't grasp. I'm afraid of corrupting him, you see. Like a virus.

My mother used to say that some people were born to be happy and some weren't and if you were one of the unlucky ones, there wasn't a whole lot you could do about it. It went through me like a knife when she said that.

I was eight years old and we had just walked past our local crazy man in the street. I don't know what his name was, but everyone knew him by sight. He stamped along the pavements and waved his arms about and muttered expletives to himself and shouted in shops for no reason.

We all knew to steer clear. And here was my mother saying that a life of happiness or unhappiness was determined at birth. That frightened me to death. I knew which she was and I didn't want to be the same.

My mother didn't have a bad life, but something deep inside her was broken and whatever I did, however hard I tried, I couldn't fix her.

One of my clearest memories of childhood, perhaps my first, is of my mother sitting at the bottom of the stairs and crying, her face buried in her hands, her shoulders shaking. Silent, like an old film. I must have been three or four. I was terrified and the worst of all was that there was absolutely nothing I could do.

I sat beside her and wrapped my arms round her leg and tried to give her a cuddle but she didn't seem to notice me. After a while, she pulled away and disappeared into the kitchen and I sat there a few moments longer, miserable, listening to her blow her nose, then light the gas and fill a pan with water, carrying on like the martyr she always was.

The hall was poky and there was no fitted carpet, just a shabby rug. Cold air came up from the cellar between the floorboards and made me shiver. But I stuck it out for a while. It was an instinctive offering, a bargain with God. I made a lot of deals with God as a child. *I'll suffer this cold if you sort out my mum.* He couldn't. She was born to be unhappy. *What if I'm the same?*

It took a while for me to feel strong again, after the car accident. The physical aches, of course, but also the shock. I love little Gracie, how could anyone not? If she hadn't come through . . . well, it doesn't bear thinking about. I don't know how I'd have lived with myself. I'm tough, but I am human, whatever her crazy mother thinks.

Then, one Saturday morning, I was leaving my yoga class when Richard called me on my new phone. It was a relief to have a new number, believe me. Well worth the hassle. Suddenly, for the first time in a long time, the only calls I was getting were from Richard or close friends. Calls I actually wanted.

"Where are you?" Richard sounded stressed. "Fancy a drink in the park?"

A bit odd, but why not?

We sat huddled together on a bench and he produced sangria in a screw-top bottle. He'd mixed it himself at home and brought proper glasses and everything. I should have realized something was up. One of my favorite love songs is about a couple drinking sangria in the park, just hanging out, happy together. Richard is so thoughtful, it's overwhelming.

So we drank the sangria and watched the ducks on the pond. And the kids. A small girl with wild eyes wobbled as she struggled to ride her bike. Her father ran along behind, steadying the frame, cheering when she finally pedaled off on her own. A toddler, still unsteady on her feet, tried to throw bread to the ducks but dropped most of it. I looked away.

Richard's cheeks were flushed. The sangria had gone to his head. He got to his feet, packed away the bottle, and wrapped the glasses carefully in a kitchen towel. That care, that attention to detail, made me smile.

"Right," he said, straightening up. "Lunch. Shall we try the Chinese over there?"

I smiled. "You hate Chinese food. You always say it's greasy."

"You like it." He shrugged. "They do dim sum. Come on. I'll be fine."

He'd planned the whole thing. I only found that out afterward when, halfway through the meal, the waiter brought a single spring roll on a plate and Richard started fussing, pushed it toward me.

"That's yours."

"I didn't order spring rolls." I stared at it. One spring roll? What kind of order was that? I picked up the plate and handed it back to the waiter. "Sorry. Wrong table."

The guy shrugged, looked across at Richard.

"Leave it. Thanks."

I pulled a face. "Richard, it's not mine. I didn't—"

"Please. Ella. I ordered it. For you."

I stared at him as he reached forward, picked up the spring roll with his chopsticks, and held the end to my mouth.

"Try it."

I steadied his hand—he was never very good with chopsticks—and bit into the end, humoring him. My teeth touched metal and I sprang back.

"What the—Richard, there's something in it."

I was thinking: a bolt or a screw or who knew what. Then I saw his face. Excited, anxious, beseeching. I felt sudden panic as light dawned.

"It isn't . . . ?"

He gave a sheepish smile, pulled open the doughy wrapper, and lifted out a ring. A damn great solitaire, sticky with sauce. Before I could stop him, he'd scraped back his chair and was down on one knee, right there in the middle of the restaurant.

"Ella. I love you so much. Please. Will you do me the honor of marrying me?"

The whole restaurant was looking. I couldn't speak. His eyes were so full of love, of hope, I couldn't bear it.

"Get up."

"Ella?" He looked uncertain. "You haven't given me an answer."

"Of course I will!" My heart thudded, blood surged in my ears. I don't know what I felt. Overwhelmed, for sure. Embarrassed. And panicked. "Now get up."

He beamed, shuffled forward, and pressed the warm, wet ring onto my finger, then kissed me lightly on the lips, a discreet, public kiss. When he sat back on his chair, the waiters, watching in a huddle from the service area, gave a ragged round of applause.

I shook my head. "I can't believe you just did that."

Richard reached for my shaking hand. The ring slid, unfamiliar, down my finger.

"It's an auspicious date today." The tension that had hung about him all morning was gone. He looked happy. "They helped me choose it. The eighth, super-lucky, apparently."

"Really?" I didn't know what more to say. I thought of Richard in a jeweler's shop, picking out the ring. Coming to the restaurant and planning the spring roll surprise. I thought I knew everything about him but I didn't. I couldn't look him in the eye.

Later, as we lay together in bed, the ring, washed now, sparkled on my bedside table.

"Richard, are you sure about this?" I asked him. "I mean, really?"

"Totally, absolutely, one hundred percent." He tightened his arms round me. "I love you, Ella. I want to make you happy."

That's what chilled me. It brought back that memory of my mother, crying at the bottom of the stairs, and my three- or four-year-old self, chilled to the bone, striking a bargain with God that He never kept, and the terror, which had never left me since, that maybe I was the same as her and the same as the crazy man who yelled in shops, and that maybe there were people like Richard who were born to be happy in this world and I was simply not one of them.

CHAPTER 25

Jennifer

As well as sending flowers, Matt phoned every night that week. Sometimes he was at work and we only managed a quick chat. Other nights, we talked for an hour or more. He discussed articles he'd read in the paper and the new film he wanted to see and told me about the homeless man, Barney, who sat on the pavement near the hospital holding a cardboard sign reading "Smile!" Matt picked up a cappuccino for him on his way in, when he bought his own coffee. Barney was very exact: skinny cappuccino, two sugars.

And when Matt wasn't talking, he listened. I wasn't used to anyone showing interest in me, in my day, in my opinions. It took me a while to get used to it. He teased me when I hesitated before answering or asked him: "Really? Do you really want to know?"

We arranged to go out again that weekend, for a quick dinner and then a film. I was still nervous but excited too. I counted down to it. Planning what to say, what to wear. And then, that afternoon, Dianne called—my one and only decent babysitter—and said she was so sorry, she had flu.

I texted Matt to cancel. *V sorry. Another night?*

He texted straight back. *Tonite! Can I cook at yrs?*

I stared at the screen. I was flattered, I admit it. He seemed determined to see me. But I couldn't imagine him cooking in my kitchen.

Another text appeared. *I'll bring it all. OK?*

He arrived just after seven, earlier than I expected. The spillage from your egg on toast was congealing on the front of my blouse, my hair was in clumps, and I was only halfway through reading you a bedtime story.

He carried a bulging gym bag into the kitchen and swung it onto a chair. The zip was open at one end, showing groceries.

I hesitated. I wasn't sure I wanted to leave him alone in the kitchen, in our home.

"I'm not quite ready."

He nodded. "That's OK. There's just a few things I need."

He ran through a list: weighing scales, cheese grater, knives, saucepan, wooden spoon. He looked over each item as I rooted it out of a cupboard or drawer, then lined them up in a neat row along the back of the kitchen worktop. He bent over to peer at the cooker, trying the ignition button to check that the hobs lit.

"Fine. Leave me to it." He looked directly at me for the first time since he'd come in, gave me one of his disarming smiles, then turned away again, opened his bag, and drew out ingredients with his long fingers. A packet of Gruyère cheese. Parmesan. Roquefort. Fresh pasta. He placed everything on the counter with precision.

He saw me watching and said: "I hope you like cheese."

"Mummy!" Your voice, from upstairs, was shrill.

Black pepper. Double cream. A bottle of mineral

water, then a bottle of red wine. Valpolicella. He really
had brought everything.

"I'm fine," he said. "Really."

You were sitting up in bed, your arms round your bear.
Other cuddly toys jumbled along the wall. A pile of picture books sprawled across your knees. You handed me
the one we'd been reading.

"Where were we?"

"Has he come? Is he downstairs?"

"If you mean Matt, yes, he is. He's going to cook
Mummy's dinner."

You looked thoughtful. "Why?"

I shrugged, opened the book. "Because Mummy's
hungry. Now, let's see what happens, shall we?"

I curled on the bed beside you and put my arm round
your shoulders and you leaned in, your head against the
soft pad of my arm. I started to read.

"Is he a doctor?"

I broke off, looked down at you. "Matt? Yes. In the
hospital. Remember?"

I went back to the book. Your expression was preoccupied for a while, as if you were thinking this over. Finally,
your attention returned to the story.

When we reached the end, you cuddled down with
your bear and I tucked you in.

"Good night, my love."

A faint clatter of pans from downstairs. The rising
smell of garlic.

"Where's Grandpa, Mummy?"

"Grandpa?" I reached out and stroked your soft hair. "I
don't really know. I think he's having a long sleep."

You hesitated, considering. "If I go to sleep, will I
see him?"

"You might. If you dream."

You lifted your head from your bear, your face creased. "What if it's a bad dream?"

"Then shout out and I'll come upstairs and chase it away."

You smiled, pulled your bear close again, and put your head on its stomach.

I got up. As I crept away toward the door, you said: "Matt won't play with my railway, will he?"

"I'll make sure he doesn't."

"Promise?"

"I promise. Now go to sleep."

I gave myself ten minutes to brush my hair, change my blouse, spray a little perfume.

Downstairs, Matt was in full swing. He'd taken my apron from its hook on the back of the door. It was so short on him that it barely covered his groin, slightly absurd where it strained round his waist and yet endearing. He was standing at the stove, tossing spaghetti in sauce with the wooden spoon in one hand and a salad server in the other. The tiles at the back of the cooker were splattered. The kitchen was warm with steam, rich with cheese, with garlic, with homeliness.

He looked round, used his forearm to brush his mop of a fringe out of his eyes.

"Glass of wine?" He gestured to the worktop.

The Valpolicella was open, breathing. Two wine-glasses sat beside it. He must have found them in the end cupboard, a dumping ground for things I didn't use. They had broad rims and colored green stems. A Christmas present, years ago, when Richard and I were still a couple and people bought everything in pairs.

"I'd pour you one but I'm just—" Matt's hands rose

and fell as he tossed the spaghetti on the hob. Whatever he was doing, it looked complicated. I poured us both an inch of wine and hovered there, warming it in my hands. He'd rolled back his sleeves and the muscles in his forearms bulged as he worked. I leaned back against the counter, admiring them. He looked like a TV chef, all confidence and quick, competent movements.

"I'm nearly done. Five more minutes and it goes in the oven." He nodded to one of my casserole dishes, greased and ready beside him. "You go and sit down. I'll be through in a minute."

I sat on the settee and crossed my legs, then, self-conscious, got up again and moved to one of the arm-chairs instead. I sipped the wine, looked through to the kitchen. Matt bent over the casserole, spooning the pasta, then tipping up the pan and scraping out what was left.

The wine tasted rich and full. The oven door closed. The kitchen tap ran in a furious stream. *My God, he even washed up.* I sat very still. It had been so long since some-one had cooked for me, I could barely remember how it felt. It was a relief to have someone else take control.

"Everything OK?"

He stood in the doorway, wiping his hands on the apron. I opened my mouth to ask him to use a towel, then closed it again.

"I think so. All quiet upstairs."

He pulled off my apron, came through with his glass. "You read a good story."

I must have looked baffled because he pointed to the monitor. Of course. I'd forgotten. He must have heard every word.

"One of life's joys," I said to the mantelpiece. "Reading stories."

He perched on the arm of the settee with the air of a man who had his mind on the oven. "I heard her ask about her grandpa."

"My dad. She asks about him sometimes. Wonders where he is."

"Ah."

"It's not easy, being three. Life, death, what happens to people. She's got a lot to figure out at the moment." I hesitated. "And it'll be divorce, next."

"Divorce?"

A long pause. "Richard's putting pressure on. We're not actually divorced, you see, just separated. I suppose I always thought maybe—" I felt my mouth twist and stopped, studied the carpet, then took a few breaths. "He and . . ." I couldn't say her name out loud. "Anyway, he says he wants to marry her."

My breathing sounded loud in the room.

Finally, Matt said: "How does that feel?"

"Not great." I looked into my glass, my stomach tight. "But, you know, what can I do? If that's what he wants."

After a while, I dared to raise my eyes and found him watching me. His expression was gentle.

"You really try, don't you? To do the right thing."

"I try." I lifted the glass to my mouth but didn't drink, lowered it again. "I don't seem to manage very well."

A piece of green Lego lay under the table. A scrap of torn paper. A raisin.

The alarm on Matt's watch went off and he fiddled with it.

"Saved by the bell."

"Not at all." He gestured toward the kitchen, got to his feet. "I'll be five minutes."

I sat in silence and thought how strange all this was,

how little I knew this man and yet how much I felt understood by him. Noises drifted through from the kitchen as he bustled about in there. It was peculiar to hear another person clattering my dishes, opening and closing my cupboards and drawers.

Finally, he appeared in the doorway and called me through. I entered the kitchen and stopped in my tracks. It looked like someone else's kitchen, a happier one, full of life and warmth.

The kitchen table, usually so grubby, was covered with a fresh white linen cloth. He'd set it for two with the Royal Derby crockery. It was a wedding present from Richard's mother and kept in the cupboard for special occasions, which meant it hadn't been used for years. Linen serviettes, pleated restaurant-style, stood upright on the side plates.

"Have I done the wrong thing?" His hands were in my oven gloves. He stood, poised, by the oven door, his eyes on my face. "I hope I haven't—"

I shook my head. "No, it's just—" He'd made such an effort. For a moment, I thought I might cry.

"Come on. My cooking's not that bad."

I crossed to the table, set down my empty glass, and sat, my hands clumsy and large in my lap. He bustled round me, serving his pasta with a flourish. The top was crusty with baked cheese.

"It smells wonderful."

He reached over and re-filled my glass.

"I love cooking," he said. "Well, I love eating. Maybe that's it."

He wound spaghetti in the bowl of his spoon like a pro. "Anyway, I didn't want to miss seeing you this evening. I was looking forward to it too much."

I concentrated on eating, my eyes on my plate.

"I thought we could still watch a film later, if you like? I brought some videos..."

I shook my head in disbelief. "You think of everything, don't you?"

He looked pleased. "Maybe not everything."

He started to talk about an experimental play at The National. He'd seen it at the weekend, he said. Very Ionesco. It was a name I remembered from my English degree but hadn't thought of since. The only theater Richard liked was Noël Coward.

Matt sat back in his chair, inhabiting the space as if it were his own kitchen, his own home. His hands drew pictures in the air as he talked. I wondered who'd been to the theater with him or if he'd gone alone. He didn't say.

The sight of him, here in my kitchen, was a wonder to me. When he leaned back, he almost touched the fridge, which was empty apart from Diet Coke and TV dinners and plastic containers of preschooler food. It was decorated on the outside with crayoned pictures fastened in clumps by magnets showing faraway places. Places I had dreamt of visiting before you came along, before I married Richard.

When he got to his feet to offer seconds, I suddenly said: "It must seem dull to you."

He looked round, eyebrows raised: "What must?"

"All this." I hesitated, embarrassed. "Living with a three-year-old and never going out."

He shook his head, brought the hot dish back to the table to spoon out more.

"You do go out."

"Not much. I used to." The rising steam made the kitchen shimmer. "I used to go to the theater, to the cinema. I used to have friends, you know. I was a normal human being. But then—"

"I know. I get it, Jen." He dropped a spoon of pasta onto my plate and smiled. "I think you're amazing. You adore Gracie. Of course you do. Of course she comes first. And anyway, it won't be forever."

"What won't?"

"Just"—he hesitated—"the way things are at the moment."

"What do you mean?" I just wanted Matt to keep talking, to find out what he thought about me.

He twisted his fork in the spaghetti and started to eat again.

"You do what you have to do. That's all. I take the long view." He waved his fork in a sweep of the kitchen. "It's a privilege to be here. Don't you see? We'll go to the cinema another day."

He sounded as if he'd really thought about it. His tone was so gentle, so thoughtful, that my eyes moistened and I had to bite down on my lip.

I stared down at my plate. "OK, but I do wonder why you're bothering."

"Then I can't explain." He sat beside me at the table. "Now, make me happy. Finish your pasta."

Later, he produced dessert. Two slices of chocolate cake, the upmarket type that you buy by the slice in a patisserie.

As we ate it, I asked him more about his work. He seemed more comfortable talking about the shift system and the quirks of his colleagues than about actual cases.

"It must be hard," I said. "Working with sick children."

I thought of you, such a tiny scrap of a person, lying on that hospital bed, all tubes and machines. I didn't know how anyone could bear that, day in, day out.

"You just have to be professional." His tone was sad. "It

has its rewards." He paused and seemed to retreat into a memory. "Some children respond dramatically once you hit on the right treatment. It seems miraculous, sometimes. And the look on their parents' faces when that happens..." He smiled to himself.

"They must adore you."

He gave me a sideways look. "Let's just say, I get a lot of whiskey at Christmas."

"And single mums eager to meet after hours?"

"One or two." He raised his eyebrows. "Even dads, once in a while."

I laughed. "I've been meaning to ask you something. Why can't I find you on the Internet? Haven't you written any cutting-edge research papers or anything?"

He pulled a face. "You've been looking? I'm flattered."

I tutted. "Don't tell me you've never searched for me."

He spread his hands. "Of course. But what did I find? Just some stuff you'd written about personal development and setting goals. No scandal at all."

"I could have told you that." I narrowed my eyes. "The hospital website's useless—everything is password-protected."

"You tried?"

"Of course. I wanted to read up about you."

He laughed. "They've got a terrible photo of me up there. Doesn't do me justice at all."

"Still, I'd like to see it."

He shrugged. "The hospital worries about giving out information about doctors. And they're probably right. It's better to keep a low profile."

He was looking past me, toward the darkness of the garden.

"Why?"

"Some cases are very painful. You know?" He finished his dinner and set down his knife and fork.

I sat back in my chair, watching him, waiting.

"There was a little girl last year. Bernadette. Bernie, they called her. She was perfect—blond curly hair, long eyelashes, you can imagine." He paused.

"What was wrong with her?"

"Meningitis. I had her transferred to ICU in a matter of hours but she deteriorated so rapidly, there wasn't much we could do."

"How awful."

He got to his feet, gathered up our plates, and clattered them as he stacked the dishwasher.

"Anyway, let's move on." When he turned back to me, his face was resolutely cheerful. "Time for a film?"

I made coffee and carried it through to the sitting room. He handed me the films to look through.

I was still reading the covers when Matt leaned over and touched the corner of my mouth with his finger, lifting a stray flake of chocolate. He held it to my lips to eat and, without thinking about it, I took the tip of his finger in my mouth too and drew on it. He froze. I sensed the tension in him, the tremble in his muscles. I shivered and reached again with my mouth for his finger and drew on it a little more firmly, teasing the tip by making a warm circle with my tongue.

He lifted the videos from my hands and set them on the coffee table, then opened his arms to me. His mouth was firm and moist and tasted of chocolate and, as it closed on mine, I was the one grabbing at him, reaching my arms round his broad back to clutch at the folds of his shirt, hurrying him along even as he tried to steady me. He eased me backward onto the settee and lifted my shirt, put his strong hands on my hips and kissed his way slowly between them. I arched my back and sucked in my stomach.

He lifted his head. "Just relax." He looked more closely, arrested by something in my expression. "Is it too soon?" He hesitated. "Should we stop?"

Stop? He had to be joking. Suddenly, lulled by wine and good food, my problem wasn't uncertainty; it was frustration. It had been a long time. Richard and I hardly bothered with sex after you were born. With the new lumpen look of my pouched stomach and fallen breasts, I didn't think I could ever feel desirable again.

Matt was studying me, his eyes intense. "I want to look after you, Jenny. You know that?"

"Do you?" I blinked.

"We're two of a kind," he whispered, "you and I. You feel it too, don't you? We're good together."

He turned his face back to my stomach and I felt the warmth of his tongue on my skin. After a few minutes, he unbuttoned my jeans, slipped them down to my knees and, pinning me there, pressed his mouth between my legs.

I sank back into the settee and groaned. Images rose and fell through the alcohol in my head—the sensible black panties I'd put on that morning and which he was now peeling away, the rough wool of the rug in my parents' house where my first serious boyfriend, Jimmy Brent, had taken my virginity when I was eighteen, and you, my love, lying on this same settee on my chest, downy haired and smelling of milk and the most perfect, beautiful creature I had ever imagined.

When I couldn't bear it any longer, I pushed him off and scrambled to unbuckle his belt, tug at his jeans. He lifted himself on top of me and we rocked together, creaking the settee springs. The clock chimed on the mantelpiece and I counted with it as far as three and then gave up.

I clung to Matt's shoulders, his back, as if I were pulling myself out of a pit, out of hellfire itself, and when I came, I heard myself cry out "God in Heaven!" and then struggled through the fog to remember who had said that, close in my ear, whose voice was it, before remembering it was Richard, there in the hospital, when you came back to me in a rush of life and I fell into his arms, surrounded by rushing doctors and beeping machines. My God in Heaven.

"Are you all right?" Matt's voice was breathy in my ear.

His weight, collapsed on top of me now, pressed the air from my chest and it was a relief to be crushed. I didn't have the power to answer him. I lay with my face in his neck, shuddering, sloppy with crying, coming back to myself from whatever place he'd taken me, limp and ready to sink into sleep against him.

He raised himself on his arms to look down at me. Cool air flooded in.

"Are you OK?"

I nodded, wiped a hand across my eyes, and settled him beside me, lying tightly together on the settee, arms wrapped round each other to stop ourselves rolling off onto the floor and buried my face in the sour-sweet smell of his neck as my breathing slowly slackened.

CHAPTER 26

I woke up in darkness with a stiff neck and a dry mouth. Your blanket, which usually lay across the back of the armchair, had been unfolded and spread over my waist. The settee creaked as I moved and remembered where I was, what had happened. I was alone on the settee and lay still for a moment, listening.

A rustle of movement. I lifted my head. No sign of Matt. The kitchen was dark. The noise came again. A creaking sound, coming from the monitor, from your bedroom.

I pulled myself to my feet, and put on the panties and jeans that still lay in a heap on the carpet. Matt's clothes had gone. I peered at the clock. Twenty past twelve. It felt later. The road outside was silent. I knew every rickety floorboard, every creaking joint in that house. Heaven knows, I'd spent enough hours creeping round it in darkness, first when I was pregnant and restless at night, sneaking down for bowls of cereal at two in the morning, then, once you came to join us, the blur of day and night as you fed and cried at all hours.

The only sound as I made my way with care up the stairs and across the landing to your bedroom was the pump of blood in my ears. I always kept the door ajar so I could easily check on you. I slid through the doorway and stood for a moment, adjusting to the deeper darkness of your bedroom with its heavy curtains and blackout blind.

My hand flew to my mouth. The black shape of a figure, a man, was solid in the armchair by your bed. Silent and still, hunched forward in the shadows.

I whispered, without thinking: "Richard?"

"It's me." He rose to his feet, quietly crossed the room. "Matt."

I stared, then felt a sudden surge of anger. "What the hell are you doing?"

He looked embarrassed. I pointed to the door and stood there, glaring at him as he left, then went to check on you. You were on your back, sound asleep, your arms sprawled above your head, your hair wild on the sheet. I stroked your cheek, my fingers trembling, tucked the duvet round you, and headed back downstairs.

He was standing in the middle of the sitting room. He strode across as I entered, put his hands on my shoulders. His eyes were apologetic.

"I'm so sorry. I was looking for the bathroom. I saw the door ajar and I went in to check on her." His eyes, on mine, were anxious. "I didn't mean to intrude. I'm sorry."

I was still shaking. I thought of him, sitting silently in the darkness beside you. "How long were you there?"

"Not long." He hesitated. "Ten minutes, maybe. I didn't mean any harm."

He hung his head and looked down into the lattice of his fingers. A long silence. The clock chimed half past.

"I miss Katy." His voice was quiet.

"Your daughter?" I sat down in the armchair across from him, my eyes on his face. My hands were tense and I folded them in my lap. He didn't look threatening. He looked defeated.

"She's seven now."

I sat on in the silence, waiting, willing him to explain.

"It didn't end well. She—Katy's mother—she was very depressed after the birth and started taking anti-depressants. They weren't good for her. She had a"—he hesitated—"a sort of breakdown."

"What happened?"

He looked exhausted. "She became really paranoid. I could see it was the medication but she wouldn't believe it, she wouldn't listen to me. She imagined all kinds of things. That I was undermining her all the time. Once someone says that, it's hard to carry on. Her parents were sympathetic, they could see what was happening, but it was hard for them too."

I went to sit beside him, put my arm round his shoulders. "That's awful."

He leaned in toward me and let out a deep sigh.

"Well, anyway, she ended up leaving and taking Katy with her. She was four at the time, not much older than Gracie is now."

"Was there someone else?"

"No." He shrugged. "Not that I know of. She just said she wasn't happy. You know, the usual stuff. She wanted her space, thought she'd be better off alone."

"And what about Katy?"

"She doesn't let me see her."

I frowned. "She can't stop you, can she?"

He blew out his cheeks. I thought how gentle he was with you, how he made you laugh. He'd be a devoted father, I could tell.

"You're her father. You have rights too."

"Through the courts?" He sighed, shook his head. "Not easy. She was never diagnosed with anything, just baby blues. And family courts, well, they tend to side with mothers, not fathers. My brother, Geoff, is a policeman, a detective. He talked to a few people. A lot would come down to her word against mine."

He hesitated, his face tight. "I just don't think I could face it."

"So you don't see her at all?"

He shook his head, ran his hands over his face.

"I get snippets of news about Katy. She's learning the violin. Doing well at school. She would, she's bright. Our mothers speak to each other, once in a while. They're Katy's grandmas, after all. But that's it."

I stared at the shadows on the wall, the reflections through the curtains from the streetlights. He was such a caring man, so kind. I thought of the way he'd comforted me when you were so ill, helped me to pick myself up again.

"Is that what brings you here? Because Gracie reminds you of her, of Katy?"

He shook his head. "You bring me here. The way you are, the way you love Gracie. My ex was never like that. Never like you."

He turned to me, opened his arms, and drew me to him. His breath was warm in my hair. "I'm sorry. I wanted to talk about it earlier. I suppose, if I've seemed a bit cautious... well, the timing never seemed right."

I nodded. It had felt as if a piece were missing. Now I had it.

"You must miss her terribly."

"Not my ex. I hated her for a while. Not anymore. But

Katy—" He paused. "It's hard. Hard for me. Of course I miss her. It tears me apart. But I try to tell myself not to be selfish. If I went into battle with her mum, kicked up a fuss, what would that do to her? Kids can't cope with all that. It's confusing."

He paused. He turned away from me as if he were wrestling with himself and didn't want me to see.

"But I try to keep some sort of contact. I send her presents, you know, for Christmas and her birthday. But I don't know what she has, what she likes. I don't even know if she gets them." He paused. "Or if she even remembers me."

"That's terrible."

His jaw was clamped shut and I saw his struggle to collect himself before he could speak again. "Perhaps that's why I understand a little bit of what you're going through. You can't bear the thought of anything happening to Gracie. I see that. I suppose I can't bear the fact I lost Katy, in a different way."

I hesitated, tried to imagine it. "Maybe, one day."

"Maybe." He nodded but his face was without hope. "I think that, sometimes."

"I'm so sorry. I don't know what to say." I reached out and stroked his cheek. "And I'm sorry I was angry. It was just—"

"You were right to be. I should have explained."

He shrugged on his coat.

"I should go. Get some proper sleep."

In the hall, we kissed and it was a new kiss, less electric and a little sadder, as if we knew each other differently as a result not just of the sex we'd shared but because of what he'd told me.

Before I crawled into bed, I came into your room and

sat there in the armchair. My eyes slowly adjusted to the darkness. I tried to see it all through his eyes. The framed pictures on the walls, old-fashioned scenes from nursery rhymes: Humpty Dumpty tottering on a wall, a fine lady on a white horse, the princess and the little nut tree. The shelves of stuffed toys and storybooks. The creams and wipes and thermometer and bottles of medicine lined up on the top shelf, out of your reach.

You were curled round now, your arms clutching your bear. I leaned forward until I could hear your soft breathing, so close that I could smell your hair, your skin.

I tried to imagine it. To imagine Richard taking Gracie away from me and never being allowed to see her, to hold her. I thought of Matt going alone into toy shops twice a year, into department stores, struggling to choose presents for a little girl he no longer knew. Not knowing if she opened them.

He was right. I couldn't bear to lose you. You weren't just what made life worth living. You were my life.

CHAPTER 27

The next couple of weeks were pleasantly warm and we spent our afternoons at the park. I pushed you on the swing or bounced up and down at the other end of the seesaw or played hide-and-seek in the bushes.

You were far more fun to be with than the other mothers and nannies who sat with hunched shoulders on the benches, gossiping and drinking their takeaway coffees. As I listened to your giggle and looked at your lovely, laughing face, for the first time in a long time, I felt truly happy.

I still worried about you. Some nights, I lay awake in bed until late, watching the shadows of passing cars swing across the walls and worrying about everything you'd said. About Mr. Michael. About Catherine, your imaginary friend with red hair. But at other times, during the day, my breathing eased. You were my life and now, tangled up with us both, there was Matt too.

He had made himself a regular fixture. We went out often—to dinner, to the theater, to the cinema. Once or twice, to cut back on babysitting, he came round to cook. The days varied to match his rota but that didn't matter to me. I was always here.

We found ourselves in that mad, heady phase of falling in love when we couldn't get enough of each other, couldn't stop talking, could barely tear ourselves away each evening. Was it like this with Richard, at the beginning? It must have been but I couldn't remember it.

Slowly, Matt began a battle to win you over too. At the weekend, he sometimes took us both out. For an afternoon on a steam railway, run by volunteers. To a fun fair with a mini-carousel and dodgems. To a new petting zoo. He always had a surprise in his bag when we met up: a chocolate bear or a packet of sweets or a small toy. You seemed to love him as much as I did.

Some evenings, you specifically asked, as I tucked you up with your bear and kissed you good night: "Are you seeing Uncle Matt?" Your voice was excited, as if you were pleased for me.

I didn't push it. I wasn't sure how you'd feel if he stayed all night and was still here at breakfast. Besides, I quite enjoyed the fact that we parted like teenagers in the small hours, sexed up and crumpled, sleepily kissing good night at the door. Somehow it was more romantic than waking up side by side in the morning with bad breath and messy hair. The time for that would come soon enough.

But through it all, the memories of the strange things you'd said just wouldn't go away.

"Can I talk to you about something? It's bothering me."

We were lying on the sitting room floor in each other's arms, post-dinner, post-sex, under a throw. Matt's body was strong and warm and smelled pleasantly of fresh sweat.

He tipped back his head to look at me. "What?"

"This is going to sound mad. OK?"

"OK."

"Gracie says she met a little girl, that time she went off and saw an angel. Mr. Michael."

"When she was"—he hesitated—"unconscious?"

"Yes." I swallowed. "She calls her Catherine. Says she's got ginger hair. Anyway, she said she was Ella's daughter, you know, Richard's girlfriend? I thought that was odd because she can't have children. Richard told me."

Matt tensed. "Does Gracie know that?"

"I think so. She does now." I paused. "And there's something else. She said Ella sent Catherine to St. Michael."

Matt gave me a sharp look. "What's that supposed to mean?"

"I don't know." I paused. "Gracie's very intuitive. I wonder if she's picked up on something. Maybe a sense that Ella doesn't like children. Doesn't like her around. And this is her way of telling me." I considered. "After all, what sort of mother wouldn't do anything to hang on to her own child?"

"Not one like you." He lifted his hand and stroked the line of my chin. "You're an amazing mum."

"I don't know about that." I kissed his fingers. "Weird though, isn't it?"

"Very."

"Why would she say that?"

He lifted himself onto his elbow and looked down at me. His chin was dark with stubble. "How much do you know about Ella?"

"Not much. Not really." I swallowed, tried to put my sense of foreboding into words. "I keep thinking . . . maybe this is Gracie's way of warning me."

He studied my expression. "Warning you about what?"

"That she doesn't feel Ella wants her. Maybe doesn't even feel safe with her."

He nodded. "You're really worried, aren't you?"

"Maybe I'm being stupid." I hesitated. "But why would Gracie make it up? What if she's right? If Ella does resent her being around? How can I let her spend weekends with them if I'm not sure?"

He kissed the tip of my nose. "Richard's her father. He might not be a very good one, I mean, given what happened between you two. But he's good with Gracie, isn't he?"

I nodded, thinking of them horsing around, having fun.

"So he's got a right to see her, hasn't he?" His voice was gentle. I thought of his situation, denied access to his daughter. It was cruel.

"He has." I paused. "But she hasn't."

His eyes were on mine, watching me. I saw my face reflected there, pinched and anxious.

"I don't trust her. What if she's unkind to Gracie, as a way of getting back at me?"

He hesitated. "Why would she want to do that?"

I shrugged. There was hatred between Ella and me, there always had been, but I didn't know how to put it into words. "I just don't trust her."

He sat up. "You really feel threatened by her, don't you?"

I nodded miserably.

"But you know what Gracie's saying makes no sense. If Ella can't have children."

I sat up beside him, thinking. "Is there any way of finding out?"

"If she's infertile?" He looked baffled.

"Not that exactly. If she's had a child. If Catherine could possibly be real."

He widened his eyes. I reached out, put my hand on his shoulder and stroked it. "You're a doctor. Can't you get access to birth records or hospital records or something?"

He frowned, looked away. I sensed his unease.

"Please? Just to put my mind at rest."

He didn't answer for a moment, then turned back and kissed me lightly on the lips. "It's not exactly ethical. But if it means that much to you, I suppose I could try."

He wrapped his arms round me and pulled me close to him. When he spoke, his breath was warm on my neck. "I'd do anything for you, Jen. You must know that by now. Anything."

He got to his feet, padded through to the kitchen, and came back with a pen and a piece of paper.

"Write down what you know about Ella and I'll check the NHS database. And I'll ask Geoff too. He owes me a favor."

"Your brother?" The police officer.

"Keep it to yourself, won't you?" He gave me a sharp look. "He shouldn't really." He paused. "Well, neither should I."

He pushed the paper into his pocket, kneeled on the floor in front of me, and stroked his hand down my thigh. I felt better already, less alone.

"Try not to think about it," he said. "Until we know a bit more. Can you?"

*   *   *

Later, as he gathered together his clothes and got ready to leave, he said: "I was thinking. Maybe we could go away somewhere fun for a weekend. The three of us."

I hesitated, trying to imagine it. "Where?"

He shrugged. "What do you think? Euro Disney?"

"Gracie really wants to go to Venice." I thought of your eager face, asking where it was. "Something about meeting this imaginary girl again."

He laughed. "Is that what she said? Love it." He was still smiling. "Hate to break it to you but it sounds to me as if she's having you on."

I frowned. "You think so?"

He nodded. "Not in a bad way. Kids do that. She's a smart girl. She picks up on things. Maybe she's heard about Venice somewhere and thinks that's her best chance of getting you to take her."

I wasn't convinced. You always struck me as such an honest child. "Maybe."

"Gracie'd love Euro Disney. She hasn't been, has she? Well, then. We could take the Eurostar, stay a couple of nights."

He smiled down at me and I tried to smile back. I wasn't convinced. Once you got an idea in your head, there was no moving you.

"Or a posh hotel here, if you like? A country house with an indoor pool for Gracie and open countryside."

I couldn't answer. He drew me closer and kissed the top of my head, rocked me for a moment in his arms. Suddenly, he pulled away and looked me in the face.

"You really want to take her to Venice, don't you?"

I nodded. I was embarrassed. It felt ungrateful, but I really did. I thought it might settle you, lay all this to rest.

"Well, it is a great city." He hesitated, looking down at me. "If it'll make you happy, then sure. Let's go."

"Really?" I buried my face into the warm, musky creases of his neck and hugged him. "Thank you." Here was a man willing to love me and Gracie too. As if she were his own.

"She'll love it." He drew back. Our faces were almost touching. "All those boat trips. The world's best pizza. Ice cream. No cars."

When I kissed him, his lips smelled of coffee and red wine.

At the door, as he pulled on his coat, he said: "Let's do it. I'm serious. Not this weekend—I'm on call—but the one after that."

"About the cost...I mean, is Venice expensive?"

He put his hands on my shoulders, kissed me lightly on the lips. "My treat. Doctor's orders. OK?"

He was gone before I had the chance to argue, leaving me standing there, heavy with wine and food and sex.

In the kitchen, I cleared away and stacked the cutlery, the plates, mugs, and wineglasses in the dishwasher. My movements were slow. My body still carried the feel of his fingers, his mouth. I saw my reflection in the dark window and lifted a hand to rake through my disheveled hair. My cheeks were flushed and my eyes looked wide and brighter than they had for a long time. Since Richard left and I thought I was finished with all this.

I leaned over to sling the empty wine bottle in the recycling and, as I moved, I saw a sudden streak of light behind me, reflected in the dark glass. I spun round. Nothing but a shadowy, empty kitchen.

I gripped the edge of the sink and leaned into it to catch my breath. I closed my eyes. I was tired, that was

all. It was nothing. It must have been a shaft of light that
bounced off the curve of the bottle.

But as I steadied myself, my fingers trembled with a
more visceral feeling. A feeling that something of my
father was there in the quietness with me, watching as I
bowed my head and gathered my strength.

Venice, he seemed to say. *Beware, my child. Beware
what you may find.*

CHAPTER 28

Ella

Richard's buoyant this evening. He comes rushing home to drop news at my feet, a dog bringing a stick to its master, tail wagging, eyes imploring, desperate to be stroked. He starts before he even takes off his coat.

"Guess what? She's seeing someone."

No need to say her name. She haunts us like Banquo.

I pull a languid face, acting cynical. I try to make him laugh, when he talks about her. There's no point in discussing her any other way. Richard knows full well what I think. He should toughen up, not let her manipulate him the way she does.

"Whoopity-doo. Some desperate single parent she met at nursery? I can just see him. Paunchy, balding, his wife died and he's all sad and lonely. Don't tell me: His little Ermentrude and Gracie are best friends?"

Richard smiles, shakes his head. "Someone she met at the hospital. And it sounds serious. He's taking her to Venice next weekend. Gracie too."

I start, putting my hand to my stomach, feeling

suddenly sick. He doesn't see. He's too busy unbuttoning his coat, hanging it in the hall, heading through to the kitchen to fix us both gin and tonic.

"What's for dinner?"

He lifts the lid of the pan on the stove and smells the Bolognese sauce, sticks a spoon into it, and turns to me as he tastes. I am leaning against the doorway. My face says too much.

"You all right?"

"What's his name?"

"She did say . . ." He frowns, trying to remember. "Why?"

I can't answer. He moves round the cupboards, pulling out glasses, adding ice, pouring gin. The new bottle of tonic cascades in a fizzing plume over his hands when he opens it and he swears, dashes to the sink, looks down, cross, at the spray across his trousers.

When he's mopped them with a tea towel, he comes over, hands me a drink. I gulp it.

"Mark? Mike?" Already he's heading past me toward the sitting room and the lure of the television news. Over his shoulder, he adds: "Good luck to him, I say. I hope they're very happy. Now maybe she'll leave us alone." He considers. "Just as long as Gracie likes him." Then, his tone slightly wounded as he settles on the settee: "Anyway, thought you'd be pleased."

I don't know how I get through dinner. I can barely eat, but he doesn't seem to notice, he's too focused on the crisis in the Middle East or Sudan or wherever the hell it is. I don't care.

All I can think is: *it's him. It must be. And she has no idea*.

Later, I run a long bath and take the radio into the

bathroom with me. I turn it up loud and lie flat and low in the landscape of bursting bubbles, my hair floating in tendrils round my head, the oval mask of my face just protruding above the water.

My breathing is shallow and quick. I try to press myself down into the smooth, hard plastic of the bath, to hide myself away. I'm afraid to close my eyes. I'm afraid of the darkness that waits for me there, that draws me always back to Venice and the dreadful days there I've struggled so hard to forget.

CHAPTER 29

Jennifer

"It's amazing, Matt." I stand in a daze at the long windows. "It's unreal."

The louvered shutters are fastened back, revealing the broad sweep of the Grand Canal in Venice. The sunlight glimmers and gleams in streaks across the moving water below, stirred into life by a dozen boats of all sizes, passing at all speeds. A low breeze carries the tang of brine. Voices call, distant, soft with lilting Italian. On the far side, the fabric of the tall, thin buildings that face ours is crumbling with age.

Matt, coming up behind me, slips his arms round my waist and kisses the top of my head.

"See that big dome, there on the left?" He lifts a hand to point. "On that spit of land, sticking out into the water. That's Santa Maria della Salute. One of the plague churches. Sixteen something."

I crane to see. "Plague churches?"

His breath is warm in my hair. "It came on the ships. Decimated the population. Anyone who showed signs of it was shipped out to an isolated island, out there in the lagoon. Rather a brutal sort of quarantine but it worked. When it was over, the survivors built churches to thank God. That's one of them."

I twist round to him. "How do you know all this stuff?"

He smiles and lowers his face, touching the tip of his nose to mine.

You run in from the adjoining room, eyes shining, and throw yourself between us.

"Mummy, come on!" You tug at my hand, pull me after you into the small second bedroom. Bear sits on the pillow, propped up by pink satin cushions. An oil painting, an old-fashioned scene of a regatta on the Grand Canal, with the Rialto in the background, hangs grandly over the bed. Your shoes, already kicked off, lie on a sheepskin rug. Your coat is abandoned on an antique chair with a plush red seat and gilded wooden back.

I smile to myself. "Do you like Venice?"

You nod, jump onto the bed, and bounce there. "It's springy."

I wonder how much of this you'll even remember.

"We must say a big thank-you to Uncle Matt. Remember? This is his treat."

I look round at the antique furniture. The walnut wardrobes with ornately carved doors and gold handles. The polished side tables with spindly legs. The mirrors with massive frames, which bounce reflections of the sunshine from one to another across the room. Heaven knows what it all cost. Matt just waved me away when I offered to pay our share.

"Can we go out?" You're on your feet again, manic with excitement. "Can we?"

I nod. "Let's go and explore."

*   *   *

That first afternoon, Matt takes us to a café in St. Mark's Square and we sit right there at the edge of the piazza, gazing out across the vastness of the square toward the basilica. A string quartet plays behind us, fighting against the noise of declaiming tour guides and the chatter of tourists. Matt orders drinks in Italian from a waiter.

When the glasses arrive, you point past your cloudy lemonade to our glasses, your forehead crumpled with interest.

"Fizzy orange." You look at me. "Is that yours?"

"They're spritzers." Matt lifts his glass to show you. Light pours through the glass, turning the color to fire. "They're for grown-ups. Don't think you'd like them."

I take a sip. Sparkling white wine and water, ice cold. And another taste too within that, something bitter.

"What's the orange?"

"Ah. A secret ingredient, known only to Venetians." He leans closer as if he's confiding a great truth. "Aperol."

We share a smile, just from the pleasure of being there, together. The sun throws shards from the marble surfaces around us, bouncing off the expanse of paving stones. I fumble in my bag, find my sunglasses, and put them on.

You watch, then ask: "Are we on holiday?"

"Yes, my love. We certainly are."

You look out across the square. Small children totter there, reaching for pigeons. Older ones, closer to your age, chase them, sending them scattering into the air in a flurry of feathers, only to settle again a little farther away. Here and there, hawkers sell snacks and ice creams and cold drinks. Distantly, their cries drift across: *Panini! Gelati! Bibite!* To the right, at the foot of the Campanile, tour groups cluster, waiting for guides who hold aloft flags or furled umbrellas.

You break in: "Can I go and play?"

I look at Matt, unsure.

"Of course." He points. "Just stay in this big square, OK? Where we can see you."

"OK." You slip down from your chair and set off, a tiny figure running out into the vastness of the piazza, as count-less small children have done before you and will do in years to come.

"She'll be fine. No traffic." Matt reaches for my hand, there on the table, and covers it with his own. "Happy?"

I nod. "It's amazing, Matt. I can't believe it."

"It's special, isn't it?" He looks grave. "I love this place. It's either a miracle of faith or a miracle of engineering, depending on your point of view."

"What do you mean?"

"Look at it. Look at what they built on a swamp. All this, here where we're sitting, it's resting on a bed of nails. Tree trunks, thousands of them, driven into the lagoon. That's all that's holding us up."

I laugh. "Really?"

"The Venetians are a pragmatic lot." He grins. "Smart and self-sufficient. They have a saying here: 'Venetian first, Italian second.' They stick together. That's how they've survived this long."

A hawker skirts the café tables, showing off the tour-ist souvenirs crammed onto his cart. Postcards. Glossy brochures of Venice in half a dozen languages. A string of brightly colored plastic masks with curved beaks and streaks of glitter down the cheeks. We watch him pass.

"We should come next year," Matt said. "For the carni-val. *Carnivale*. It's all about masks. Disguise." He draws his fingers across his eyes, play-acting. "Here you can be anyone you like. Do anything you like."

I raise my eyebrows. He leans forward and kisses me. His mouth is soft and the kiss makes my body ache for him. Tonight will be our first proper night together. The first time we share a bed like a normal couple. Fall asleep together and wake in the morning in each other's arms.

He says in a low voice: "Thank you for saying yes—for agreeing to come."

"I'm the one to say thank you." I wave at the piazza, at the drinks. "All this."

He shrugs. "If we're going to do it, might as well do it properly."

Out on the square, you've befriended another child and the two of you run in wild circles in the sunshine, chasing each other, lacing an invisible thread back and forth through the crowd. Even from here, I feel your excitement, your sense of freedom.

I pause, wondering if it's the right time for an awkward question. I sip the spritzer.

"You said you'd been before?"

He looks away into the middle distance, slow to answer. My stomach contracts. I can't leave it there. "Holiday?"

Finally, he turns back to me, lifts my hand from the tabletop, and encases it in his own. *Here it comes.* I have a sudden urge to lean back, to pull my hand away.

"I came here several times but ages ago. A good friend at medical school, she was Venetian. Maria-Eletta. There aren't many of them left, true Venetians. They've all moved out. She came from a very old family, been here for centuries. Very proud."

He twists and makes a vague gesture back toward our hotel and the Grand Canal.

"They have an amazing old house on the Grand Canal, farther down than us. Been in the family for generations.

All high ceilings and antiques and sweeping staircases. The bedrooms had tiny wrought-iron balconies over the water. We used to sit there for hours and drink coffee or these"—he points at the drinks—"and just let the world slide by. You know what it's like when you're young. You think you're immortal."

I don't answer. He seems lost in the memory of it. Of her.

"The house had a particular smell. I don't know if I can describe it." He hesitates. "Our hotel's got it too. A sort of worn, fusty smell of age and salt water and crumbling walls."

I sit quietly, absorbing this, thinking of the old houses opposite our hotel with their decaying brickwork and imagining Maria-Eletta. A lover, presumably. A brilliant young doctor with the romantic soul of a true Venetian. I wonder again, for the hundredth time, why he's bothering with me.

"What happened to her?"

He pulls a face. "She came back. We lost touch."

He lifts my hand to his lips and kisses the tips of my fingers, one by one. His lips are cold from the spritzer. "Anyway. Long time ago now."

"Amazing."

He catches the tone of my voice and smiles. "Venice is amazing. She wasn't."

That evening, after we put you to bed, we order room service and sit late over dinner. Matt orders a bottle of our favorite, Valpolicella. My head thickens with the rich food and wine. We leave the shutters thrown open and cool salt air blows in from the water below. Neither of us speaks very much. I'm preoccupied, thinking of the night ahead. Perhaps he is too.

Later, we stand together at the open window, looking out at the Grand Canal. The buildings across the water gleam with falling light, chopped into stripes by half-closed shutters. The reflections dance on the choppy surface of the canal. The water beneath is black and deep.

The breeze reaches in to us, carrying the tinny strains of music and raucous voices. A few moments later, a tourist boat glides past. The deck is strung with colored lights. People stand along the rail and some wave, giving a general drunken salute to Venice as they pass.

Matt holds me in front of him, pressing my back and buttocks close against his chest, his stomach, his groin. His arms reach round my body and his hands, warm where the breeze is cooling me, touch my breasts. He trembles against me and bows his head. His lips kiss their way along my neck, my ear. His fingers unzip the back of my dress and pull it loose from my shoulders and it falls to my feet and pools there. He unclasps my bra, reaches round to cup my breasts.

He turns me to face him and puts my hand on his groin. The salt air chills our skin, exposed now to the night, and we press together, craving each other's warmth. He slips off my pants and presses me against the open shutter. The panels clatter shut behind me.

He goes down on his knees and his lips move to my stomach and I stand leaning back against the smooth wood with one hand caressing his hair, the other on his shoulder. I have at once a glimpse back into the room behind him, now dense with shadow, and, if I shift my head only slightly, a view out into the night, straight down the open mouth of the Grand Canal, past the grand, ornate dome of Santa Maria della Salute and far beyond to the open lagoon itself.

It's a scene as rich and beautiful as a painting and I imprint it on my memory, even as my legs start to buckle under me and he reaches for me and guides me to the floor.

Across the canal, the double doors to a broad balcony are flung open and, in a rush, a crowd spills out, loud with drinking.

I whisper: "They'll see us."

"Let them," he says in my ear, and his voice is hoarse, and I realize I don't care either; I'm flushed and free and already revived by Venice, this eternal city, finding again here my younger, undamaged self, reckless and joyful, the self I feared forever lost.

Later, when we are both heavy with tiredness, he lifts me onto the soft double bed and pulls the counterpane over us. He holds me close, warm against his chest, my head on the muscle of his arm, and lulls me to sleep.

CHAPTER 30

Something tugs my arm. A hand, pulling, a low voice whispering. My head is thick and dull and I struggle to come round. Cool air on my skin and the taste of salt.

"Mummy."

I open my eyes. Your face hangs beside me, level with the edge of the bed, pale and eerie in the half-light. Memory floods in. Venice. We're in Venice. And Matt is there in bed beside me, breathing deeply.

I put out a hand and stroke your hair. "It's nighttime, Gracie. We need to go back to bed."

"But, Mummy . . ." Your voice is high and thrilled.

"Shhh. Very quiet."

I manage to slide my feet to the floor, then ease out the rest of my body and straighten up, point across to the connecting door.

You stare. "You haven't got any clothes on."

I put my fingers to my lips. The gilded edges of the chairs and wardrobe gleam. The breeze blowing in from the lagoon is chilling. I steer you back to your own room and climb into the narrow bed, make room for you beside me. You put your cold feet on my legs to warm them and reach for your bear.

"Did you have a bad dream?"

You shake your head. "She's here." Your eyes are gleaming. "I can feel her."

My stomach clenches. "Who?"

"Catherine!" You shake with excitement.

I stiffen. "What are you talking about?"

You still look pleased. "Catherine, silly Mummy. If Auntie Ella is her mummy, is she my sister?"

"Auntie Ella hasn't had children. You know that. Now go to sleep."

I try to rest your head on my shoulder but you struggle, sit up. My tone has become cross and you look indignant.

"But why?"

"Why what?"

"Why are you saying that? I dreamed about her and then I woke up and I heard her. She's here, Mummy. In Venice. Like she said." You stop, read my expression more closely.. "What?"

"I'm just tired, Gracie. You've been dreaming. That's all. A dream. Now settle down and let's go to sleep."

"But—"

"Hush, Gracie. That's enough."

Your lip trembles and for a moment you look about to cry but you swallow it back and just frown. I wrap my arms more tightly round you and hold you against me, trying to calm my breathing. Your skin is hot. Maybe you're coming down with something. You lie still for a moment.

"Mummy, will you miss me when you die?"

"Gracie." I twist round and try to make out your face.

"What kind of question's that?" Your eyes are anxious. I sigh. "I'm not going to die. Not for a long time."

"Not until you're very old?"

"Not until I'm very old. You'll be grown up then."

Your eyes fill. "I don't want you to die."

"I'm not going to die." I hold you close, rock you in my arms, press my face against the top of your head, and breathe in the clean scent of your hair. "It's all right, Gracie. Mummy's here. Go to sleep."

Your limbs slacken and your breathing slowly deepens. I lie in the silence, trying to understand you. Waves of light, reflections from the stirring water down below, ripple across the shadowy ceiling.

As I finally fall backward into sleep, I'm gripped by a strange sense of timelessness, of confusion, as if the solid lines that usually contain us are warping and shifting, leaving us drifting, any age and all ages, in a world without form.

CHAPTER 31

We start the next day with a lazy breakfast of coffee and hot brioches on the hotel terrace, overlooking the Grand Canal. You kneel nearby on a low wall and hang your arms over the rail, watching the passing boats and waving at the tourists inside. You say nothing more about Catherine and I don't mention it to Matt.

Matt places his chair close to mine, his hand reaching often to stroke my hand or the back of my neck as we sit, lazy. The air is fresh on our faces.

"I thought we could take the *vaporetto*," he says. "Out to the islands. They have glass-blowing workshops on Murano. Gracie might like that. Plenty of room for her to run around. Or there's Torcello."

I nod, only half listening. He seems happy to take charge and it's a relief to sit back and let someone else organize.

"And this afternoon, do you think Gracie would cope with the Palazzo Ducale, the Doge's Palace? It's stunning. You can't come all the way to Venice and not see it. We needn't stay long. The artwork is fabulous. Just the ceilings alone."

I try to imagine you staring at painted ceilings. You'll probably last about five minutes. But Matt seems so earnest and if we give you a busy morning, you might be worn out by then.

I smile. "It sounds great, Matt. All of it."

The clouds are low and dull and it's still too early in the year for most tourists. The first *vaporetti* we see look almost deserted as they glide past. We take a boat that's heading straight out into the lagoon and sit huddled together on a wooden seat at the bow, overlooked by the crew in their elevated glass cabin.

Your nose wrinkles as you face into the salt breeze, your hair flowing out behind you. You're excited and your eyes gleam. It's the same fervor I saw in you last night when you talked about Catherine. I should be excited too but, watching you, I feel cold with foreboding. I tighten my grip on Matt's hand and press closer to him.

We pull steadily away from St. Mark's and the mouth of the Grand Canal and head out into the open swamp. A low mist rolls across the water, veiling everything from sight. The horizon slowly vanishes as water and sky meld together in a formless smudge of white. I have a sense of floating, of becoming untethered, unleashed from the land, from the city, from the modern world.

As the mists thicken, the crew quietens the engine to a purr. It's the only sound in the muffled air. We creep slowly forward as if we're explorers, navigating the unknown. One by one, wooden stakes, hammered into the water to mark channels of safe passage, emerge from the banks of cloud. Each seems a relief, a blessing, handing us forward from one to another through the invisible dangers on all sides.

Now we are far out, in open water. The wind whips low and stings my eyes. Matt rubs my arms and reaches to put his jacket round my shoulders. You delight in it. You jump down from the seat and stand forward against the rail, leaning over, trying to reach the dark water far below with your trailing hand.

"Be careful, Gracie."

"Relax." Matt smiles and reaches sideways to kiss the tip of my nose. "She's fine."

The men running the boat, dark-skinned Italians, call to you as they work and laugh amongst themselves.

Matt has taught you to say "thank you" in Italian—"*grazie*"—and you consider it your own special word because it's so like your name. Now you say it endlessly, to everyone. One of the men, younger than the rest and thick-set, feeds you sticky red sweets in shiny paper and you're so delighted that I don't have the heart to stop you eating them.

Eventually, when I'm stiff with cold, the solid outline of a dock appears and the crew, gathered now on the small deck, set about the business of coming alongside. Matt takes your hand as we bump to a halt and the two of you jump off together onto solid ground.

A boatman, a young Italian inked with tattoos, gallantly takes my hand and straddles the gap to help me disembark. The water sucks and laps as the boat knocks against the wooden platform.

"*Attenta, signora.*" The boatman nods to me, smiles. He is young and sure to break foreign hearts when the tourists arrive in earnest. For now, he makes do with charming me. His voice is a song of Venice, drawing out the vowels as if they were operatic. *"Benvenuta a Torcello."*

You run on ahead down the long, straight path alongside a canal. The island seems tiny, a narrow, largely featureless strip of land that offers little choice but to go forward. I fall into step beside you and you reach for my hand.

"Where's this again?" What I really mean is why are we here.

"Torcello." He looks happy and I think how at home he seems here. "This is where it all began."

I look round doubtfully as we walk on past deserted cafés, restaurants, and small shops selling canned drinks and postcards and guidebooks. The strains of a solitary radio drift through the air, playing a jaunty Italian folksong.

"Does anyone even live here?"

"Hardly anyone. They've all moved out."

Away from the water, the air becomes heavier and more humid. A fly buzzes in my face and swerves away. Insects buzz at our feet in the scrubby marsh grass. Overhead, birds swoop in from across the water and cry.

We approach a small, shabby square. It has an air of neglect, of abandonment.

"There."

Matt nods toward two buildings that stand side by side across from us, dominating the piazza. Their walls are made of worn, dull bricks that suggest great age, and the facades are marked out by prominent crosses. The nearest has a colonnade with a low roof, covered with curved terra-cotta tiles.

A square bell tower rises from the far end of the other, higher building. It soars above everything else on the island.

"That's what we've come to see. *Cattedrale di Santa Maria Assunta*."

His pronunciation is slightly Anglicized but, like the boatman, his tongue lingers over the music of the Italian. I squeeze his hand.

You're already there before us, a tiny figure waiting outside the arched entrance, tilting back your head to crane up at the walls.

"This was the first church ever built here in the lagoon when settlers first came, all those centuries ago." Matt turns to check my expression and hesitates. "I know it doesn't look much but come and see inside."

Matt buys entrance tickets and we head into the gloom. The mood changes instantly. The sounds of life outside, of the birds, the insects, fall away to silence. The salt air is replaced by the fug of an ancient, crumbling building and the cloying smell of spent candles and incense. The church has only just opened for the day and we seem to be alone.

I lean in to Matt as he joins me, dropping my voice to a whisper.

"How old is it?"

Matt shrugs. "It goes back to the seventh century, to the start of Venice. I'm not sure which bits are original." He looks round. "The mosaics are ten-something."

He steers me forward down a narrow aisle. It ends in a high dome, encrusted with gold mosaics. In the center, a towering figure of the Virgin Mary in flowing blue robes gazes down at me. The infant Jesus sits in her arms, a chubby hand raised as if in blessing.

Matt whispers: "This is what Venetians were busy making while we were being invaded by Normans."

I don't answer. I can't. I stand, enthralled, staring up

into the vast sweeping curve of the dome. The Virgin
Mary's tall, slim figure dominates the entire space, isolated in a sea of shining gold. Her face is gentle and her
hands, cradling her child, are full of love. I bite my lip.

"It's beautiful, isn't it?" he says quietly. "I knew you'd
feel the same."

When I can finally tear myself away, I turn to find you.
It isn't a vast church but it's dark with shadow and hidden
spaces. Matt, sensing my sudden anxiety, turns to look
too. He touches my shoulder.

"You stay here a bit longer. I'll find her. She wouldn't
leave without us."

He strides off at once down the aisle and I turn back to
the mosaic, tracing the shapes with my eyes and trying to
fix it in my memory. I can't concentrate. Whatever Matt
says, I'm worrying. I need to know where you are.

I skirt the main body of the church, hoping to cover
different ground from Matt. The windows here are high
and small and the columns of dusty light finding their
way through the plain glass barely penetrate the darkness.
I walk on, peering behind sculptures and ornate thrones,
reluctant to call out to you and disturb the silence.

Then I hear it. A giggle. Ahead, in the shadows. Low
and stifled.

I creep forward, craning to see. "Gracie?"

Silence. Then the light, high-pitched giggle again. I
follow the sound, sensing the barely audible shuffle of a
small body creeping to find a new place to hide.

"Gracie, come out."

I find myself at the bottom of wide steps. It's the
entrance to the bell tower. A notice, giving basic information and the price in four languages, is tattered. A man sits
beside it on a wooden stool. He's elderly and unshaven.

I hesitate. "Excuse me, did a little girl just go up there?"

"*Campanile*," he says, pointing up the steps with a nicotine-stained finger.

I hold out my hand to show your height. "*Bambina*. Girl."

He shrugs. I don't know if he understands me or not but he gestures with an open palm for me to pass, to go and see for myself. The thought of you running up there to hide and possibly falling sends me rushing forward.

The stone path is broad and rises gently, falling to steps at the corners. I climb at speed. Blood pumps in my ears and within a few minutes, my breathing is hard. Here, away from the body of the church, I dare to call out.

"Gracie!"

The high giggle bounces down along the curve of the wall.

"Gracie, it's not funny."

I press on, determined to catch up with you but you seem always ahead. Fitter than me and more nimble. After a while, I stop for breath and strain to listen. Silence. Then the whisper of quick, shallow breathing drifts down to me from somewhere above. I race on.

I'm tired and cross now. *It's not funny, Gracie. It's naughty and it's dangerous. What have I told you about running away? You're old enough to know better.*

Just when the aching in my chest is becoming unbearable, I make a sudden turn and all at once the steps give way to the brightness of daylight and the outside world. Fresh salt air hits my face. I spill out onto the top of the tower and stand, leaning heavily against the wall, blinded by speckled patterns of light as my blood races. I struggle to breathe. Then I turn, scanning the corners of the tower, baffled. I'm alone. It's deserted.

I walk back and forth across the stone floor. The perimeter is enclosed by wire. There's nowhere to hide. You are nowhere to be seen. But I heard you. I sensed you. I followed you.

I am only dimly aware of the spectacular view out across the lagoon, stretching into the mist, of the breeze cooling my flushed face and lifting my hair from it. I stand at the tower wall and peer down, narrowing my eyes, frightened of seeing what I know is impossible. Perhaps you've somehow climbed, penetrated the mesh, and fallen. Could that be possible? But there's no tiny broken body far below. Nothing. My legs, exhausted now, give way and I sit on the cold stone, exhausted and suddenly afraid.

I find you both in a café on the far side of the piazza. You are sitting together at an outside table, keeping watch for me. Matt lifts his hand in a broad arc of a wave as soon as I step out of the cathedral and back into the light.

You don't look up. Your head is bowed over a sundae and you are busily scooping up chocolate and vanilla ice cream. I see as I approach that it's nearly gone. You must have been here all along.

"You OK?" Matt gets to his feet as I join you. His face creases with concern.

I shake my head, sitting down.

"I'm sorry." Matt looks confused, guilty. "I thought you wanted some time to yourself. Gracie had had enough so I thought we might as well..." He hesitates, uncertain, says again: "Sorry."

"OK." I let out a long breath, not knowing how to explain what happened, what I heard. The giggles. The child's quick breathing.

"I thought she'd gone up the tower. I went up after her."

He lifts his eyes to the tower, square and dark against the sky, and he frowns. For a moment, he looks so troubled that I reach at once for his hand and grasp it, eager to pull him back to the present and to me.

CHAPTER 32

It's the middle of the afternoon by the time we return to Piazza San Marco and go to queue at the entrance to the palazzo. We're all tired. You whinge, pulling on my hand and saying as we inch our way forward toward the entrance: "I don't want to see it, Mummy. I'm tired. I want to go home."

I'm starting to get a dull headache, brought on by the humidity and a glass of wine at lunchtime and I'm inclined to agree with you but Matt seems determined to take us round it.

Inside, you trail up the marble steps without enthusiasm, a dead weight dragging on my hand. You fuss and twist and run away down echoing corridors every time Matt tries to point something out. I run after you, apologizing to Japanese and German and every other sort of tourist as we barge past, interrupting them in their quiet contemplation of Venetian paintings and sculptures.

My head throbs and I can feel myself getting short-tempered with you and cross too with Matt for dragging us in here and with myself for letting him. After all, it isn't really a palace; it's an art history museum and you're not even four.

Finally, I decide to call a halt and tell Matt that I'm sorry but you're too tired and I'm taking you straight back to the hotel. He's somewhere ahead of us and I take you firmly by the hand and urge you forward to find him, even as you struggle and protest. We plow on, you dangerously close to a tantrum, when you suddenly shake me off and stop in your tracks. I feel your mood change in an instant. You stand, stock-still, just staring.

"Look, Mummy." Your voice falls to a whisper. "Look."

The painting is striking. I stand close beside you and gaze.

It's in muted colors and clearly centuries old. The bottom two-thirds show naked, long-limbed figures against a dark background. Their bodies contort as they gaze in reverence backward and upward, guided and encouraged by others, suspended around them, who are robed and winged.

But it's the top third of the painting to which the eye is drawn, the object of the figures' gaze. It shows a whirling vortex of light, growing in brilliance as it twists in a cone toward pure white at the far end. A tunnel of brightness.

I crouch down beside you, putting myself at your level. You can't take your eyes from it, just reach a hand sideways to find mine.

"That's it." Your voice is hushed. "What I saw." A long pause until finally, almost to yourself and in wonder: "How did he know?"

Your face is radiant. I look again at the painting, dramatic with fifteenth-century religious fervor, then again at your ecstatic expression.

"That's what you saw?"

"I went down that tunnel." You lift your free hand and point at the light. "That's where Mr. Michael is. And Catherine. Don't you see? Down there." You turn to me and break suddenly into a broad smile. "The man who did this painting," you whisper in my ear, as if you've stumbled at last upon a great truth, "he must have gone there too."

CHAPTER 33

That evening, Matt announces that he wants to see if he can find a little family hotel-restaurant he remembers, off the beaten track. If it's still there, he says, it has the most amazing pizzas. He seems suddenly obsessed with finding this place, as if it really matters to him, and I'm afraid to ask why.

We set off with a map. We're venturing far from Piazza San Marco and we soon leave behind the main tourist routes and find ourselves twisting and turning through a maze of increasingly narrow side streets. At times, these give way without warning to hidden squares, built round modest churches with low lights.

We enter a series of paths along the edges of minor canals that are so gloomy that I call you back and make you hold my hand. The water here smells stagnant and forbidding, its surface barely visible in the darkness. I draw you away from the edge, frightened that if we fell in, we'd simply disappear into nothingness.

There are few streetlights in this forgotten stretch and

the buildings look decayed and deserted. Arches and doorways are toothless with missing bricks and bowed by the weight of history. Matt walks on with purpose but his map is useless in the darkness.

Finally we emerge, as if by miracle, into a small piazza. A typical Venetian campo, Matt says, looking round as he gets his bearings. He's clearly delighted and leads the way with renewed confidence to a tall, narrow house on its edge. It's barely identifiable as a hotel. It looks dilapidated and cramped but full of character.

Downstairs, restaurant tables spill out onto the pavement. A middle-aged woman, prematurely thick around the waist, sits smoking at a corner table, reading a newspaper. Matt leaves us and crosses to greet her.

She raises her eyes with little interest at first, and then feeling floods into her face and she jumps up, kisses him on both cheeks, and embarks on an animated flow of Italian. Her eyes shine but her expression becomes wistful as she talks.

After a while, he gestures toward us and she looks over fleetingly at me, then more closely at you, pressed against my side. Her eyes are curious but I see none of the warmth in them with which she greeted Matt.

He comes back to claim us and steer us to a table.

"Sorry," he says, smiling. "*La patrona*. I wondered if she'd still be here."

I think of his student friend, Maria-Eletta, and wonder if there's a connection here that he's politely omitting to mention.

"She certainly remembered you."

He is already leaning over the pizza menu. The woman has picked up her newspaper and retreated inside, leaving us alone. A much younger woman takes our order.

Matt is suddenly subdued and I sit quietly beside him, wondering why. The pharmacy on the corner is still open and every now and then a bell jangles as the door closes on customers. Dusk deepens around us. A wrought-iron streetlight, holding three ornate lanterns, casts lengthy shadows across the paving stones.

You sit with us while we all eat, folding the edges of your pizza slices into curves, delighting in being allowed to eat with your hands.

When you've had enough, you jump down from your chair and, while Matt and I linger over our wine, you make your own game of hopping and skipping across the campo's flagstones. You buzz with life and, as I watch you, a lithe figure in your buttoned-up coat, I think back to the painting we saw together, to its twisting tunnel of light and the naked figures reaching for the perfect brightness ahead.

Matt leans closer and reaches an arm round me. "I'm sorry. I've been lousy company tonight."

I take his hand between my own. "Are you OK?"

He nods and draws me closer to him. His body is firm and warm against mine and I'm comforted by it but still uneasy. Something about this place, about talking with that woman, dampened his mood and I don't understand why.

"You were upset, weren't you, this afternoon?"

I hesitate. His tone is sympathetic and I want to respond to it, to talk about you and your strange reaction to the painting, but I'm also reluctant to change the subject and move on.

"She was so struck by that painting," I say, remembering the emotion in your face. "Maybe she's right. Maybe the artist did go through something similar."

"Maybe he did." Matt shrugs. "Experiences like that, however you explain them, must have been around for centuries. We might call them near-death experiences. Maybe they just called them visions."

"When did you say it was painted?"

He pauses. "About fifteen ten. A superstitious age. They all painted religious stuff."

I don't answer. Your light, high voice drifts across the campo on the breeze. You're chattering to yourself, lost in your own world. Your hair flies round your head as you leap in and out of the shafts of light thrown across the paving stones by the lanterns, jumping between light and darkness, light and darkness. I have a strange sense of you jumping also in time, back and forth through the thin, shifting veil between past and present, between this world and the next.

Mist is gathering along the far side of the campo, rising from the canal, creeping in from the lagoon. It blurs the edges of buildings there and swallows the shops beyond the canal.

You run back to me. Your eyes shine with the excitement of being outside so late.

"Is it nighttime, Mummy?"

"It's very late, my love."

"It's dark!"

I just nod, reach out a hand, and tickle the back of your neck. You have a habit of stating the obvious sometimes, as if you just enjoy the pleasure of making conversation.

"Soon," I say, "we'll go back to the hotel and then it's straight to bed."

You skip off again. This time you head toward a narrow hump-backed bridge over the canal in the far corner of the campo. It is already becoming engulfed by swirling mist. I narrow my eyes and struggle to keep you in sight.

Your voice drifts clearly through the still air. *One. Two. Three.* You count the stone steps up one side of the bridge, run back and forth across the top, then come back again, springing off the bottom step with a bound.

"This time tomorrow," I say, "we'll be back in London." It seems impossible.

Matt pulls me closer. When I encircle him with my arms, his back is broad and strong.

He kisses my cheek. "I don't want it to end."

You start to climb the steps again, this time hopping with your feet together. I hold my breath as you reach the top of the bridge and, for a second or two, disappear into the hanging fog, only to reappear again.

An Italian couple, strolling by, call out to friends and stop to talk. The song of their voices, the lilting music of their words, washes over us.

Matt lowers his voice. "It works, Jen. You and me. Don't you think? And Gracie too."

I nod. It's been a happy weekend. For the first time, I've had glimpses of the three of us as a unit. As a family.

He clears his throat. "I know it hasn't been very long."

Part of me wants him to stop there, to leave things as they are and not risk spoiling them. Another part wants him to carry on.

"I love you, Jen. You know that, don't you? We belong together, you and me. I sensed it the first time we met."

He cups my chin with his hand and turns my face away from you to him. His lips close for a moment on mine, stopping my breath.

"I don't want to rush you." His eyes loom large, streaked with low light. "But I want to take things a step further. Will you think about it? I want to look after you.

You and Gracie. I want to wake up with you every morning, not creep out of the house at night as if we don't really belong to each other."

I pull a little apart from him.

"Jen? What is it?" His voice is gentle. "Is it too soon?"

I shake my head. "It should be," I say. "How long have we known each other? A matter of weeks. That's no time at all." I hesitate. "But that's not how it feels."

"How does it feel?"

"Like a dream," I say, in a low voice. "If you'd told me a few months ago that I'd be sitting here in Venice with a doctor, talking about being together—" I break off.

"Think about it. Please."

He moves in and kisses me.

"I love you so much, Jen. I don't know how I'd carry on without you."

I close my eyes.

When I open them again and look round, you're standing on the curved back of the bridge, barely visible in the thickening mist: a slight, shadowy figure leaning forward over the wall and peering down into the canal.

I look more closely, then pull away from Matt and sit up straight.

"Is there—"

The fog swims round you, at times obscuring you, at others giving you back to me. I get to my feet. My heart pounds. It may be no more than streaks of light shimmering in the mist but it seems to me, as I gaze, that there's something or someone beside you, a presence even slighter than your own, there at your side. I blink, straining forward to get a better look.

"Is that someone with her?"

Matt doesn't seem to hear me at first. Then he understands and says: "With Gracie?" He too sits straighter, cranes forward. "I can't tell."

"Can't you?"

I push past the table and stride toward you. I am suddenly afraid, gripped by the same fear that chilled me this morning on the boat and again as I stood high on the bell tower, looking out across the vast expanse of the lagoon, and thought you gone.

I quicken my pace. The fog deepens and you are lost for a moment. Then I hear it. A stifled giggle drifts across the campo toward me. It is followed a moment later by the soft, light breathing of a child. The same sounds I heard so clearly as I raced up the bell tower.

The mists sway and thin in the breeze and you emerge again, leaning away from me now, over the far wall of the bridge. I shiver and run toward you. As I draw near, I catch the low murmur of voices.

"Gracie?"

You look up, alarmed, and shout at once: "No, Mummy. Go away!"

You stand squarely on the narrow bridge, guarding it from me. I try to peer past you, into the darkness.

"Come away now. It's late."

You stamp your foot, furious. "No! You're spoiling everything."

"What?" I've almost reached you now, my arms open, but as I move to embrace you, you pull away. "What's wrong?"

"You made her go away." You hit out at me, arms flailing. "Why, Mummy? Why did you do that?"

"Calm down, Gracie!" I try again to hold you but you lash out and struggle, barely able to contain your rage. "It's all right."

"It's not all right." Your face crumples, close to tears. "She was here and you've frightened her away."

"Who?"

"Catherine."

"Gracie." I shake my head. As I look past you, all I see is a wall of dense fog, streaked with light bouncing off the fast-moving water below. "It's very late."

You lean over, peer down at the black stream gliding through the darkness. Your pale face, reflected there, shimmers.

"We need to go." I hold out my hand for you to take. "Come on."

You burst into sobs, fall to the ground, and bang your fists, your feet.

I stand, helpless, watching you.

"Gracie. Sweetheart. Get up."

I lean over you, lifting your shoulders even as you struggle against me, trying to pull you to your feet.

"No, Mummy. You don't understand. She's gone again. It's your fault. Why did you come? Why?"

I can't answer. I manage to hoist you up into my arms, battling to contain you as you scream and kick and shout: "No! No!"

I carry you down off the bridge, away from the water and back onto solid ground. As we cross the campo toward him, Matt stands motionless, watching us approach, his face pale.

CHAPTER 34

"Have you got bear?"

You opened your bag to check, nodded. Your face was solemn.

Richard held up your coat, trying to push your arm into the first sleeve.

"Daddy will look after you. But if you need me, you know you can phone. All right, my love? Any time at all, day or night."

Richard said into the coat: "Maybe not night." Your second arm found its sleeve and he reached round you, zipped up the front. "We'll be fine, won't we, sausage? We'll be too busy having fun."

"She's got two lots of pajamas, just in case. And make sure she cleans her teeth properly, won't you? Not just the front ones."

Richard didn't answer. I knelt down to you and opened my arms, squeezed you tightly for as long as I could until you wriggled free. "Don't forget how much I love you."

You didn't answer. You were busy with your gloves, finding the right holes for each finger.

"All the way to the moon and back," I whispered into your soft hair. "And a bit more."

"Come on." Richard put his hand on your shoulders, reached to open the front door, and steered you out. I stood there on the threshold, sick to my stomach, watching as you climbed into the back of his car and he fastened you into your seat. Ella, resplendent in the front, twisted back to talk to you.

I waved as he pulled away and eased into the road but you didn't even look. When I shut the front door, the house was unbearably silent.

It felt strange, setting out alone that evening. As I got on the train, I expected the other passengers to stare. I missed you so much, my love. Such a physical sense of your absence. I sat quietly on my own, without your small, fidgety body on the seat beside me, climbing back and forth over my knees, craning to look out of the window. I had to remind myself not to point out the power station, the police car flashing alongside the railway, the horses in a dark field.

I got out my phone and texted Richard. *All OK?*
No answer.

Matt had chosen the restaurant, a little Italian bistro in town, hidden away down a side street, close to Waterloo. I left myself plenty of time to find it but even though I arrived early, he was already waiting.

My heart skipped when I looked round the restaurant and saw him there. Handsome and kind. He'd taken a cozy table in semi-darkness at the back. A tea light candle burned in a glass holder. The tablecloth was starched linen. Heavy doors swished as the waiters, stout Italian men in old-fashioned uniforms, strode to and from the kitchen, releasing smells of basil and tomato and the rich aroma of simmering meat.

"Darling." He kissed me on the lips, pulled out a chair, and settled me beside him. He was already drinking from a bottle of Valpolicella and a waiter leaned forward to pour for me. I lifted my glass to touch his.

"Memories of Venice," he said. "And many more holidays to come."

I looked round. The walls were crowded with heavy black-and-white photographs. Italian piazzas and villages on hilltops. Pictures of small-town celebrities: boxers and politicians and actors. I thought back to the first time we went out to dinner properly together, in that noisy, crowded restaurant. It wasn't very long ago and yet it felt it. I was so nervous then and knew him so little. Now we were already a couple.

The waiter handed me a menu and I opened it. The names of the dishes were all in Italian and I smiled, trying to remember what Matt had taught me in Venice.

"Well!" He smiled across at me. "Here we are again." He reached for my hand.

A moment later, the waiter interrupted to announce the specials and Matt ordered for us both. I asked him about work and he started telling me about his patients that week—a little boy with a heart condition and a ten-year-old just diagnosed with leukemia. His eyes grew intense as he described their cases, giving more medical detail than I could understand.

I sat quietly as we ate and drank more than my share of the wine and let Matt do the talking. He seemed more at ease with me since Venice. More willing to trust me, to confide in me about his work. It was clear, just from hearing him, how much he cared about his patients. I let the wine loosen my limbs and gazed at him. Despite all my worries about you, about what you were doing, what Ella had given you to eat, if you were missing me, I was happy to be here with this extraordinary, loving man who doted on me.

The waiter cleared away our plates. Matt leaned forward and took my hand.

"I missed you this week." He stroked my fingers. "How are you doing?"

I shrugged, feeling embarrassed that he had so much to tell me and I had so little.

He looked thoughtful. "You're worrying about Gracie, aren't you?"

I tried to smile. "Is it so obvious?"

"It must be hard." He pulled back as the waiter set dessert in front of us. A rich chocolate mousse, one to share. "She needs time with her father."

I nodded. Ella was the one I didn't trust. We picked up our spoons.

"Look." He pointed his spoon at me. "Of course you'll worry. You're an amazing mother. But it'll do you both good. She needs time with Richard. And you, madam"— he leaned forward and kissed the tip of my nose—"you need time with me."

When he disappeared to the toilets, I checked my phone. Nothing. I started another text to Richard—*All OK?*—then deleted it.

We were almost at the end of a second bottle of wine. I was flustered that evening, anxious about you, self-conscious about being out at all, and I barely remembered drinking it. The waiter leaned in, a linen napkin on his arm, and poured the last of the bottle into my glass. My fingers fumbled the glass as I lifted it and I spilled some, then mopped at the mess with my napkin, making it worse.

Matt reappeared. "Paid." He wafted away my thanks with his hand. "My treat."

When I got to my feet, the table swayed. The waiter steadied my elbow as I headed toward the door. Outside, the air was cool and fresh. I stood still for a moment, feeling it on my cheeks, thinking of home and sleep.

"Let's not rush back." Matt seemed suddenly full of energy. "Come on. Do you know DDs?"

I shook my head. Matt, taking my arm, was already hailing a cab.

"How often do we get the chance, Jen, really? Come on."

DDs was a double-fronted club just off Shaftesbury Avenue. Stylishly dressed couples, some of the girls barely out of their teens, queued inside a rope. A thick-set bouncer in a tux guarded the door.

Matt winked. "Watch."

He pulled out his wallet and flashed something at the bouncer, who unclipped the rope and lifted it aside for us. I hesitated before following him inside. The taxi ride had left me feeling queasy.

The club was all darkness, scored with crisscross lines of colored lasers. It pulsed with noise. The vibrations reached for me as soon as we entered and rose up through my legs to my stomach. Matt steered me up a short flight of steps to a low balcony and a young man in a torn T-shirt with the rippling chest and biceps of a body builder escorted us to a table with a red shaded lamp. Matt said something in his ear and he nodded and disappeared.

We settled side by side in cushioned seats and looked out across the dance floor. It was heaving with gyrating bodies. They swam in and out of the moving lights, arms high, faces sweaty, eyes stupid with alcohol or drugs or both, like some modern vision of Dante's Inferno.

I thought at first, *My God, I'm too old for this*, but as my eyes started to adjust to the dark, the faces became clearer and I saw how many of the people around us were actually middle-aged or older.

The young man came back with two glasses of champagne and Matt paid at our seat with a card. He raised his glass in a toast.

"To nights out!"

My head was already swimming with Valpolicella and I had to concentrate to wrap my clumsy fingers round the champagne flute and touch it to his without spilling it. The champagne was icy on my lips and in my throat. I took just a sip, then another, then turned back to the dance floor, focusing my eyes on a distant point as I tried to steady myself. The music throbbed inside my head.

Bubbles burst somewhere deep in my stomach and a sour trace of acid rose into my mouth. Sweat moistened my hairline. I peeled off my jacket and rolled my sleeves up. Matt drummed his fingers on the tabletop in time to the thudding music and the banging traveled along the surface and into my bones.

I tried to sit back. I wondered how soon I could ask to leave, how we could get home quickly. I thought of you. Maybe you'd woken up and were crying, calling for me, and I wouldn't even know. Why had I had so much to drink? I shook my head and the lights flew so rapidly, I had to blink to stay upright. Perhaps it would be better if I moved, if I splashed water on my face.

I took hold of the rail that ran along the edge of the balcony and used it to hoist myself to my feet. Matt looked up and I managed a vague nod before turning and groping my way back along the narrow walkway to the entrance.

The lights in the ladies' were dazzling after the club interior, and I stood at the sink for some time, blinking, running cold water on my wrists and dousing my face. It was a relief to escape the worst of the crashing noise. I looked ghastly, my skin sallow and my eyes unfocused.

I swayed, gripped the edge of the washbasin to stop myself from falling. Time to head home. I'd go straight back to Matt and say I was really sorry, I just didn't feel well, it must be something I'd eaten. I nodded at my reflection and saw the pale face bob, then turned and went into a cubicle.

I sat inside with my head in my hands, trying to hold myself steady. My eyes throbbed. My hands came away slippery with sweat. I wanted the headache, the sickness, to go away and to be well again and to be with you, to hold you and see you settled in my arms, sleeping, as if you were a baby again. Safe and close.

My feet juddered on the tiled floor. I opened my eyes, braced myself against the seat, and managed to get to my feet, stood for a second getting my balance before opening the door and stepping out.

CHAPTER 35

The lights were strobing. The club jumped and shifted in the jerky beams. I groped my way to a handrail and stood, gripping it tightly, trying to keep my balance in the thumping music and popping light. I stared across the gyrating bodies on the dance floor. Each moment was separated, frozen. A series of photographs of raised arms, grinding torsos, locked limbs.

One revealed Matt, in the background, on his feet. I focused, trying to piece together the set of jerking pictures. He was half turned, leaning forward, talking intently to someone. To a young woman. His body obscured her face but I caught glimpses of her curves. Tall and slim and encased like a sausage in a tight, figure-hugging sheath. Sexy.

I felt my way along the handrail toward them. The floor was sticky with spilled drinks. Matt's body was tense as he leaned in to her. The strain showed in his hunched shoulders and the jabbing movement of his hand as he talked through the music.

I found my way across the edge of the seating. As I climbed the steps up to our seats, I lost sight of them behind a row of pillars. At the top, I turned, closer now, then stopped dead as I saw the woman's face. Her. The last woman on earth I wanted to see. Ella.

She shifted her gaze and saw me. For a moment, our eyes locked. She didn't have the grace to look embarrassed, just stared me down with a hostile, superior glare. I stared back and she turned away, all disdain, and began to stalk off on her high heels, this woman who had wrecked my marriage, whose dangerous driving nearly killed my daughter.

Rage took me. I broke into a messy run, banging against the backs of the seats as I closed the gap between us, reached her, grabbed her arm to swing her round to face me.

"Why're you here?" I paused. "You followed me, didn't you?"

Her eyes showed surprise, then became cold. She reached calmly down to prize my sweaty fingers off her sleeve, brushing away all trace of them.

"What were you saying to him? Leave us alone. Haven't you done enough?" I plunged on, my mouth out of control. "You can't bear to see me happy, can you? Is that it?"

She made again to turn away from me. She simply pretended she couldn't hear me, that I didn't exist. The more composed she looked, the more she infuriated me. I barged into her.

I called through the blast of noise from the speakers. "Who's Catherine?"

She stopped in her tracks and swung round. Beneath all that makeup, her cheeks turned gray. *You were right,*

*my lovely girl. You were so right. Why did I ever doubt
you?*

"So it's true. You had a child, didn't you?" Every word
hit home now. Each one pierced her. She couldn't move.
She stood there, rooted, and took the blows.

Matt stepped forward and put his hand on my arm. He
tried to pull me away, but I threw him off. Someone else
took possession of my tongue and I couldn't have stopped
if I'd wanted to.

"Even Richard doesn't know that, does he?" I don't
know where the words came from. They just tumbled
out, fueled by the wine and the hate I felt for her. She was
capable of *anything*. I just knew it. "What did you do to
her? Did you hurt her, like you hurt Gracie? Too wrapped
up in yourself to consider the safety of a poor, defenseless
child?"

Her eyes were wide, staring. The emotion in them was
raw but hard to read. Fear, perhaps. Or panic. Or just fury.

Her arm flashed out. She struck me hard in the chest
and I tottered. The room tilted sideways and slid as I
crashed, unguarded, to the floor. Pain stung the side of
my face as it caught the hard edge of a chair. White shards
flashed through my eyes and burst like fireworks. I groped
blindly, stunned.

Matt moved quickly to stand between us, shielding
me. He had his back to me but I saw her say something to
him, her mouth twisted and tight. Then she bent over me.
When she spoke, the words were hot against my ear.

"You're not fit to say her name."

And she was gone.

Matt reached for my arm and heaved me to my feet.
He looked pale. He picked up his jacket, held me upright
against him, and guided me slowly toward the exit.

In the taxi back home, I pressed close to him, feeling sick and grateful for the darkness. My head was spinning with alcohol and confusion. My ears still buzzed and whistled after the noise. My cheek throbbed.

"What did she say to you?"

"I don't know." He shrugged. "She was drunk."

"Something about me?" My mind was whirling, trying to work out what had happened. She must have seen us come in and waited her chance to approach Matt. To cause trouble. "What?"

"I couldn't even hear." He stroked my hand. "She didn't make much sense." He paused. "Anyway, we don't care, do we?"

I saw again the sheath dress, the heels. "You do realize who she is?"

He nodded, avoiding my eyes. "She said."

I hesitated. "What's she doing out anyway? Is Richard with her?" My voice was rising. "Who's looking after Gracie?"

Matt shook his head. "She was with a group of girls. Quite a rowdy crowd. A hen do, maybe."

The taxi braked suddenly and I slipped forward, tumbled off the seat. Matt crouched down and lifted me up. His hands were strong and warm and his eyes kind.

"I'm sorry," he said. "It's my fault. You were right. We should have gone home after dinner."

He settled me against him, his arm firmly round my shoulders. The streets were crowded with young people, drinking, jostling, chatting in jumbled clusters. I wondered if you'd fallen asleep quickly and if you'd wake in the night and call out for me and if Richard had remembered the monitor.

"Forget her. She doesn't matter, does she?" Matt

whispered in my ear. His breath was hot. "We're happy, aren't we? We've found each other. Nothing can spoil that." His hand, resting on my arm, shifted until his fingertips stroked the curve of my breast. "Let's enjoy every minute." His lips closed on the soft skin of my neck.

CHAPTER 36

We spent Sunday morning in bed, then pottered to a local café for a fry-up. I kept my body as close to Matt's as I could, conjoined by sex and sleepiness and the laziness of a slowly dispersing hangover.

He finally left in the afternoon and I was just sorting out the washing and putting the house straight again when you arrived home. You came tearing into the house—bear under your arm—as I opened the front door. You were on fire with excitement.

"Mummy, Mummy, I've got bunk beds!"

"Bunk beds?" I looked back to Richard, who was wiping his feet on the mat, his face turned to his shoes.

"She's always wanted them."

"I know that." I blinked, already cross. "And we always said no because they're dangerous. What if she falls out in the middle of the night?"

"She won't." Richard shrugged, avoiding looking at me.

You skipped round the kitchen, calling out to me: "There's a hidey-hole underneath the stairs! Full of toys."

"You should have talked to me about it first," I said to Richard. "I'm her mother."

"And I'm her father." He moved into the hall and set down your bag there. "It's perfectly safe, OK? It's got proper carpeted stairs for climbing up and down and a big lip on the top bed. She couldn't fall out if she tried."

We were talking in low voices and you came running back to find out what was going on.

"Mummy!" You stopped in your tracks, stared at my face. A red weal stretched across my cheek where I'd hit the edge of the chair. I thought I'd done a good job concealing it with makeup but you weren't fooled for a second. "Was it a wolf?"

You lifted your hand and I stooped to let you touch it, tracing the lines with your finger.

"I had a bang, Gracie. That's all. Silly Mummy."

You looked doubtful. "Will it get better?"

"Of course it will. Now take your coat off. You can have a quick play and then it's bath time." I held up my hand. "Five minutes."

You disappeared into the sitting room.

When I turned back to Richard, he narrowed his eyes, looking too at my bruised cheek.

"Your girlfriend gave me that. Did she tell you? She just happened to bump into us." I drew sarcastic quote marks in the air around the words "just happened."

"My fiancée."

"Oh, please."

He hesitated, shuffled his feet. His brown lace-ups looked cheap compared to Matt's shoes. I thought of him in the evenings, sitting cross-legged on the kitchen floor, surrounded by brushes and tins of polish, one hand inside a shoe and the other patiently buffing the leather.

"Ella was very upset when she came home."

"She was upset?"

"Look, I don't know what happened—"

I opened my mouth and he held up his hand to stop me.

"And I don't want to know. I said the same to Ella. I'm not interested. Leave her alone, Jen. Please. This isn't about us anymore. It's about Gracie. You two need to get along, for her sake. All right?"

I wanted to defend myself, to point out that Ella was the one who'd bothered us, who'd gone out of her way to cause trouble, but I saw his face and swallowed it back. It wasn't worth it. He'd never believe me anyway. I took a deep breath.

"You told me she couldn't have children."

He looked taken aback. "What's that got to do with it?"

I hesitated. I knew Richard and he didn't look guilty or embarrassed. Quite the opposite, in fact. He looked indignant, as if I were the one being mean.

"Richard." I didn't know how to tell him my suspicions. "I think Ella had a daughter."

"What're you talking about?"

"Ask Gracie. She says she's seen her. Ella's daughter."

Richard looked cross. "That's ridiculous."

I pulled a face. "But Gracie—"

"What? She's three, for God's sake. She wants to pretend she's got a sister. That's all."

I opened my mouth and closed it again. How could I tell him about the look on Ella's face, her utter shock? About Venice and the strange giggling inside the bell tower. About the shadowy presence beside you in the mist.

He went into the sitting room to say goodbye to you, then pushed straight past me to the front door. He hesitated there and turned back.

"I'm sorry for what happened, Jen. Believe me. I never wanted to hurt you." He hesitated. "But I'm starting to wonder if I knew you at all. I never had you down as silly. Or cruel."

Afterward, I joined you on the sitting room floor where you had the bricks out and were building a multi-story garage for your cars.

"So, sweetheart." I tried to join in, to win you back. "How was your sleepover? Did you have a nice time?"

You didn't answer, just scrabbled through the box of bricks looking for the piece you wanted. I moved in closer and added a few bricks of my own to your wall.

"How was Auntie Ella? Was she fun?"

You nodded without looking up.

I reached round you and kissed your hair, inhaled its fresh, lemony smell, and tightened my arms in a hug.

"Don't, Mummy." You fought me off, cross. "I'm busy."

CHAPTER 37

On Wednesday, the weather lifted. It was bright and typically English: warm in the sunshine, cool in the shade. When I picked you up from nursery, we headed straight to the park on the far side of the river, the sprawling one with ducks and rose gardens and zones for everyone, from the skateboarding youths you stopped to watch, eyes wide, to the dog walkers and the joggers in Lycra.

We spent an hour at the play area, on the big-girl swings without backs, which you still tended to fall off, on the see-saw, and on your favorite, the roundabout. I ran round, turning it for you, getting dizzy and out of breath, as you beamed.

We ate ham and cream cheese sandwiches on a bench by the river and counted boats. Small racing yachts with white sails. Rowers, schoolboys mostly, wrenching their way in packs against the tide. The strains of the cox's voice, made monstrous by a megaphone, bounced across the water like skimmed stones. A police launch bounced at speed through them all and made waves that tipped and tossed the sailing boats, the rowers, and made us laugh.

You pushed down from the bench after a while and took the remains of your last sandwich to the rail along the steep embankment to the river below. You threw bits of bread, aiming at the stray ducks below on the water but attracting a sudden swirl of seagulls who made a cloud round your head and frightened you into dropping the lot.

"London seagulls," I said. "Cheeky."

I pulled out an apple, polished it on my trousers, and bit into it. The gulls moved on and you wandered along the rail, a hand trailing on the bar, looking down at the river. You looked suddenly old in your cream coat, a proper child now, lost in your own thoughts. A girl, already growing away from me and getting ready for school. I tried to imagine dropping you off at the school gates and walking back to an empty house. I sucked juice from the apple and chewed. Richard was right. I'd be ready to go back to work by then. I needed to get earning again and, besides, I'd need to fill my days and not just count the hours until I could be there at the school gates, looking for you.

I closed my eyes and saw Richard there, standing so awkwardly in the sitting room we'd furnished together, as a couple, all those years ago. The same sitting room where we had fallen asleep, slumped against each other, a thousand times. Where I'd nursed you, stroking your downy head with the tip of a finger, utterly content, feeling as if I had at last joined the human race, joined the cycle of life. Matt was right. It was time to move on. Let him marry her, if that's what he wanted. He could find out the hard way what she really was.

Ella was brassy. I thought of her tarty dress at the club. She couldn't bear to see people happy. She was that kind of person. Destructive. She'd taken Richard from me. He

was so naïve when it came to women. He couldn't understand why she and I hated each other. I knew what she
was up to. She wanted to drive a wedge between me and
Matt, if she could. Well, she couldn't.

I thought of Venice and the smell of the salt air from
the lagoon and the firmness of his body as he reached
for me. I missed him, now, sitting here in the sunshine,
more than ever. He'd done so much for me, for us. It was
a miracle that he'd walked into our lives the way he did.

Someone passed, walking a panting dog, and blocked
the sun for a moment. I opened my eyes, looked for you.
The rail stretched along the edge of the path, empty. I
pushed the last sandwiches back into my bag and got to
my feet. No sign of you, no flash of cream coat, of shoes
with light-up heels.

I took a step to the rail, half smiling at myself for
worrying. Of course you were there. I'd see you any
minute. You were testing me again, making a point about
how grown-up you were, how independent. You never
went far.

I stood at the rail, the peeling paint pricking my fingers, and scanned the river below, fearing you'd somehow
climbed or fallen through. No cream coat. I started to
walk down the path.

"Gracie!"

You liked hide-and-seek. Maybe that was it. I peered
into the bushes along the verge, green and full-leaved
now.

"Where are you?" I tried to make my voice a singsong,
to keep it a game. A bush stirred and I spun round, ready
to smile, ready to see your face, laughing at me. A large
dog, collar jangling, sniffing as it ran out onto the path.

I quickened my step, shouting every few steps:

"Gracie!" Reached the end of the path where it gave way to a mud trail toward the swings. My heart was loud in my ears, my breath short.

Beyond the final bushes, the grass opened out and gave a clearer view ahead. I narrowed my eyes, concentrated, searched the walkers, the dogs, the youths, the children, for your small figure in cream. The park looked empty. What if this was it? What if I never found you? My legs trembled and a cold sickness rose through my stomach into my chest.

"Gracie!"

I tried to tamp down the panic. You weren't a baby. You were nearly four. I was panicking. In a short time, any minute, I'd see you, I'd run to you, it would all be over and seem absurd, a story to tell people. It was only a matter of minutes, I'd say, but it seemed like forever. I could almost hear your voice in my head, saying: "Silly Mummy!"

"Gracie!"

I turned, walked back to the section of rail opposite the bench where I'd last seen you. If you came running back to find me, it would be here. I climbed up on the bench and tried to see through the trees, the foliage. A middle-aged couple came past, Labradors at their heels, and gave me an odd look.

"My little girl," I said. "Have you seen her?"

The woman frowned.

"She's in a cream coat."

The man shook his head and they walked on.

I climbed down and sat heavily on the bench. The strength drained from my legs. I looked down the path one way, then the other. Just vacancy, stretching on forever. I felt utterly lost. I must be sensible, keep calm, but for a moment, I lost all sense of what to do. Should I set off round the park, walking briskly, searching? It was a large park. How much did I cover? How far should I go?

Or should I sit here, half-hidden from the lawns by the bushes, and try to stay calm, trust you to find your way back to me?

My breathing was so shallow that my chest ached. I pulled out my phone. A mechanical voice told me that Matt's mobile was switched off.

I left a message: "It's me. Sorry to bother you but could you call me back? Please."

I already imagined myself feeling a fool when he called, later, and we were already together, crisis over. I'd laugh about it, about how flustered I'd been, honestly, what a hopeless mother.

I got to my feet again, paced back to the end of the path and this time headed out down the dry mud trail toward the swings. Of course. You'd be back on the roundabout, on the seesaw. I almost ran to the gate and into the playground. It was clouding over and the swings were quieter now. I scanned the equipment. Ran round the grassy mound to check the baby swings, to look inside the play train. Nothing.

I sank to the grass. It was cool and damp through my jeans. How long had it been now? Ten minutes? Twenty? I didn't know. I pulled my diary out of my bag and looked for the number of the hospital, then dialed it. My hands shook.

Switchboard. The woman who answered sounded mechanical. A foreign accent. East European.

"Doctor Matthew Aster, please."

"Who?"

I stiffened. "Matthew Aster. Pediatrics."

A pause, then the call clicked onto music. I got to my feet, restless, and started walking round the edge of the playground, scanning the park.

The woman finally clicked back onto the line. "No doctor with that name."

"A-S-T-E-R." I spelled it out with exaggerated care, trying not to lose my patience. "Pediatrics. You know, children?"

"I know that." She sounded shirty. Tap, tap as she checked. "I can't help you."

"Can you at least put me through to the department?"

"Are you a relative?"

"A relative?"

"Of the patient?"

I wanted to reach into the phone and shake her. "I'm not trying to reach a patient! I'm trying to contact a doctor. Doctor Matthew Aster."

"I'm sorry, there's no—"

I ended the call, pushed the phone back in my pocket. Stupid woman. Anyway, Matt might have picked up the mobile message by now, might be trying to call me back.

I left the playground, rushed back toward the riverside path. I was almost at the bench when I saw you, a daub of cream, crouched down low right at the far end of the path, close to the entrance to the park. You were bending forward, your forehead pressed against the bottom bar of the railings, peering at the river below.

I broke into a run. As I got close, you must have heard my thundering feet, my panting. You glanced round, unconcerned, saw me, then looked down again.

"Gracie!" I put my arms around you, tried to pull you to me in a hug. "Where were you?"

You fought me off, annoyed at being interrupted. "Look."

You pointed down at the river. The fast-flowing water was brown with churned mud. A stick swirled past, followed by a piece of clear plastic, swollen, rising and falling in the current like a jellyfish.

"What?"

"Wait." You stared down, transfixed. "I saw her."

I sucked in my breath, trying to be patient.

"Who?" I knew the answer before you spoke.

"Catherine. She waved to me."

You seemed so separate from me. So calm.

"Don't be silly, Gracie. There's no one in the water."

You weren't listening. Your mind was elsewhere. My heart thumped. The panic, the running, and now this, your strange stillness.

"Gracie." I crouched low, took hold of your arm. "Don't ever run away like that again. You hear me?"

You ignored me, focused on the flowing water.

I reached more firmly for your shoulders and pulled you round to face me.

"Gracie, listen to me. Mummy was very worried. We've talked about getting lost, haven't we? It's dangerous. Very dangerous."

You stared back, cross. "I wasn't lost, Mummy. I was here."

I put my arms round you and pulled you to me again, relishing the soft warmth of your body against mine in the few seconds before you struggled free.

About half an hour later, as we walked back home, hand in hand, my phone rang.

"Everything OK?" Matt.

"Fine." I was exhausted. All I wanted just then was a cup of tea, a chance to sit down in the knowledge that you were there, safe, at home. "Long story but we're fine now."

"You're sure?" He sounded concerned. "I'm sorry. I only just got your message. I was worried."

"Me too." I swung your hand in mine as we walked. "I lost Gracie. That's all. But I found her again."

He went very quiet. "And you're OK?"

"I'm fine. I'll call you tonight."

When I hung up, you said: "I wasn't lost!"

"I couldn't find you, Gracie." You seemed to have no sense of the fact you'd run off and how frightened I'd been. "I was worried."

"But I wasn't lost," you said again, indignant now. "I was right there."

CHAPTER 38

That night, I came downstairs after reading you a story to see a dark shadow against the glass of the front door.

I went into the sitting room and peered out through the side window. Matt stood on the doorstep, with flowers in one hand and a bag of groceries in the other.

When I opened the door, he said: "Hello, gorgeous. Surprise." He handed me the flowers. The neck of a bottle of wine poked out of the shopping. "I come bearing gifts."

"You shouldn't have." I moved out of the way to let him in. We stood close together in the hall and kissed. I thought of the TV dinner in the fridge. Much, much better to have Matt here.

"Missed you." He pulled back and looked into my eyes. "I was worried. You didn't sound yourself this afternoon."

I nodded. "It was a bit of a shock."

In the kitchen, I sat on a chair and sipped wine and felt my shoulders relax. He tied my apron round his waist, pulled groceries from his shopping bags, and set to work, washing and chopping mushrooms, yellow and red peppers.

I liked watching him work. It was the same pleasure as watching any devoted craftsman. He was so intent, so absorbed in his tasks, so quick with his hands. It was sexy as hell but in a soothingly lazy way, all the passion still to come, and it was comforting to be there with him in the light, in the warmth, watching those same capable hands that healed sick children.

It reminded me too of being a child, hanging around in the kitchen at home. My mother made terrific pies, with crunchy crusts and fluted edges and she used to give me pastry off-cuts to roll out and cut. The bottoms for jam tarts and pastry people with currants for eyes and waistcoat buttons.

"Earth to Jen." He paused to look at me, his knife poised. "You're miles away."

"Sorry." I nodded, smiled. "How was your day?"

He shrugged. "Intense."

I'd guessed that from the vehemence of his chopping. Some days his cooking seemed a kind of frantic therapy. Those days, we had a lot of diced vegetables.

"Tough case?"

He shifted his floppy fringe from his eyes with the top of his arm. "A three-year-old boy. Pneumonia. I think we caught it in time but only just." He sighed, set his knife on the board, and pushed the pile of chopped mushrooms off, into a bowl. "He was critically deoxygenated on admission."

I nodded, tried to look wise. "What did you do?"

"Gave him oxygen, basically. He's a strong chap though. Responded well." He looked round, suddenly self-conscious. "Sorry."

I shrugged, sipped my wine. "Don't be."

He sliced open a pepper, started to de-seed.

I swallowed, watching his hands. "When I called the switchboard, they couldn't find you."

"Really?" He was bent over the chopping board. "Did they page me?"

"I don't know. I don't think she got that far." My memory was obscured by a fog of cold panic. "She wouldn't put me through to pediatrics. I remember that."

"Natasha, probably." He looked round. "Did she sound Bulgarian?"

I considered. "Something like that."

"And a bit chippy?"

"Definitely."

"That's Natasha." He laughed. "People are always complaining but they won't get rid of her. She's ruthlessly efficient, well, most of the time." He fell to dicing peppers at speed. "She seems to think it's her job to stop people bothering us. Not ideal. Especially if people are upset to start with."

I wandered over to the worktop. "What's the recipe tonight?"

"Ratatouille and pork casserole, à la Matt."

"Ah." I bent low and kissed the backs of his hands. "My favorite kind."

"Anyway"—he turned, kissed me quickly on the lips, not ready yet to be distracted from his cooking—"if you need me, mobile's best."

CHAPTER 39

When Friday the eighteenth came round, I dropped you off at nursery, as usual, went to the shops, and then found myself heading across to St. Michael's. I wasn't sure until I walked in that I'd really go. It was just something about Angela. I didn't want to let her down.

I arrived early and sat for a while in the stillness of the church. The morning light streamed through the stained glass. Multicolored columns splashed onto the gravestones set amongst the flags that made up the floor. St. Michael, locked in his eternal battle with the serpent, gazed down at me as I said my own quiet hello.

Just before eleven, I went back into the bright, living world of the café. Angela looked up as I appeared and smiled at me. She was dragging tables together to make a long central spine down the room and scraping the chairs as she arranged them round it.

A queue of elderly women stood at the counter, ordering cups of tea, scones, and pieces of cake from the young woman there. I went to help Angela. By the time we'd finished, the elderly ladies were settling into their seats, ten or eleven of them altogether and one solitary man. No sign of any younger people.

Angela went up to the counter and gestured to me to join her at the table. When she returned, she set a cup of tea in front of me and a piece of coffee and walnut cake.

"On the house." She looked flushed with pleasure. I wondered if she'd really expected me to come.

"Now, everyone." She tapped her teacup with her spoon to call for silence.

The rows of lined, thickly powdered faces turned.

"We have a newcomer today." She indicated me with her hand. "This is Jennifer. I hope you'll make her welcome."

The ladies exchanged whispers, looked at me with interest. One of those closest to me nodded and smiled.

They bowed their heads as Angela said a prayer.

"Bless us, Lord, as we gather here in your name and feel your presence."

I lowered my head, embarrassed. I couldn't imagine what Matt would say if he knew I was here.

"Help us to understand your purpose in taking home to your kingdom those we love and miss here on Earth."

I stared down at my teacup, at the untouched cake, wondering how soon I could escape.

"Help us to trust your promise of eternal life and to remember your triumph over death. O death, where is thy sting? O grave, where is thy victory? Amen."

When she finished, the women dissolved into chatter. My knuckles whitened as my hands gripped each other in my lap.

The lady beside me said, rather loudly: "It takes a bit of getting used to, doesn't it?"

I hesitated, not sure what she meant.

"Bernard and I were married for forty-one years. There isn't an hour goes by that I don't think of him. It's been thirteen years now but, do you know, every night, I set two places at the table. One for him and one for me." She smiled, showing crooked teeth. "Silly, isn't it? I know he's gone. But it's a comfort."

"I'm sorry." I didn't know what else to say. I reached for my fork and took a mouthful of cake. It was sweet and light, homemade, and reminded me of my mother's baking.

The lady watched me for a few moments as I ate. She leaned toward me, bringing with her the scent of talcum powder and a flowery perfume.

"So what's your story, dear?"

I blinked. My confusion must have shown in my face.

She prompted: "Have you lost someone?"

"Well, my father." My hand shook and I set down the fork. "But that was a long time ago."

"Awful." She tutted sympathetically. "You poor thing."

She reached out and patted my hand. Her knuckles were swollen with arthritis.

"Well, you're very welcome here, dear. We've all got a cross to bear, haven't we? No one's spared."

I didn't answer and, a moment later, she turned to reply to a question from someone on her other side. I sat quietly for some time, letting the sounds of conversation wash over me and focusing on my tea and cake.

After a while, Angela turned to speak to me.

"All these ladies have lost loved ones. Husbands. Brothers and sisters. Even children. It does help to talk about it."

I didn't know what to say. I turned, looked out, beyond

the end of the table, into the darkness of the church. I could almost see you there, a shifting shadow, a small, fragile figure, kneeling on a hassock and stretching forward, running your fingers over the stone flags, reading the engravings as if they were Braille.

"I worry about Gracie." I thought of the women gathered here, burdened by their losses, their grief. "I keep thinking how close I came to losing her." I hesitated. "I don't feel I can keep her safe anymore."

"When you talk about Gracie, your whole face changes. Do you feel it?" She gave me a thoughtful look. "I see God there."

My cheeks felt hot. I shifted my weight on the chair.

She considered me. "If I say love, is that an easier word?"

I swallowed. "My father adored my mother and when he was feeling sentimental, he'd say: *I love that woman more than life itself.* Tears in his eyes. I was only a child. I thought it was just a figure of speech. But now I understand."

Something inside me loosened and words started to come.

"You know that myth about the goddess whose daughter was abducted and taken down to Hell and she grieved so hard that she brought winter on the world?"

"Persephone," Angela said. "And Demeter."

"Exactly. I'd do that. If I had to."

She smiled. "I doubt you'd find her in Hell."

I took a deep breath. "I do struggle to believe in Heaven. Literal Heaven. Somewhere with radiant light where you meet God and people who've already died." I shook my head. "So how do I deal with my own little girl saying she's been there, telling me things she couldn't possibly know?"

We sat in silence for a moment, an island in the general hubbub of conversation.

One or two ladies pushed back their chairs, hauled themselves to their feet, and tottered away. Several leaned heavily on sticks as they disappeared toward the toilets. Others gathered at the counter to order a fresh cup of tea. Those who were left continued to chat.

"There's probably a rational explanation," Angela said. "She might have overheard something. Or absorbed information without even realizing. She's a perceptive child."

I nodded. "I suppose so."

"That's one theory." She carried on talking to me as she nodded across to ladies who were starting now to disperse, to say their goodbyes. "Or you stop trying to rationalize. You let go. That's the thing about faith. It isn't about proof. It's about making a choice. Choosing to believe.

"From all you've told me," she went on, "I believe your daughter did go to Heaven, that she really did meet St. Michael and was blessed by him. Maybe you think of that as an actual place, a place where God is. Or, if that makes you uncomfortable, think of it as love. As the universal love that is all around us, that survives us."

Chairs scraped. A voice rose in thin, elderly laughter. She leaned in closer to me.

"That love your father felt for your mother, that you feel for your daughter . . . I don't think it ends with death. There's more than just nothingness." She paused, considering. "That's what I choose to believe. But what you choose is up to you."

I sat very still. Something hard inside me shifted and my mouth trembled. I couldn't answer. I looked through to the church again but all I could see was darkness and weak shafts of colored light.

"You know, perhaps Gracie came back to you because it wasn't her time. Or perhaps your love for her was so strong, so overwhelming, that God showed mercy to you both by sending her back."

An animated woman interrupted by tapping Angela on the shoulder and she turned away to talk to her.

On the far side of the table, the elderly man shuffled to his feet and started, with slow, deliberate movements, to thread his arms into the sleeves of his coat. The young woman from behind the counter came out into the café and started to separate the tables again, re-ordering the café as if our meeting had never been.

CHAPTER 40

By the time I headed to nursery to collect you, the skies had clouded over and the clouds looked heavy with rain. I was thinking about lunch and what to feed you when my phone rang.

"Jen. I need to see you."

"Matt?" My heart thumped. Since the accident, unexpected calls frightened me and he sounded anxious. "Are you OK?"

"Fine."

Traffic thundered past on the main road and I strained to hear him. "What?"

"I said, what about this afternoon?"

I frowned, struggling to understand what was so urgent. We'd already planned to meet up over the weekend. "I'm on my way to get Gracie."

"Please, Jen." His tone was sharp. My stomach contracted. "There's something you need to know."

We arranged to meet in a soft play center at three o'clock, just a ten-minute walk from the house. We hadn't been for a while and you were delighted. You ran in, shedding your coat on the ground behind you, as soon as we entered through the turnstile. You were always bursting with energy, even after a morning at nursery. My biggest challenge each day was finding new ways to exhaust it.

By the time Matt arrived, you'd pulled off your shoes and were tumbling on the miniature bouncy castle. Your hair was wild with static as you threw yourself back and forth. It was an effort for me not to interfere, not to caution: "Be careful, Gracie! Mind your head!" I saw so many dangers unraveling. You were so perfect, so precious, I found it hard not to imagine we were only one clumsy landing, one twisted neck from catastrophe. Perhaps all mothers are the same. Perhaps, after all we'd been through, I was worse.

It was term time and just before the end of the school day and the center was quiet. The air was punctuated by the tinny notes of a children's television program, the mechanical beeps and squawks of ride-on cars and trains and the occasional burst of wailing from a young child. It was a woman's world of babies and toddlers.

I waited for him in the café corner, drinking a black Americano. It was almost deserted. Just a few huddles of women who shared gossip and advice and roused themselves every now and again to change nappies or wipe noses.

The only other man on the premises was the youth behind the counter in reception. Matt, with his broad shoulders and bohemian hair, looked as if he'd come striding into the wrong building. The mothers and nannies watched him as he picked his way through the chaos to buy himself a coffee. He sat opposite me at the gray, plastic-topped table. It was gritty with spilled sugar.

You were busy now on the jungle climbing frame, heaving yourself up staircases of padded blocks, running back and forth across a rope net like a mad monkey and sliding down a tube, only to jump out and run round to do it all over again. As Matt settled with his coffee, you looked across at us and took in the fact of his arrival with a solid, steady gaze.

"How are you doing?"

His face was set and it worried me. He looked down into his cappuccino and stirred it. Chocolate powder melted into smudges in the froth.

The other women seemed suddenly quiet. I leaned forward and lowered my voice.

"Whatever it is, please. Just tell me."

He sighed. "I've heard from Geoff."

My stomach tensed. "Your brother?"

I'd almost forgotten Matt's promise to look into Ella, to ask Geoff to do the same.

"You can't repeat this. To anyone." He bent forward to me. "I only did this because I love you so much, Jen. I'd do anything for you. I leaned on Geoff to do this as a favor to me. You understand? If anyone found out—"

"I get it."

Cartoon music burst out of one of the rides as it rocked into motion.

Matt was hesitant. "It may not be the same person. I mean, there could be more than one Ella Hicks." He spoke carefully, weighing each word. "She did have a baby. A girl. Found dead in her cot."

I couldn't breathe. Teeny-weeny. You were right.

"What happened?"

His eyes were on mine. "Febrile convulsions."

"What does that mean?"

He shrugged. "Seizures. They're not often fatal but they can be."

Auntie Ella sent her to Mr. Michael because something bad happened so she couldn't stay with her mummy. That's what you said.

"Was it her?" I swallowed. "Was it something she did?"

Matt hesitated. He seemed too reluctant to answer.

"I don't know," he said at last. "The coroner's report wasn't conclusive." He paused. "But convulsions can be the result of injury. Of being shaken."

The air swam and I closed my eyes, grasped at the edge of the table. He reached for my hand at once and encased it in his own as if he were trying to protect me.

I saw you, a newborn, with your scrunched-up face and perfect, tiny hands. How could anyone hurt a baby? And a mother, what mother harmed her own child? It was obscene.

"Are you OK?" Matt's voice was close and warm.

I nodded, pulled my hand free, and wiped my eyes with my fingers. "I'm sorry."

When I opened my eyes, he looked anxious. "I'd never hurt you, Jen. You know that, don't you? You mean the world to me. You and Gracie." He paused. "I just thought you needed to know."

"Of course." I reached in my sleeve for a tissue. "I do."

My body was heavy on the seat. Exhausted. *How did you know, my love? How?* I didn't understand. How could she do such a thing? I shook my head. And what about your safety? How could I ever leave you with her again? "What did they do to her? I mean, was she charged or anything?"

His eyes stayed on my face. "The police interviewed

her. It's all there, on record. But they couldn't prove anything. In the end, the coroner gave a verdict of death by
natural causes. That was it."

I almost didn't bother with the next question. I knew
the answer. "What was the baby's name?"

He paused. "Catherine."

"Catherine."

You were right, my love, all the time.

A toddler, barely walking, stumbled over to our table
and stood there, staring up at me with unblinking eyes.
A voice called: "Holly!" and she turned, considered her
mother's outstretched arms, teetered back to her.

I felt a sudden physical need to hold you and looked
over, trying to search you out in the cloud of moving
children. There you were, hanging upside down from
bent knees, your legs hooked over a metal bar, your hair
streaming to the ground like water. My love, where did
you go, in those awful moments of lifelessness, as the
paramedics rushed you to intensive care? How could you
know these strange unknowable things?

"Jen?" Matt came around to my side of the table and
sat next to me on the cushioned seat, so close that his
thigh pressed against mine. I put my hand on his leg and
he wrapped his fingers round mine. "Jen, darling, are you
OK?"

"What do I do?"

"Do?"

I thought about Richard. He was a kind man. A gentle
one. That woman had manipulated him from the start.

"What if they have a baby together? She might do it
again." I breathed deeply. "And what about Gracie? She
might hurt her."

He squeezed my hand, shook his head. "You can't do

anything, Jen. You know what? I think you're right. I think she *did* kill her baby. But medically that's so hard to prove. The evidence just isn't conclusive."

I sat very still, trying to take it all in. My feet, under the table, juddered against the hard, shiny floor.

His hand, round mine, tensed. "You know now. You know what she is. Let's forget about them. Leave them alone. Focus on our own life together."

"Richard needs to know."

"Really?" He pulled away from me. "What are you going to say? You know Ella killed her daughter because an angel told Gracie when she was in Heaven? Do you know how crazy that sounds?"

I couldn't answer. He was right. It sounded absurd.

He raked his hand through his hair. "I'm sorry, Jen. I didn't mean—"

He reached an arm round me and drew me closer against his chest. We sat like that for a while. The children's cries, the grating mechanical music filled the silence.

Finally, he said: "Richard's a lawyer, isn't he?"

"Solicitor."

"See this through his eyes." He paused. "So much of what we know is hearsay. Things Gracie has told you. Maternal instinct. A question of faith. None of that's evidence."

"Yes, but even so—"

He winced, awkward. "From what you've told me, he already seems to doubt you, to think you're"—he hesitated, feeling his way—"overwrought. That you've got a grudge against Ella."

I sighed. He was right, of course. I did hate Ella. And Richard was already exasperated with me.

"I know that's not true," Matt went on. "I'm just saying. You can't tell Richard. Or anyone else. They'd never believe you."

I shrugged. "So what do I do?"

He looked at me closely. "Why do you have to do anything?"

I swallowed. "For the baby. Catherine. She deserves justice."

"In a court of law?"

"Yes."

He sighed. "You're not listening to me." He shook his head. "You have no evidence she did anything wrong. The coroner already gave a verdict. OK?"

I looked at the scratches along the surface of the plastic tabletop. A knife, maybe. A metal toy.

"I just think—" I broke off, trying to find the words. "Richard's making a life with this woman. He needs to know what she is."

"He's in love with her."

I frowned, turned away. You ran across to the dressing-up baskets and rifled through the capes, hats, aprons there.

"And you can't mention Geoff. You give me your word? He doesn't even know I'm telling you."

"He'd get into trouble?"

"Trouble? He'd lose his job."

We drank our coffees. The center started to get busier. A small boy astride a pink plastic car banged into our table, reversed, struggled to get clear.

We tried to be normal for a while, chatting without enthusiasm about nothing much. You and our plans for the rest of the day. His late shift at work.

When we finished our coffees, I said: "You should probably make tracks."

He put his hands on my shoulders and turned me to face him, right there on the bench.

"I love you, Jen. You do know that, don't you? I adore you." He spoke in a low voice. He was so close that his breath, coffee-scented, was warm against my cheek. "I want to spend the rest of my life looking after you. You see? You and Gracie. My two gorgeous girls."

I nodded, moved in closer to touch my lips to his, conscious of the mothers and nannies all around.

"I love you too." I mumbled the words into his neck.

You were in the toddler area, building towers out of colored foam blocks, then knocking them down again. Now, as Matt reached to hold me, you stopped and lifted your eyes to watch. Your expression was knowing.

His voice was in my ear. "I want to be with you always, Jen. I know it's a lot to take in. Just think about this." He paused. "I want to us to be a proper family."

I didn't move.

"My place is great for me. But it's tiny. Far too small for three. Why don't I move in with you? We were made for each other. I know we were and I think you do too, don't you?" He kissed me chastely on the top of the head, pulled away. "Let's do it. Soon."

Your eyes hadn't left us. Across the play center, even with the cries, the beeps, the noise, you seemed to know exactly what we were discussing, to hear and understand every word. I blinked, my eyes on yours. How could you be so wise? How could you know about Catherine and be privy to these strange secrets from the past? Unless of course everything you'd told me from the start, however incredible, was actually true.

CHAPTER 41

That night, at bath time, you said, from nowhere: "Do you like him as much as you like Daddy?"

I had just lifted you into the bubbles and was drawing shapes on your back with my finger. It was a guessing game, my mother did the same when I was a child, but at this age, there wasn't a lot of guesswork. Half the time, you told me what to draw before I started.

I carried on, pretended not to hear.

"It's got a big body and four legs like this and a large head with big flapping ears."

You didn't move.

"And a very, very long trunk."

You twisted round, delighted. "An elephant!"

I tried to look amazed. "How did you know?"

"Another one. Do a bunny."

I dipped my finger in the bubbles again.

"This one is really hard."

You tensed, eyes forward toward the taps, bracing your back as you concentrated.

"So. This one is small with long floppy ears. One. Two. And big feet. And a small round tail called a scut."

"A bunny!"

"Yes!"

You beamed.

Later, we snuggled together in the armchair by your bed. You were wrapped up in a big, warm towel, then wrapped again in my arms. Your pajamas, your favorite ones with the Dalmatians, lay across the back of the chair, waiting until we'd finished our cuddle.

"I love you, little Gracie."

The ends of your hair were still damp and I rubbed them dry in the folds of the towel. You wriggled, twisted sideways to lie across my lap like a baby. Sometimes you liked to play babies when we were alone. I rocked you, put my lips to your cheek, your hair. You smelled clean, of lavender soap and scented bubble bath. You kicked as you settled and your tiny pink feet came free from the towel.

"What story do you want? Have you chosen?"

You turned your face up to mine and that look came in your eyes, a knowing look, older than your years. "Is he downstairs?"

"Who?"

You didn't answer, just looked at me, as if to say: *you know exactly who I mean.*

"If you mean Uncle Matt, no, he isn't here tonight. Just Mummy."

"If you marry him, will he be my daddy?"

I hesitated, tried to find the right words. "Daddy will always be your real daddy, Gracie. Uncle Matt is Mummy's special friend. He's been very kind to us, hasn't he?"

"In Venice?" You squirmed until you were sitting upright again, reached for your pajamas, and began to put

them on. I fought back my urge to help you. It only caused
an argument.

"Yes, in Venice. And when he takes us out and buys us
treats."

You considered. "Daddy buys me treats too."

"He does. Daddy loves you very much, Gracie. He
always will. Whatever happens with Uncle Matt."

"So I'll have two daddies?"

"In a way."

"And two mummies. You and Auntie Ella?"

"Possibly." I struggled to keep my face neutral. "Into
bed now."

You finally let me tuck you up and I lay beside you
while we read a couple of stories together. I switched off
the light and sat in the armchair. You lay on your stomach, hunched forward with your forehead buried in your
bear, your legs drawn up under you.

"Shush." I made the word a long, steady sigh, which
formed a wave of white noise through the quiet room.
Gradually, as my eyes adjusted to the semi-darkness,
familiar objects grew. The nursery rhyme pictures. The
shelf of medicines, of stuffed animals and dolls, of books.

We moved you in here when you were just six months
old. I didn't want to. I wanted your cot to stay in our room,
by my side of the bed, but Richard was adamant. He
nearly broke his back, carrying the armchair up from the
sitting room. If we're going to spend half the night in here,
he said, we may as well be comfortable. He didn't know,
then, how much of the time you'd end up sleeping in our
bed, curled up with me.

You sigh, turn onto your back, bear abandoned, arm
sprawled above your head. I lean forward for a closer look.

You look so beautiful, my love, you always do. I sit

there for some time, listening to the rise and fall of your breathing and marveling at you. Your skin shines clear and fresh. Your fair hair is splayed on the sheet. Your eyelids flicker as you dream and I wonder where you've gone to, what you're seeing and feeling in sleep.

I try to imagine a baby girl called Catherine with ginger hair. Ella must have sat beside her as she slept and kept watch, as I'm keeping watch over you. She must have nursed her and changed her and stumbled out of bed, night after night, more asleep than awake, to lift her out of her cot when she cried and rock her back to sleep. How could she not adore her, protect her? I shake my head. Was it really possible that she'd lost her temper and shaken her so hard that she'd hurt her? How could any mother do that?

When I climbed in beside you in your hospital bed, amid the wires and drips, to hold you as tightly as I dared, to bring you back, you felt so frail, so lost. You had the bones of a bird. I blinked, remembering, then lowered my face to yours until I was so close that I could hear the puff of your breath.

I love you, little Gracie. If anyone tries to hurt you, ever, I don't know what I'll do. I close my eyes, wrap my arms round myself, and shudder. I'll do anything to save you. I know I will. Anything it takes.

CHAPTER 42

For days after that, all I could think about was Ella and that poor baby, Catherine, and what she did to her. It was unbearable. It made me shiver each time I thought about how much you'd known, so long before I did, and the innocent way you'd described your new friend with ginger hair.

Richard suggested dates for a holiday in July. He wanted to book, he said, to take you away to Spain. The three of them. Sea and sand and buckets and spades. You'd love it.

When I tried to stall, to say I wasn't sure, I needed to think about it, his tone turned cold. *There's nothing to think about, Jen. You took her to Venice with your boyfriend. What's the difference?*

How could I explain? How could I tell him that if Ella was capable of doing such a monstrous thing to her own child, she might hurt you too? I couldn't sleep for worrying.

Matt was right. I knew it. If I wanted to stop her, I needed evidence. And finally, my chance came.

The following weekend, Richard invited you for another sleepover. This time, instead of letting him collect you, I insisted on taking you to their house myself. It was your idea, I lied. You were desperate to show me the bunk beds. You'd talked of nothing else.

Richard sounded hesitant. I knew why. She didn't like me visiting their house. But I insisted and he didn't have much choice.

I played one of your CDs in the car and while you sang along in the back, your voice high and off-key, I tried to relax, to steady my breathing and think through what I needed to do. The car stuttered and jolted through heavy traffic.

When Richard first left, he moved into Ella's flat. I picked up bits and pieces from little things he said, from the background noises when we talked on the phone. It was a tiny flat in the heart of the city, throbbing at night with live bands and rowdy drunks outside.

You were only just walking then but even at that age, you seemed fascinated by Ella, with her tight clothes and glittery shoes. It led to petty battles. Sour notes from me when you returned one day with your thumbnails painted red and, another day, with the temporary tattoo of a winged horse on your thigh.

It was a second-floor flat with steep stairs. A nail salon on the first floor. Two men above who worked nights in a bar. It made me laugh at the time. Bitterly, of course. It was hard to imagine a place less like Richard—my dear, stay-at-home, prematurely middle-aged husband. But then, he wasn't anymore, was he?

Eventually, the two of them took the next step and moved into a small Victorian terraced house in the suburbs, closer to us. A big lifestyle change for Ella. I assume

Richard persuaded her. They needed more space and a second bedroom for you. He tried, I give him that. I'd seen it from the outside once or twice when I dropped you off but she'd never invited me in.

Now I turned off the main road, with its parades of grocery shops, newsagents, and dry cleaners, and the streets became residential and quiet. A smart young woman, earphones in her ears, pushed a buggy. A traffic warden passed, strolling, watchful, punching registration numbers into a handheld device. Farther down the road, there was a clatter of metal as builders unloaded poles from the back of a truck.

The blood banged in my ears as I approached number forty-two and found somewhere to park. When we got out, I paused at the hedge for a moment, looking it over. The gate was latched. The lid of the bin was pushed up by a bulging bag inside. Upstairs, the bedroom curtains were drawn back but the windows were dark.

Richard answered the door. You ran in past him, your bear under your arm, shouting hello to the quietness. A moment later, you shed your coat, leaving it on the floor, and went clomping up the stairs as fast as you could.

Richard and I looked at each other. His face was strained.

I managed to smile. "What about these bunk beds? Can I have a look?"

"I told you." He shrugged, stood aside to let me squeeze past. "They're perfectly safe."

I crossed the bare-wood floor of the hall, wondering if I was supposed to take off my shoes. The door to the left stood open and I paused for a glimpse inside at a large, open-plan sitting room. The walls and carpet were cream, the furniture all glass and metal. It was sparse and modern, a stark contrast with our home, which was a clutter of tired wooden furniture inherited from family over the years or picked up secondhand. Our interiors weren't designed, they just evolved.

I looked at the pristine surfaces and imagined you crayoning on the walls or running over the carpets in muddy shoes and thought what pleasure it would give me if you did.

"No Ella?"

"She's popped out."

I bet she has. Waiting until the coast's clear. He didn't offer me a drink, just pointed the way up the stairs after you, as if he wanted this over and done with as soon as possible.

There was a small first landing with a bathroom and a closed door. I carried on to the next level, following the sound of your voice as you called to me.

There was no doubt which room was yours. You'd already kicked off your shoes and were crouched on a fluffy pink rug in the shape of a bear, playing with a patchwork elephant. The walls were cream, decorated with framed pictures of fairies and princesses. Behind you, against the wall, were the new bunk beds with their carpeted stairs. The duvet hung over the edge of the top bunk. The cover showed rainbows and unicorns.

The lower bunk was piled with stuffed animals. A spotted horse. A family of rabbits in dresses, with patchwork ears. A teddy with a pink bow. Everything looked brand-new. I set your overnight bag down in the corner and went to sit beside you.

"Look, Mummy!" You scrambled to your feet and crawled across the lower bunk to disappear into the hidey-hole under the stairs. Your voice came out: "Where am I?"

"I don't know," I said, playing along. "Where's Gracie gone, Daddy?"

Richard stood awkwardly in the doorway, his shoulders hunched. He didn't answer. He looked embarrassed. The expense, perhaps. Your room here was so much more extravagant than I could give you at home. The liberal splashes of pink were tacky but you were three; of course you loved it. I knew exactly who was behind it all. It was another weapon in her battle to seduce you, to win you over.

I smiled at him. "Do you mind if I play with her for a bit? I won't stay long." I lowered my voice to a whisper to add: "She's been so keen to show me."

"If you want." He didn't look pleased but he gave in and turned away. I listened to his heavy footsteps on the stairs, heading back to the ground floor.

As soon as he'd gone, I whispered to you: "Gracie, I need you to be very good. Can you do that? Mummy's got to go and do something."

You poked your head out, uncertain. I kissed your nose.

"You play quietly here with elephant and horse and teddy," I said. "Until I come back. OK?"

I left you chattering to your toys while I crept across this second landing to the main bedroom at the front of the house. I faltered on the threshold and steadied my breath.

My eyes went at once to the bed. A king-size, unmade, the duvet thrown back, as if someone had just climbed out. The sheets crumpled. I crossed to it, found my feet caught up in a furry bedside rug. Hers. Not Richard's style. I rubbed the edge of the sheet between my fingers. Cool and crisp. Good quality cotton. Our sheets at home were soft with over-washing.

There were fitted wardrobes down one wall. I opened them quietly, door by door, and looked inside, checking the floor space for boxes, for files.

His suits hadn't changed much but he wore pure silk ties now in brighter colors and bolder designs. Pale pink and blue shirts hung alongside the white. That was her influence.

Her wardrobe had slinky cocktail dresses. At least six. Two long evening dresses, shrouded in dry cleaner's bags. Waterfall cardigans in cashmere. An angora wrap. Crisp shirts and blouses in all shades. Beneath, neatly arranged on a chrome rack, about a dozen pairs of evening shoes. Long spiked heels and spaghetti straps.

I closed the wardrobe doors and got on my hands and knees to check under the bed. A noise, just outside the house. The click of the front gate. I scrambled to the window to look, standing back against the curtain to peer down. The postman's red trolley stood on the pavement.

Downstairs, the letter box clanged, then a smack as post hit the mat. A moment later, the postman went back down the path and wheeled his trolley forward a few paces to next door's gate.

My stomach was tight, my skin hot. I stood still, listening. Richard's tread on the wooden floor as he crossed the hall to pick up the letters. My heart thumped. The footsteps faded again, back to another part of the ground floor. I needed to be quick.

The bedroom was unnaturally bare, so unlike my own. I had a whole suitcase full of your baby things. Then there were my old diaries, boxes of school reports, photographs. I even had a box under the bed with souvenirs from our wedding, right down to the ribbon from the cake.

I crossed to the chest of drawers and rummaged through the drawers. Tights and stockings in packets. Richard's cotton boxer shorts and boxes of cuff links.

Then a drawer of her silky underwear. I tried not to imagine her wearing it. Not to imagine Richard taking it off. I reached a bottom drawer when my fingers felt something different, something cool and hard. I crouched down and pulled out the drawer as far as it would go. It was her overflow space, filled with suspender belts, jewelry boxes, handkerchiefs, and purses. I lifted them out in handfuls. Right at the back was a slim, clear plastic folder.

I thought at first that the photographs, in plain cardboard mounts, like old-fashioned school portraits, were remnants from another generation. The pictures were black and white but seemed muted. There was also a stillness about them, a timelessness. I sat there on the carpet, gazing at them.

They were Ella's features but transformed by such tenderness that I barely recognized her as the woman I knew. Her shoulders were covered by the lacy sleeves of a nightdress or bed jacket. Her hair was loose round her neck.

In one, she gazed with wonder at the baby in her arms. The scrunched face of a newborn with closed eyes. Another picture showed the baby's tiny hand curled round her manicured finger. The final image was of the baby, clothed in a sleep-suit and a delicate lace-edged bonnet, fast asleep in a Moses basket. A printed slip inside the frame read: Celebrating the birth of Catherine Louise. The date was eight years ago. The final item in the folder was wrapped in tissue paper. A tiny lock of ginger hair.

I tore the paper label off the back, with the name, address, and telephone number of the photographer, and shoved it inside my pocket. The intensity of feeling in Ella's eyes made me physically sick. It was impossible to reconcile that love with the knowledge of what she did to her, so soon after these pictures were taken. I shook my head. The photographer who framed those artistic portraits would be just as shocked.

"Richard?"

Her voice, calling, down in the hall. The slam of the front door behind her. I stuffed the pictures, the hastily re-bundled hair and tissue paper, back into the plastic folder, threw the handkerchiefs and jewelry boxes on top, and closed the drawer. It shut with a bang that sounded deafening in the quiet.

A creak from the stairs. I bolted across the landing, back to your room.

"Where were you, Mummy?" You looked cross. You didn't like being on your own.

I picked up the first stuffed toy I saw and started to talk to it, pretending we were in the middle of a game.

"Yes, Mr. Elephant," I said, "of course you can have tea too. Do you take milk?"

My breath was short and the words came out in gasps. You narrowed your eyes.

"What, Mummy? What are you doing?" Then you looked past me, and smiled. "Auntie Ella!"

She stood there, in the doorway. Watching me. Her eyes were cold.

You jumped up and ran to hug her, and her eyes softened as she folded her arms round you and hugged you back.

I felt my cheeks flush. The stolen label from the back

of the pictures burned inside my pocket. I was afraid to move quickly in case it fell out. I thought of the plastic folder, shoved back so quickly, and the belongings heaped on top, left in disarray.

The silence stretched. She waited, her forehead tightened as she looked down at me. Finally, she said: "I think it's time you left. Don't you?"

CHAPTER 43

When I reached home, I copied out the name and address of the photographer from the sticky label and hid the paper in a drawer. I didn't want to risk losing it. Then I made myself a cup of tea and sat alone in the emptiness of the kitchen, considering the label.

It was true then. You and Matt were right. Ella did have a daughter, Catherine Louise. A baby with a shock of ginger hair. This woman, Stella, had documented it. I sipped my tea, thinking. This was the evidence I'd wanted that Ella really did have a child. But how could I prove what she'd done to her?

I fingered the label. These pictures were taken years ago. Stella, whoever she was, might have closed down by now or moved away. Perhaps she would have forgotten Ella, just one of hundreds of clients over the years. Or have nothing to tell me anyway. It was all possible, I knew that. But I had to try. My hands shook as I picked up the phone and dialed the number.

It rang out and I was about to give up when a young woman answered. Her tone was a bored singsong.

"Stella's Photography, how can I help you?"

I took a deep breath. "I'd like to make an appointment please. To see Stella. As soon as possible."

A rustle of paper as she turned the pages of a diary or appointments book.

"I'm afraid she's fully booked today." Pause. "She's in tomorrow. After lunch. Perhaps around three?"

Later, I took the bus into central London to meet Matt.

I gazed out of the window, distracted by the vibrancy of the outside world. I missed you. You had such a capacity for living in the present, for being excited by the smallest, everyday things: the stripes of a zebra crossing, a cat sunning itself on a flat roof, a small boy on a scooter.

Matt stood at the entrance to the shopping mall, waiting for me. His hands were deep in the pockets of his coat. His chin was dark with twenty-four hours of stubble. My pulse quickened at the sight of him.

"Darling." He opened his arms to me and I disappeared into a hug. He held me so tightly I could barely breathe. When he finally loosened his embrace, he kissed me.

"Missed you so much." He lowered his head and kissed me again, this time for even longer. "Thank you for doing this." He took my free hand and tucked it away in his pocket inside his own. His fingers, warm and strong, enveloped mine. "Toy shop?"

"Lead on."

I stood ahead of him on the escalator and he wrapped his arms round my waist as if he couldn't bear to be parted from me for a minute.

It was a large, brightly colored toy shop with animated displays in glass cases. Small children stood with their noses pressed against one, watching trains whirr through tunnels and over bridges. Inside the next, there was a fairground made of play bricks. The roundabout, complete with small figures, was slowly turning, a set of swings rocking mechanically back and forth. A small girl looked lost in it.

Matt set off down an aisle, picking up boxes, looking at them briefly, then pushing them back on the shelf. His shoulders were tight and hunched. I watched, sad for him.

He wouldn't talk to me about Katy or his ex. There was so much I wanted to know about them both but I'd learned not to ask anymore. If I tried to, even the vaguest question, he frowned and his mood darkened. So I was very conscious, as I trailed after him, that I was setting out across thin ice.

I found him at the far end of the shop, frowning at a display of jigsaws.

"How old is she going to be? Eight?"

He nodded quickly, walked a little farther away.

I tried to imagine you at eight. Tried to imagine missing all those years between now and then and the pain of choosing gifts without knowing what to send.

I caught up with him again and stood at his shoulder. He stared down at the picture of a little girl on a box, her blonde hair tied back in a ponytail, her face beaming as she played with a doll's tea set.

"Maybe a bit young?"

He didn't answer. He looked utterly miserable. I wondered how he'd managed to do this on his own, year after year.

"What about something to make?"

I walked on down the aisle, scanning the brightly colored boxes, the shiny mass-produced plastic. Paints and

felt tips and crayons. Stamps and molds. I picked up a
junior tapestry kit with a picture of a pair of kittens.

"I had one of these." Mine had shown a cat sleeping
in the doorway of a country cottage with roses round the
door. A gift from an aunt and uncle. I smiled to myself. I
hadn't thought of it for years. It kept me busy for a whole
Easter holiday and we'd framed it afterward. It must be in
a box somewhere. "I loved it."

He came to look, turned it over, his voice doubtful. "I
don't know."

I put it back, moved him on to sewing kits. Make a
fabric doll. Sew a set of doll's clothes.

"What about this?" I turned it over. "Age seven to ten."

He frowned. "I'm not sure."

It wasn't like him to be so indecisive. He seemed frightened. Afraid to get it wrong. This was his only link to his
daughter until Christmas, assuming she was even given
these gifts. I wanted to help but I didn't know how. I had
no idea what she might like and, from the way he was
behaving, neither did he. I put my hand on his arm and
gave it a squeeze.

"Let's keep looking."

We moved on to the next aisle.

"A game?"

I tried to remember being eight. I played a lot of board
games with my father. He was patient. I realized now that
he must have been tired when he came home from the
lab but he always had time for me. He spent a long time
teaching me chess.

I reached up, past the stacks of drafts and chess and
classic family games and lifted down a box. The glossy
picture showed a family of actors, a beaming mum and
dad and a perfect boy and girl sitting between them, all

waving their hands and exclaiming in delight. It didn't look like any family I'd ever seen. Matt's face, taking it all in, was dejected.

I pushed the box back, moved him on past more games and a bank of jigsaws and came finally to a small display of books.

"*The Hobbit*." I took it down and handed it to him. "Loved it. Didn't you?"

He thumbed through in silence.

"Just the right age for it too. Eight."

He stopped, looked more closely at one of the old-fashioned line drawings. "Maybe." He didn't sound convinced.

"And you can write a message in the front with the date. She'll have it forever."

He hesitated, thinking this over. "She might already have it."

Of course she might. He could say the same about any book I suggested. About any game we found. He closed the book.

"I don't think so." He put it back. "I'm being a bit useless, aren't I? I'm sorry."

I reached up to him, kissed his cheek. His forehead was tight with worry. It was clear how desperately he wanted to get this right and I loved him for it.

"It's OK."

We had almost exhausted the shop when he pulled out a box. Make your own charm bracelets. A girl smiled out, her chin cupped in her hands, her wrists resplendent with pink and white loops of plastic.

"What about this?"

I took it from him, read the blurb on the back. It was a mixture of beads and miniature charms. I had no idea whether she'd like it or not. It was a blind guessing game. I said: "Well, there's a lot to it."

He took it back, looked again at the picture, at the smiling girl.

"It's not too babyish?"

"I don't think so."

He sighed. We chose a card and a sheet of Happy Birthday wrapping paper, decorated with pink cupcakes, and he finally queued to pay, weighed down by the burden of it all. His shoulders were hunched and he seemed so vulnerable, so fragile. It was a side of him I hadn't seen before and I felt a surge of affection for him, for this man who had appeared from nowhere and inserted himself in our lives, who tried so hard to look after me when he saw me struggle.

Afterward, he found me at the door of the shop with his plastic bag in hand and we ventured together into the bustle of the shopping center. He looked dazed. I threaded an arm round his waist and hugged him and his face, when he turned back to me, was sad.

"Thank you." He kissed me on the tip of my nose. "No one's ever done that with me before.

"Let's get some lunch."

"I've got padded envelopes at home." I nodded down to his bag. "You write the card and I'll sort the rest."

"That's sweet." He smiled. "Thank you."

That evening, I left Matt in the kitchen, where he was chopping and stirring and steaming, and went for a long, hot bath. I lay soaking, surrounded by bubbles, and thought how unfair life was. That Ella, blessed with a beautiful baby girl, could care for her so little and yet Matt, clearly besotted with his daughter, was so cruelly forced apart from her.

I picked up the set of ducks on the side of the bath and set them free to bob round the islands of my knees. I wondered if you were asleep in bed now, tucked up under your rainbows and unicorns with bear. I missed you, my love. Always. The house was never the same without you in it.

I read an article once about a mother with terminal cancer who bought and wrapped Christmas and birthday presents for her young children, all the way through to their twenty-first birthdays. I often thought about that.

First, about how anyone could bear to do such a heartbreaking thing. Then, about what I would choose for you, if I knew I were being taken away, leaving you to grow up without me. It struck me as a courageous act, that woman's desperate attempt to defeat time and to stay present in her children's lives for all those years into the future. And yet it was strangely melancholy too. What if the gifts were the wrong ones? If the children simply didn't grow into the people she expected them to be, without the tastes, the interests she imagined? Like Matt, she simply couldn't know.

"I was beginning to think you'd drowned."

Matt was sitting at the kitchen table, looking over the newspaper. The air was rich with the smell of chicken and the strains of one of my old CDs.

"I didn't know you liked Springsteen."

"I didn't know *you* did." He raised his eyebrows. "Saw him in concert three times. Amazing."

I smiled, imagining him as a younger man. I remembered how desperately lonely the evenings were before he came along, the silence and the solitary glass of wine and the early nights. And how normal it seemed now, to have him here in my own kitchen.

He opened an arm to me and I perched on his knee, wrapped my hands round his neck and kissed him.

"You smell nice," he murmured into my neck. "You've been away far too long."

"Sorry." My body felt clean and relaxed in sloppy trousers and shirt and I shifted my weight as he ran a hand under my shirt and across my skin. "What time's dinner?"

"Soon. If you stop distracting me." He lifted me down, got to his feet, and lit the gas under a pan. "About ten minutes."

I took scissors and tape from a drawer and went through to the sitting room to wrap the bracelets craft set, then sealed the present and birthday card in a padded envelope.

I called through: "I can post Katy's present tomorrow for you, if you like?"

Before I went back into the kitchen to join him, I sat for a moment, looking at the parcel, trying to imagine the young girl who'd open it, what she'd feel as she tore off the paper, what she remembered, if anything, of the father who'd chosen it with such love and such pain.

CHAPTER 44

Matt was working a late shift on Sunday and left straight after lunch. I pottered around the house, stacking the dishwasher and putting a wash on. I made your bed and arranged your toys along the bottom. A few more hours and you'd be home again. Then I picked up the photographer's address and set off.

The bell jingled when I pushed the shop door open. The girl behind the counter didn't lift her head. She bent forward over a magazine, her nails painted vivid pink. Her hair was long and swept up in a ponytail, tied with a green ribbon.

The interior was shadowy after the bright sunshine of the street. I made a show of looking at the frames: wood, plastic, metal, multi-frames, singles.

I crossed to the display wall toward the back. Portraits by Stella. She offered several styles. Young children playing, dressed up as pirates or princesses. They laughed, open-mouthed and joyful as only a small child can be, looking up and slightly to one side, their attention caught by someone or something offstage. I wondered how many shots it took to get those perfect photographs and thought with a pang how gorgeous you'd look.

Others were more formal, portraits of families sitting together in posed groups, children with slightly strained faces, in the protective hoop of their parents' arms.

The final section was artistic. The face of a girl, about your age, on the far side of a bubble, just before it burst. A boy, a chubby toddler in a sailor suit, reaching for a falling balloon. It was hard to believe the images weren't faked.

"Can I help you?" The girl, finally. She spoke without moving.

"I've come to see Stella. Jen Walker."

She blinked. "Have you got an appointment?"

"I called yesterday. You told me to come around three." She frowned. "You didn't speak to me."

"Well, whoever it was, that's what they said. Is she in?"

She sighed, heaved herself down from her stool, and padded to the back. Her heels echoed on the wooden floor as they clattered through.

Stella was about fifty, with long, unashamedly graying hair and no makeup. She strode out in baggy trousers, flat shoes, and a loose, blouson top. Her eyes were quick and her handshake firm.

"You wanted to see me?"

"I was thinking of arranging a photo shoot as a present for a friend," I said. "Could I ask you about it?"

The back room had the feel of an artist's gallery. The walls were exposed London brick, the woodwork painted a brilliant white. The ceiling gave way to a long, strutted skylight down the center, which flooded the whole area with light. Around the walls, individual framed pictures were picked out by spotlights on tracks.

Against one wall hung a screen: the pull-down, rolling type, which offered different colored backgrounds. Next to it, there was a large wicker basket that overflowed with props and children's costumes.

"May I have a look round?"

"Feel free." She settled at a long desk in one corner of the room, covered with mounts and prints, and bent over her work.

I walked round, past the wedding portraits, the family shots. They were standard color prints, not the old-fashioned sepia of Ella's pictures. I hesitated, wondering if I'd got the right place. Perhaps it had kept the name but changed hands.

After a few minutes, I sensed her watching me and turned. She got to her feet and came to join me, handed me a brochure and price list.

"Was there something in particular?"

"My friend's having her first baby next month," I said. "I wanted something special for her. You did some striking pictures for another friend of ours, a few years ago. Of her newborn." I hesitated, pretended to think about it. "Well, seven or eight years ago, actually."

She looked at me more closely. "I don't really do newborns."

"Really?" I opened the brochure, looked down the prices. They started at three figures. "I'm sure she said Stella. They were such lovely shots. The baby only looks a few hours old. There's one of her in her mother's arms and another of their hands together, the baby's little fist curled round her mother's finger, you know? They were really evocative."

She didn't speak for a moment. She just stood there, staring at me with an odd expression on her face. I turned away and studied the price list, feeling my face flush. I always was a terrible liar.

"Your friend, the one who's expecting a baby," she said at last, "is everything all right?"

"Yes, well, I think so." I faltered.

Her face became stern. "Are you a lawyer?"

"A lawyer?" I blinked. "No."

"I'm sorry." She looked at me thoughtfully. "I get them, sometimes. I don't want any part in all that. Good luck to people, if that's what they need to do. Personally, I don't think it helps."

She stood for a moment, looking me over, then seemed to come to a decision. She crossed to a shelf and ran her finger along a bank of large albums there before lifting one down. It was ivory and tied with cream ribbon. She opened it on her desk, gestured me across to join her as she started to turn the pages.

"I don't put these out," she said. "Are these the ones you mean?"

I recognized the style at once from the pictures hidden away at the back of Ella's drawer. They all had the same timeless sepia tint, the same stillness in the features. Tiny babies, some of them impossibly small and fragile, some with blue veins bulging at their temples through marble skin, some wrapped round in fluffy white towels, other dressed in baby grows and bonnets, all with their eyes screwed closed.

"I don't charge for these," she said. "But I only take referrals from the hospital. The midwives know me."

I didn't know what to say. I didn't understand.

"I went through it myself, you see, years ago," she went on. "There was nothing available then but a lot of people find it helps. It gives them something to remember.

Otherwise, the whole experience, well, it can seem very unreal afterward."

She glanced at me. My eyes moved again to the photographs. Slowly she turned the pages, showing me family after family. I started to see the dreadful sameness in the pictures. How still the babies lay. Not one of them was crying. Not one had its eyes open.

"Your friend," she said. "The one whose baby I photographed. You didn't know her very well, did you?"

I shook my head.

"How did you see her pictures?"

"At her mother's house," I stuttered. "That's all. She had them on the wall."

She narrowed her eyes and looked thoughtful. "Did your friend suddenly drop you after the birth? Avoid you? Some women do that, you know. Don't take it personally. You can't imagine, until you go through it yourself. The pain of being the only woman on the maternity ward without a baby. Your breasts filling with milk, just as if your baby needed it. And all those well-meaning people, people who haven't heard, phoning you, texting, asking if it's a boy or a girl, wanting names, weights, pictures." She closed the book. "It's not an easy thing to talk about."

She put the album back on the shelf. When she turned around, I was still in the same spot. My feet were rooted.

"Now you know why I don't do newborns," she said, "in the normal sense. Plenty of other studios do." She paused. "I'm sorry if there's been a misunderstanding."

She turned and escorted me to the door.

At the entrance to the shop, she said: "Born sleeping. That's what I like to say." She paused. Again, the curious, appraising look. "If you thought your friend's baby was really alive, well, I must be doing something right."

CHAPTER 45

I barely remembered getting home. My body carried me along. The rest of me was numb. Ella's baby girl. Stillborn. God, how awful. The pavement, the passing traffic, swirled and blurred as I stumbled on.

I couldn't make sense of it. Was it true then, after all? Was there really some medical problem, a reason she couldn't have children? My palms sweated.

And I believed Stella. There was no reason for her to lie to me. *Stillborn*. How did she bear it?

I remembered the calmness in the baby's face. I'd thought she was just sleeping, but it was more than that. I saw it now. It was true. She was already at peace.

I thought again of the pictures. Of the tender look on Ella's face as she held her newborn baby, Catherine Louise. She knew, even as she looked down into that scrunched face, that she'd already lost her baby. That those tiny eyes would never open and fasten on hers. What courage it must have taken to hold back her grief, her anger and cradle her dead baby's body with such love. I kept walking, my hand on my stomach, trying to imagine it, oblivious to the world around me.

My thoughts were jumbled, confused. I thought of the strangeness in her eyes when she saw me teasing you, cuddling you. It was there too when you ran to her and hugged her. A hardness I always read as loathing. Evidence of her bitter hatred of us both. Now, knowing what she'd been through, what she'd lost, it seemed something else. Something far worse. Pain.

At home, I crawled into the crumpled, unmade bed and pulled the covers over my head, trying not to feel, trying only to hide. I shook for some time, my eyes screwed closed. Then a fresh blow hit me. I sat bolt upright, my hands to my cheeks.

What about the medical reports? The seizures? How could both things be true? I drew up my knees, wrapped my arms round them, and hugged them to me. Had Matt's brother, Geoff, made a mistake, looked up details of the wrong case?

I stared at the wall, struggling to figure it out. *Was there more than one Ella Hicks?* It wasn't such an unusual name. I hesitated, forcing my brain to work. But both with babies called Catherine, born around the same time and both dying? I shook my head. It didn't add up. Someone was lying and I didn't think it was Stella.

I moaned, lay back on the bed and curled into a ball. I saw it all again. The club. Ella, there in front of me. Her face when I'd taunted her about Catherine. My body flushed hot with shame. *I didn't know, how could I? What had she thought of me?* She was very upset when she came home, Richard had said. His face was stern. *I didn't have you down as cruel.* I put my hands to my face, trying to scrape away the memory, too ashamed even to cry.

Later, when Richard dropped you home again, I couldn't look him in the face.

I waited until he left, then lifted you into my arms and pressed you against my chest, holding you tight even as you struggled, my wet face pressed into your hair. My own sweet girl, the day you were born was the most miraculous, the most wonderful day of my life. The thought of anyone losing their baby, just as their child's life was meant to begin, made me tremble and I clung to you as if you were the only solid creature in this sad, swirling world.

Before you went up to bed that evening, we crayoned together at the kitchen table. You were happy and full of stories about the weekend. You told me about the little boy you'd met in the park. You'd grabbed his hand when he tried to run through the open gate and escape onto the road.

"He was so naughty, Mummy," you said. "I held his hand very tightly like this because he wanted to run away. What a silly banana."

You shook your head, fondly despairing of a boy who sounded only about two. You sounded so adult that I had to look up to reassure myself that you were still only three years old, crayoning with passion, your hair spilling forward down your cheek. Your words sounded at times like a window on your future, as if time could fold and past and future merge right here in the kitchen and show me your much older self.

I crayoned slowly alongside you, struggling to concentrate. My chest was tight. I was weighed down by thoughts of Ella and baby Catherine and the sadness of what happened to them. Life seemed suddenly so fragile, so unpredictable, that I couldn't quite believe you had survived and were here with me now, and couldn't bear to think how barren my life would be without you.

All I wanted, as I made my careful strokes within the lines and let your chatter fill the silence, was to fold my arms round you and hold you close. I realized how angry I'd been. Angry with Richard for abandoning us and angry with Ella for stealing him away and frightened too that she wanted to take you next and then maybe even Matt. The people I loved most.

Now the anger fell away and I was left limp and exhausted and had to bite my lip to stop myself breaking down and sobbing in front of you. Ella had suffered, suffered much more than I had, suffered grief I couldn't imagine.

CHAPTER 46

Ella

I know exactly what she did. I heard her running across the landing, away from our room, as I came up the stairs. It was obvious the minute I saw her there beside Gracie, flushed with guilt, pretending they were calmly playing together, when her chest was still heaving. She's a terrible liar. An amateur.

I didn't bother talking to Richard about it. He'd never believe me. He doesn't have a prying, malicious cell in his body. But she and I are more alike than she cares to admit. Funny that, isn't it?

That drawer sticks. It's easy to open but there's a knack to closing it and it wasn't properly shut when I went to look. And inside, my mother's old handkerchiefs and her jewelry lay jumbled in a heap. I would never leave them like that. And Catherine's pictures shoved in their file in the wrong order. No one has the right to touch those. No one in the world, apart from me.

I know she hates me. I know she blames me for taking Richard from her. I understand that, however wrong she is. But she's gone beyond that now. She's become like him. Obsessive. Vengeful. He does that to people. Something terrible happens and they have to blame someone. To punish them. It's how they make sense of things, even if the truth is, it's no one's fault. The car crash? She *needs* it to be my fault, another reason to hate me.

And what happened to little Catherine? He always needed to lay that on me, heaping it on top of all the other hurt until I nearly suffocated. Now he's filled her mind with poison too.

Good luck to them both. All I ever wanted was for him to leave me alone, to take his grief out of my sight and leave me to deal with mine. I have dealt with it. I may not be whole but I'm still here. We're all just trying to survive at the end of the day.

I knew it was him. I knew as soon as Richard told me that she'd met a man at the hospital who was suddenly part of her life. Oh yes. I didn't need to hear the name.

I know what he does. I hear about it all the time from friends and from my mother, who refuses to end her friendship with him. I know he asks about me obsessively. He asks about Richard. He stalks us both. He has so little in his life. He can't let go of mine.

So of course he found out at once about the accident, about poor little Gracie, about Jen, the wronged wife, suddenly vulnerable and alone at the hospital. She fell right into his lap.

That's why he was hanging around the ward, walking the corridors, looking for us all. That's why he just happened to bump into her and befriend the suffering, needy mum. And she lapped it up, just as he hoped.

And then I saw him at DDs. It's not the first time he's gone there looking for me on a Saturday night. He knows it's my favorite club. I took him there myself, once upon a time. And so he takes her there to find me, to show me what he's doing. Pathetic, really.

I've thought a lot over the years about what happened with us. I've wondered, in the middle of the night, what on earth attracted me to him in the first place. I think back to my mother and the black hole inside her that I tried endlessly to fill. Maybe I saw something of her in him, thought he was someone I could finally fix, if I only loved him enough. Maybe I even liked his neediness at first, his fragility. Maybe he made me feel wanted. I don't know.

I was a mess for a while. That wasn't all his fault. Grief plays strange tricks on people. It warps their hearts. You know that children's story about the magic mirror? The one that smashes into fragments that lodge in people's eyes, in people's hearts, so they see and feel only ugliness in the world, only evil in the people around them? That's how it felt. For a long time. Until Richard came along.

I forgive him most things. The craziness. The stalking. The endless phone calls, even that string of abusive calls on the day of the accident, the ones that nearly cost little Gracie her life. I take responsibility for that. He can't help who he is, not really, and I should never have let it go on like it did.

But there's one thing I struggle to forgive. Why he took her to Venice. That wasn't for her benefit, it was for mine. I felt it. A message to me. A new way to hurt me. A cruel way of trying to force me to remember. As if I could ever forget.

I was nearly eight months pregnant when we went. It was our last holiday before Catherine came and my very last chance to fly. We stayed in a small family hotel in the backstreets, all we could afford. Matt charmed *la patrona* with his good looks and his smattering of Italian and she doted on me as only an Italian mama can care for a woman about to give birth to her first child.

By dusk, once the tour groups headed back to their hotels, we had Venice to ourselves. One evening, we strolled through to Piazza San Marco in the fading light and treated ourselves to drinks in one of the over-priced cafés there, right on the piazza. I sipped ice-cold freshly squeezed orange juice, one hand on my rounded stomach, and watched the lengthening shadows as Catherine stirred and kicked inside me. Matt was fussing beside me, warning me about the heat, the mosquitoes, and who knew what other dangers he feared.

I didn't even care. The last fingers of sunlight set fire to the gilded façade of the basilica and it was so magical, so serene, and I loved that little girl, teeming with life inside me, with such passion that I was filled with hope. Maybe it was possible. Maybe, despite everything, despite my mother and Matt and all their unhappiness, maybe *I* could be happy, after all.

The following day, we took the *vaporetto* out to the islands. We had lunch in Burano, with its multicolored houses and cafés and shops piled with lace. I bought a tiny lace-trimmed bonnet for Catherine. I still have it. It's the one she's wearing in the photograph, as she lies, so small and so still, in her Moses basket.

And then to Torcello. I'd read about the cathedral and the amazing view from the tower. He said it was too much for me, I'd be tired. I wouldn't listen. So I paid my extra lira and headed up there. It wasn't such a steep climb after all. And the view was stunning. It was a clear day and I could see right across the lagoon. The great dome of Santa Maria della Salute. The campanile in St. Mark's.

There was a breeze up there and I stood against the wire mesh with my eyes closed, feeling its fingers cool and refreshing on my face after the stickiness of the walk below. It was timeless. Sometimes now, when I need to escape, I close my eyes and feel myself there again, the salty air on my cheeks, alone on the deserted tower, my beautiful baby girl safe and well inside me, high above the world.

It happened on the way down. I don't know how. I was about two-thirds of the way to the ground. My legs were tired and perhaps Catherine's weight unbalanced me too, pitched me forward. The sheer rounded bulk of my stomach made it impossible to see where I was placing my feet.

One moment I'm coming steadily down the steps. The next, I'm stumbling and falling forward into nothingness, my hands flung wide, scraping the smooth, curved walls as I pitch past, crashing and bouncing helplessly down toward the bottom. I don't even have time to scream. I fall with such dreadful suspension—the moment stretching forever—and yet with such speed that I'm powerless to save myself. To save her.

He finds me close to the bottom of the steps, curled round in a heap. My hands and one leg are bloodied, my face bruised. When I finally hobble in to the hotel that evening, limping and half-carried by Matt, *la patrona* makes the sign of the cross on her breast and kisses the crucifix round her neck.

She and Matt huddle in a corner and I know they're discussing me. The fact he wants to rush me to a local hospital and I won't go. It's something else he holds against me, later. I'm not bleeding. I'm not in pain. Whatever's happened, I don't see how they can help. I want rest, that's all. I want to believe there's still hope.

So I lie awake all night, my hands spread across my stomach, trying to protect her, to heal her with my love. *Please God, let her be all right. Please God. I'll do anything.* I don't feel a single kick.

We took the first flight back to London the following morning and went by taxi from the airport straight to the hospital. Nothing they could do. Too late. No heartbeat.

They gave me injections and we had a desperate, endless wait until the contractions started and by afternoon, I was in labor. I suffered all that pain to deliver a baby girl who was perfect in every way apart from one small detail. She was born sleeping.

She was beautiful, you see. My Catherine Louise. Even now, there isn't a day I don't think about her. Perhaps not even an hour. And every night, every single night, I go to sleep praying to have that dream.

The dream where I'm holding Catherine in my arms and she's so beautiful and she opens her tiny blue eyes and looks up at me and she's alive, she's breathing and it was all a mistake, a terrible mistake. I live for that dream. Even now.

Then I wake up and it's one more day without her. One more day alone, without my angel, sleeping in my arms.

CHAPTER 47

Jennifer

I hardly slept that night. The bed seemed to shift and pitch. Nothing made sense. I'd made terrible mistakes, I saw that now, but I was left adrift, confused about all that had happened and what to believe. All I could think was that Geoff had lied to Matt, fed him nonsense about Ella. I longed to see Matt, to feel him hold me and comfort me and talk all this through with me, so we could work out the truth together.

On Monday, I took you to nursery and then drove around, not sure where I was going. The day stretched ahead without purpose. When I tried to call Matt, his phone went to voicemail. He'd been on late shift the day before but he should be home by now, pottering and having a shower before he made up some sleep.

I pulled into a garage, filled up with petrol, and bought a coffee. Afterward, I parked at the edge of the forecourt, sipping it and trying to decide what to do.

My hands shook. All I wanted was to be with Matt, to be held so tightly that I felt safe from all this, from Ella's

grief and your strange stories and my own sense of loneliness. I imagined him in his tiny flat, close to the Tube
station, and had a longing to be there with him, to talk, to
crawl into bed and hide away together. I finished my coffee
and punched the name of the Tube station into the satnav.

He always made fun of his little flat in central London,
about what a postage stamp it was and the fact that two of
us would have trouble squeezing inside at the same time. I
didn't care. He'd turned up on my doorstep plenty of times
without warning. I didn't see why I couldn't do the same.

I drove in to the city center, guided by the satnav, and
finally found the entrance to the Tube and the private,
leafy square just across from it. It looked different in daylight. The restaurant where we'd first met for dinner was
closed and silent. It all seemed a long time ago. A very
different time.

I turned into the square. The pavements here were
almost deserted. Many of the Georgian houses had
brass plates on the doors, suggesting corporate offices or
embassies. It was a warm day and I lowered the window
as I crawled along, looking for somewhere to park. The
outside air smelled of blossom and mown grass.

I finally found a metered space for the car and set off
on foot toward the narrow side street he'd pointed out to
me that night. I wasn't sure how I'd find the right block
but in fact, there was only one contender, a grand Victorian mansion block, hidden just off a street crammed with
bistros, sandwich shops, and offices. The entrance was set
in a horseshoe round an ornamental garden and a small,
spouting fountain with a stone bowl.

I stood by the water and ran my eyes across the array
of flats in the three-story block. Flat number twenty-two,
he'd said. Easy to remember because it was the same as

your birthday. The windows were still and dark. Many were concealed by curtains or blinds. I felt a sudden chill, wondering where Matt was and how he'd react when I appeared at his door.

The stone doorway was secured by a glass door. I put my face to it and cupped my hands until I could make out, through the reflection, a dimly lit lobby. A bank of metal postal boxes covered a side wall, most of them leaking flyers. In the center, there was a polished wooden table with a large display of dried flowers. Ahead, up several carpeted steps, the metal shine of two lifts. The whole block had a hushed, opulent look.

I tried to imagine Matt, in his expensive coat, crossing the lobby and smiled to myself. I had a sudden sense of him lying close to me, in fresh cotton sheets in a modern apartment, all glass and chrome. He would stumble to the door in a dressing gown, bed-warm and drowsy, his face prickly with overnight stubble and open his arms to me to go inside and join him.

One of the lift doors swished open and a young man stepped out. A city type in a dark suit, a Mac in the crook of his arm. The young man paused to check his mailbox, then held open the door for me to go inside.

I crossed to the lifts, feeling like an intruder. The second-floor landing had the same deep pile carpet as the lobby. I counted down the brass numbers on the doors. The landing was empty. All the doors looked identical.

I lifted the brass knocker on number twenty-two. The clatter made me jump. My pulse beat in my ears as I waited, listening. I had the same anxious flutter I once felt as a teenager when I hung round the school stairwell, hoping to catch sight of Jimmy Brent and his friends. Silence.

Behind me, the lift purred as it slid down its shaft.

A key rattled in a neighboring door, then, again, silence. I got out my phone, dialed Matt's number, and stood close to the door in the hope of hearing it ring inside. Nothing. It clicked straight to voicemail.

I lifted the knocker, banged it again, a little harder. Waited. I was deflated, embarrassed. Perhaps he was still at work.

I was turning away when the door suddenly opened, just a matter of inches, held in place by a metal safety chain. A woman peered through the narrow gap, her eyes suspicious. She was in late middle age, her cheeks floury with powder, her lips an unfashionable red.

"Hello." I straightened up, smiled. "I've come to see Matt. I'm Jennifer."

"No man. Please." She had a strong foreign accent and made to shut the door in my face. I stopped it with my foot, wondering if she'd understood.

"Doctor Aster? He works at Queen Mary's Hospital."

She shook her head. "No hospital."

I tried to peer past her into the flat. I'd envisaged a stark modern interior, all black and gray and cream with few home comforts. My stereotypical idea of a bachelor's pad. This hallway was hectic with polished wooden furniture and knickknacks. A large ceramic pot against the wall bristled with walking sticks and umbrellas. The wall above was crammed with three rows of framed pictures of all sizes, watercolors and photographs competing for space. A walking frame stood, partially folded, underneath.

"Please—" I began.

"No. You please." The woman kicked away my foot with unexpected force and the door slammed. I stood for a moment, stunned, my heart thumping.

I stood, staring at the closed door in disbelief. I was

certain he'd said flat twenty-two, the same as the door in front of me. Was I in the wrong block? Or the wrong street? I didn't see how I could be.

I was just reaching home when my phone rang and I stopped at the side of the road.

Matt's voice was breathy. "Are you OK?"

I shrugged, looking out at the traffic. "Well, not really."

"I'm so sorry. Only just got your messages. Had my phone switched off. Been a night and a half."

He sounded tired. I felt a bit better, just hearing his voice.

"Where are you?" I wondered for a moment about turning round and driving back. I wanted so much to see him, to be held.

"Still at the hospital. Won't bore you but it's been non-stop. Going to grab a shower and then sleep here."

I took a deep breath. "Matt, is someone staying in your flat?"

A couple of teenage boys trundled past on skateboards, shouting to each other. Their wheels drummed on the cobbles, drowning out his reply.

"Didn't hear you." He sounded distant, as if he'd moved away from the phone. "In the flat? Hope not. Unless I've got squatters. Why?"

I opened my mouth to say more, then closed it again.

"Has something happened?" He sounded concerned.

I tried to picture him in the hospital accommodation block, crawling exhausted into bed in some anonymous bedroom on a shabby corridor.

"Yes. I mean—" I didn't know where to start. "I really miss you."

"I miss you too. Sorry. I'd come over but—" A crackle on the line. "Love you."

I hesitated. "You too."

*   *   *

The house was empty with you at nursery. I went into your room and sat in the armchair with your bear in my arms, looking at your bed, trying to calm myself. Downstairs, I put the kettle on and stood against the kitchen counter with a cup of tea I didn't really want, looking out at the sunlight falling in shafts across the overgrown yard.

My legs juddered. I couldn't keep still. I could feel my father there with me, quietly invisible in the background as he always liked to be. And Catherine too, a baby with ginger hair who never had the chance to grow. I paced up and down the kitchen, my hands trembling on my cup. I thought about Ella and the love in her face as she looked down at her little girl.

And I thought of Matt. Of the knowing look in his eyes as he leaned forward to me across that gritty table and told me what he'd discovered about Ella Hicks and his suspicions about her dead child. Of his vagueness that night in the taxi when I asked him what Ella said to him in the club.

You deserve each other, she had told me.

The parcel, now neatly addressed to Matt's daughter, lay there on the side. I grabbed it, reached again for my coat and car keys, and headed for the door.

CHAPTER 48

The address on the parcel was in west London, a suburb about half an hour's drive away. As I drove closer, the streets looked increasingly depressed. The route took me down a main road, which was dotted with small parades of shops: kebab, pizza and burger chains, late-night convenience stores, laundrettes, betting shops.

The ground was patched with scraps of litter. The walls that bordered the road were daubed with spray-can graffiti in bright colors. I stared out of the window, feeling a growing sense of unease.

As I entered the neighborhood, I lost confidence and pulled into a burger place. It was soulless. The interior was designed not for comfort but to thwart vandals and drunks. The tables and benches were made from cheap plastic with rounded corners and were molded to the ground. The floor was covered in scuffed tiles.

I bought some chips from a spotty Chinese youth in a paper hat and sat in the window to eat. The shiny table, designed to be indestructible, was scored with cigarette burns. I looked out through the grimy window at the scruffy people waiting at the bus stop across the road. A homeless man, over-dressed in woolen hat and miser mitts, sat in a corner of the shelter, bulging with carrier bags. I wondered what kind of home Matt's ex lived in and what sort of upbringing his daughter was getting.

The house was a little farther on, a few minutes from the main road, set in a cul-de-sac on an estate. The properties were square and uniform. Nineteen-thirties, perhaps. They might have been council-owned until Margaret Thatcher put them up for grabs.

They reminded me of my childhood. Each had a short driveway and a curve of rounded bay windows across the front. The sort of rather poky house my mother would have described as a two-up, two-down.

I stopped just before number thirty-eight. The sitting room of number thirty-six was concealed by net modesty curtains. A vase with a cornflower-blue posy, flanked by two neat rows of china dogs, decorated the sill. They were the kind of ornaments my grandmother used to own, before she moved into a home and most of her possessions went to the auction house.

The next house, clearly visible over the low fence, was the same design. A small garage sat beside the house, its paint peeling. The driveway was empty.

I hesitated. My thoughts had been focused on finding the house and learning what I could about it, with the pretext of delivering the parcel. Now I faltered, unsure quite why I was here. My legs wobbled. The taste of chips was thick and greasy in my mouth. I didn't know if I really wanted to meet Matt's ex. Or his daughter.

A car slid past. It slowed, turned round at the far end of the cul-de-sac, and came crawling back. I felt conspicuous. I thought of the police officers and their warning all that time ago. No more trouble.

I unfastened my seat belt, reached for the parcel, and climbed out of the car.

The house needed a fresh coat of paint. I marched up to the front door, eager now to get this over with and go home. Perhaps no one was at home and I could just leave the parcel on the doorstep.

The curtains were drawn back and I glanced through the windows as I approached. It was dark inside but light enough to show an old-fashioned and solidly conventional sitting room. It was dominated by a brushed cotton three-piece suite, set round a coffee table and angled toward a medium-sized television set on a stand. A few magazines lay on the table in a neatly aligned pile. A mirror with a gilded frame hung over the fireplace. A pair of candlesticks stood at either end. A mantel clock with a dark wooden case sat plumply between them. It was exactly the sort of room my mother would like. *Tasteful*, she might say. *Unpretentious*. It might have waited, unchanged, for the last thirty years.

I blinked. For the second time in a day, I must have picked the wrong house, the wrong street. There was no trace of a child living here. No toys, no clutter, no books. This was not the house of a young woman, a Londoner of about my own age.

A shadow shifted. I started, jumped back. A figure there, to one side of the room, watching me. A stout woman. She disappeared. My palms made sweaty marks on the padded envelope. I turned, ready to bolt.

Before I could move, the door opened. The woman stood there in the doorway. She was smartly dressed, about seventy years old. She had short, permed hair. With one hand, she pulled together across her stomach the draping flaps of a cardigan. Her other hand held the door.

"Hello." She looked thoughtful.

"I'm sorry," I stuttered. "I think I've got the wrong house."

She reached out, lifted the parcel from my hands, and studied the address, the handwriting, then, with the same appraising look, studied me. Her eyes were faded blue, as if time had slowly drained the color from them. She looked familiar but I couldn't place her.

"You're Jennifer, aren't you?" she said calmly, reading me as if she understood everything. "Won't you have a cup of tea?"

She opened the door wider and stood to one side to let me in.

"I thought you'd turn up, sooner or later." She sounded resigned and rather sad. "But I wasn't quite sure when."

CHAPTER 49

I perched on the edge of an armchair in the hushed sitting room and followed her movements in the kitchen by sound. The whoosh of water as a kettle filled. The click of a cupboard, opening and closing. The soft suck of a fridge door.

I blinked. The parcel sat on the coffee table beside the women's magazines. Beneath, the carpet was hectic, with red and pink swirls. The cushions on the beige settee seemed carefully chosen to reflect the same shades. The wall-lights were semi-transparent glass, the bulbs held by pale-pink petals.

Jennifer. She'd greeted me by name. Had she mistaken me for someone else? It made no sense. I wondered what Matt would think if he knew I'd come.

"Do you use a teapot?"

She came in carrying a laden tea-tray, lined with a lace-edged cloth, and began the methodical business of setting out the teapot, covered with a hand-knitted cozy, two cups and saucers, the milk jug, a sugar bowl, and teaspoons. A plate of plain biscuits. Serviettes. She was entertaining, in the old-fashioned way. Making an effort.

"So many people have lost the ability to make a decent cup of tea. Don't you find? I went to New York once. A long time ago, when Harold was still alive. I asked for tea at breakfast and do you know what they brought me? A mug of lukewarm water, no saucer, with a rather dismal teabag floating in it." She tutted. "They may be the leaders of the free world but really, they have a lot to learn about tea."

She spoke softly but efficiently as if she were used to being in command of her own ship. Her back was straight and firm as she sat forward to pour the milk, then placed a metal tea strainer over my cup and added the tea. It was strong. She struck me as the kind of woman it might be dangerous to underestimate.

"Do have a biscuit." She set a plate in front of me and a serviette, folded into a triangle. "I always use loose-leaf tea. Everyone seems to use teabags. But you know what they put in those bags? Sweepings from the floor." She nodded. "It's true. I read an article about it."

She seemed perfectly at ease, crossing her legs neatly at the ankle and watching me with a half-smile as I sipped my tea. She was wearing light slip-on shoes, rather than slippers, and I wondered if I'd interrupted her as she was getting ready to go out.

I took a deep breath. "I am sorry to disturb you. I was delivering a parcel, you see. For a little girl. It's her birthday in a few days and I didn't trust the post."

She nodded as if she already knew. "Katy."

I stared. Katy's name wasn't written on the envelope, only her surname, Aster.

She smiled, watching me. Again, I had the sense that

she understood far more than I did and was giving me time to catch up.

"Let's drink our tea and have a chat first. Then I'll explain about all that."

She talked easily for a while, as if we were old friends. Inconsequential chat about the warm weather. The accelerating pace of life in London and the demise of good neighbors. The changes to the cul-de-sac since she and Harold moved there, more years ago than she cared to remember.

I listened for clues but her conversation was as carefully neutral as the three-piece suite. She clearly cherished the vanishing English art of small talk as dearly as she valued properly made tea.

Finally, as we reached the bottom of the pot, she set aside her cup and saucer, picked up the parcel, and got to her feet.

"Come."

CHAPTER 50

I followed her out of the room and up the stairs to a narrow landing. She opened the door to a box room. It was a little girl's bedroom, with cream walls and a small chest of drawers painted with stars and moons. A jewelry box rested on top. A clown doll, with a soft body and chipped china face, sat slumped against it.

A single bed, squeezed in against the far wall, was covered with a bobbled pink counterpane and a cushion with an appliqué dancing elephant. The elephant's tutu, a semicircle of starched white net, stood proud from the fabric.

A row of soft toys sat along the length of the bed, their backs against the wall. Teddy bears with red ribbons, a knitted rabbit, a giraffe, felt dolls.

It was too still, too tidy. The sunshine streaming in through the small window danced with motes of dust.

She pointed, inviting me to step inside. There wasn't a lot of room. A low table sat behind the door. It was piled with brand-new toys.

Dolls in unopened packaging. Jigsaws, still in cellophane.

A shiny box of building bricks. Packet of pristine crayons, paints, felt-tip pens. Above it all, a framed drawing of a large, ornate letter "K." On the end of the table stood a bud vase with a single yellow rose, its petals already loose and starting to fall.

I turned back to her. She was watching my confusion, her expression sad.

"Katy's room?"

She nodded. She opened the padded envelope, tore off the wrapping paper I had taped with such care, and placed the box on top of a jigsaw. The little girl, her wrists decorated with plastic bracelets, smiled up at us both. The room was lifeless.

"She doesn't live here, does she?"

"Not exactly." She frowned. "But we like to feel she's here."

She ushered me out. The door directly across the landing was open, showing a second bedroom. That one was clearly occupied. I crossed to the threshold and peered in.

The walls were a neutral beige, the carpet and curtains dark blue. The jazzy duvet on the double bed was crumpled as if it had been pulled across in haste. The bedside table was piled with books and scraps of paper.

A pair of men's trousers hung across the back of a chair. Used socks and a pair of underpants were strewn on the seat. Across the bottom of the bed, an abandoned sweater. Matt's sweater.

She stepped past me and stooped to pick up the dirty washing, then dropped it with a low sigh into the canvas laundry basket by the door. It was an automatic gesture that suggested years of repetition, years of arguments.

I looked again at the line of her jaw, the shape of her eyes.

"You're his mother."

Her forehead creased, worried. "I am."

I looked back toward the box room. "Katy's grandma." She nodded.

I shook my head, looked again at the messy male room. "He lives here?"

"He didn't tell you, did he?" She reached forward and patted my arm. "He's a good boy. Don't be angry with him. He really cares for you. I'm his mother, you see. I know. He just hasn't been himself. Not since we lost Katy."

I stepped farther into his bedroom. Along the wall to my left, partly hidden by the door, hung a long cork noticeboard. Its surface was covered with a mess of black-and-white pages, stuck with colored pins. Grainy photographs, printed off from a computer. My stomach contracted. I went across to look more closely.

Pictures of me. Walking through the shopping center. On the high street. Outside nursery. Standing in the park. Images of our home. Some taken from the far side of the road, shot through parked cars. Others from right outside the house, from the gate. They were scribbled with marker pen. Hearts drawn crudely round my face. A cartoon flower stuck in my hand, another in my hair.

Several were dark, taken at night. Dim close-ups of the shadowy front door. An image of my bedroom window, a line of light tracing the edges of the curtains. "How dare he." I turned back to her, angry now and slightly sick. A memory rose in me from those weeks just after your accident when I felt most vulnerable and had a sense of being watched, of being followed, of glimpsing a figure in the shadows, staring at the house through the darkness from across the road.

"He followed me, didn't he? Before we really knew each other. He spied on me."

She spread her hands by way of apology and inclined her head.

"He didn't mean anything by it. He just wanted to protect you. He felt it was, well, his mission." She hesitated. "He'd never hurt you. You know that?"

I didn't answer. I didn't know anything anymore.

She guided me back downstairs and into an armchair. She set a glass of water in front of me and I drank it off, my head spinning. All I wanted to do was to run out of that mummified house and go home, lock the front door, and crawl into bed. To hide away from all the confusion, the hurt, the betrayal. My legs shook and she seemed to pin me there, with her politeness, with her kindness.

"You have to understand, it's an illness." Her eyes never left my face. "He can't help it. It's a tragedy, really. He could have done so much more. He was always clever. Did well at university. And he almost qualified, you know, as a doctor." She hesitated, reading my shock. "Ah. That's what he told you, isn't it? A doctor?"

I stared, shaking with fury. I felt stupid. Tricked. Who was this man who had walked into our lives and lied to me? Who deceived me, abused me.

She went quietly on. "Matthew works in a restaurant. The smart restaurant at the hospital, on the top floor. Have you tried it? A bit pricey but very nice food. It's not a bad job. He's very reliable and he cooks well, don't you think?"

Her look was almost sly as if she knew, as if she could see him there in my kitchen, my apron round his waist, his strong arms chopping and cutting, grating and stirring. As if I should have known.

"They didn't plan the baby. But once he got used to the idea, he wanted it desperately. You've no idea. He loves children. And then, when they lost her..." She trailed off, gazing past me at the wall, unseeing. "It was devastating. And then she left him almost at once. It was cruel, really. It was more than he could cope with."

I put my face in my hands. My temples throbbed. "I should go."

"He said you were different, Jennifer. That you might understand. He told me about all you've been through with your husband, with your little girl. We're both so sorry." She hesitated, her eyes back on my face, beseeching now. "*We're two of a kind, Mother.* That's what he said. Two of a kind."

"I went to his flat." I thought of the stylish block and the contrast it made with this place. "He doesn't have one, does he?"

"Oh dear." She looked away. "No, I'm afraid not." She leaned forward, stacked the plates and cups on her tray.

I sat there, stupid with shock. She got quietly to her feet and carried out the tea things. I looked down at the swirling carpet and pictures seemed to form there. Matt, appearing from nowhere as I sat, alone and desperate, in the hospital café. Matt, appearing on the high street as I walked you home from nursery. Matt in the kitchen, capable and confident as he cooked. Matt, sitting silently in your darkened bedroom, hunched forward, his eyes sad.

When she came back, she was carrying a large box. She seemed pleasantly surprised that I was still there. She set the box on the table between us.

"What about Geoff?" I said suddenly.

"Geoff?" She blinked.

"He doesn't have a brother, does he? A policeman. A detective."

Her face seemed to crumple and she looked down, fiddled with the lid of the box.

"How could he tell so many lies?" I was on my feet, my hands balled at my sides. "Everything. Everything he's told me!"

"Not everything, Jennifer," she said very quietly. "You mustn't think that. He does care for you."

The room was unbearably oppressive. I strode through to the kitchen. Compact, neat, ordinary. The tray sat on the worktop. The cups and saucers, already washed, sat upside down on the draining board. I stood there at the sink, looking out at a small handkerchief of garden. The borders were planted with rows of white and yellow alyssum. The square of lawn in the middle was freshly cut. I imagined Matt, his sleeves rolled up, pushing a mower up and down the patch of grass, straightening the edges with shears while his mother, pottering in the kitchen, watched from the window.

I ran the cold-water tap, splashed my eyes, my face, trying to steady myself.

He was never a doctor at the hospital. He chopped vegetables and stirred soup for a living. All the stories he told me about difficult nights, about desperately ill children, they were all lies. What a fool I'd been.

I went back into the sitting room, where she was steadily emptying the contents of her box onto the table.

"Matthew painted the nursery. They had everything ready, the sweetest little booties, dresses, bonnets, everything. Then they went on that silly holiday. I did advise against it but they wouldn't listen. They rushed to the hospital and it was too late." She paused, remembering. "Poor things. Imagine. Having to go through all that. To give birth to a child who's already passed away." Her voice caught and she hesitated, collected herself. "It doesn't bear thinking about, does it? Please try, Jennifer. Try to find pity in your heart for him."

I turned to her to say goodbye. I thought of Matt and his sad little life, pictured him striding into this dim room in the evening, sitting with his mother, watching television. I shook my head. I never wanted to see this wretched house again.

"I'm sorry," I said.

She pulled out a thin cardboard folder and opened it, held it up for me to see.

"This is Katy."

I looked down at the photograph. I recognized it at once. A sepia study of a newborn with closed eyes, wearing a sleep-suit and a tiny hat with lace trim and lying in a Moses basket. A sticker on the mount said: Portraits by Stella. On the table, beside the box, nestled in tissue paper, lay a lock of ginger hair.

"Ella was his ex, wasn't she? It was his baby she lost." I pointed, my voice sharp. "Catherine Louise."

She shrugged, smiled. "*She* preferred Catherine. But we always called her Katy. It was my mother's name too, you know. And besides, Catherine is such a formal name for a baby girl. Don't you think?"

CHAPTER 51

On the way home, my hands shook on the steering wheel. I bit down on my lip to stop myself from crying. When I stopped at traffic lights, the eyes in the driving mirror were frantic. I switched off my mobile and pushed it to the bottom of my bag.

I drove as fast as I dared but I was late collecting you from nursery. Your face was tight with hurt, the teachers cross.

As soon as we entered the house, I locked the door behind me and bolted it, then went through to the sitting room and closed the curtains. You watched, wary.

"What are you doing, Mummy?"

I swallowed hard. "Let's watch television this afternoon. It'll be fun."

A moment later, the phone started to ring in the kitchen. I couldn't move. We stood there, side by side, listening to the ring. Finally, it stopped.

After lunch, I got the box of videos out and let you watch as many cartoons as you liked. You were utterly

absorbed. You clutched your bear to your chest, sometimes bouncing on the settee with excitement, sometimes
chuckling, lost in the world of your program.

As I watched with you, I could almost feel myself a
child again, watching television in the afternoon, fresh
from school, barely aware of the sounds that ran always
beneath the soundtrack, the distant thud and crash of my
mother as she moved about the kitchen, scraping and stirring and washing as she made my tea.

I took out my wallet and studied the picture of myself
as a small girl, innocent in a summer dress and sandals.
A scene from a world that was lost now. My parents close
behind me, protecting me. Their faces so impossibly
young.

I was still gazing at it when your video finished and
you hung over my knee to reach for my wallet, to see what
I was looking at.

"Mummy, what's that?"

I bent low and kissed your head, smelled your hair,
your skin.

"That's an old picture." I hesitated, letting you look
before I explained. "Guess who these people are?"

You peered more closely at the faces, then shouted. "Mr.
Michael! Look!" Your eyes glowed with pleasure. "It's
him, Mummy. Look! Why did you say he was made up?
He's real!"

I stared. I couldn't speak.

You grabbed my wallet with both hands, excited. "He's
got normal clothes!" You considered. "Where is he?
Who's that girl?"

"That's me, sweetheart," I managed to say. "When I
was about your age. With my mummy and daddy. That's
me."

You hesitated, thinking.

I pointed. "See? That's Grandma. Doesn't she look young?"

"Grandma?" You narrowed your eyes as if you were struggling to reconcile the young woman in the picture with the elderly one you knew. "Why's she with Mr. Michael?"

"That isn't Mr. Michael. That's your grandpa."

You shook your head. "I don't have a grandpa."

"You did. You just never saw him. He died a long time ago."

"Silly Mummy." You laughed. "He isn't dead. He's looking after baby Catherine and the other girls and boys."

I looked again at the young man, thinking of the father I remembered. Gentle and funny and strong and wonderful with small children.

"So you *do* know Mr. Michael." You sounded hurt now, considering. "Why did you say he wasn't real?"

CHAPTER 52

The phone kept ringing all through that long afternoon of videos and snacks. In the end, I stopped it for good by unplugging it at the wall.

When your bedtime finally came, I wrapped my arms round you, hoisted you high, and carried you up the stairs in my arms.

"Is Uncle Matt coming tonight?"

"No, my love." My voice was tight.

You sensed that something was wrong but I didn't know how to explain and you didn't ask any more questions. In the bathroom, you perched, still and silent, on the linen basket as I ran a bubble bath for you. The cascade of running water shut out other noise. The rising steam in our small bathroom drew us together and hid us, kept us safe.

You sat, waist-deep in water, unnaturally withdrawn as I drew animals on your back with the bubbles, tried to make you laugh by tickling your toes.

When you were dry and warm in your pajamas,

smelling of lavender and argan oil, I drew the curtains on the outside world and let you climb into my bed, Mummy and Daddy's big bed. We cuddled together there, the duvet tucked round us, reading as many stories as you wanted. Slowly, despite yourself, you started to yawn and your eyes grew heavy.

You fell asleep there, lying on your side, your arms clinging to your bear and my arm tucked safely round your waist. I put my face between your shoulder blades and tried to slow my heart to the soft rhythm of your breathing, to fill my senses with the smell of your skin, of your freshly washed body.

Later, I crept downstairs. The kitchen was full of shadows and I stood in the doorway, weary, letting my eyes adjust. Slowly, the shapes emerged. The kitchen table where Matt and I had so often sat together to eat. The worktop where he chopped and diced. The fridge. The silver gleam of the window over the sink.

I didn't put the light on. I was frightened of the darkness but I was even more afraid of being seen. I thought of the photographs pinned to his wall and the way he'd spied on us, day and night. He hadn't come across me by accident, that night in the hospital. I saw that now. He must have known about the accident soon after it happened. I imagined him tracking Ella at first, his ex, photographing her as crazily as he had me. Then extending his obsession to Richard, once they fell in love. And then to me and to you too, my love. He stalked us. He planned it all.

I opened a bottle of red wine and sat, curled in a corner of the settee in the darkness, cradling a glass. My body trembled.

I thought about Matt. About his focused pursuit right from the start. The chance meetings in the hospital, on the high street. I shivered. They looked different to me now, not accidental at all but deliberately engineered. The way he phoned me every evening to talk, turned up on my doorstep, invited or not, saying how desperately he missed me, promising to take care of me. Of the way he wouldn't take no for an answer when I tried to cancel. The way he constantly hurried the pace. *I love you so much, Jen. I don't think I could live without you. We belong together. I'd do anything for you.*

I'd seen it all as devotion, as proof of his love. I wanted to. I'd been so lonely. I let him into our lives. I trusted him.

I thought of him sitting in the darkness in your bedroom, silently watching you as you slept.

When I closed my eyes, I saw his poky bedroom with its tasteless beige, his mother stooping to pick up socks and underpants. The thought of it made me nauseous. I drank off the glass of wine and then another and finally the edges of the room started to blur. After a third glass, I buried my face in the cushion and sobbed.

I must have dozed. When I woke, I groped my way across the kitchen and filled a glass from the tap, drank it off. My hands trembled. I stood in the silence for a moment, trying to steady my nerves.

A sound. I stiffened, strained to hear. The low groan of our gate on its hinges, barely audible. A ting as it closed. Footsteps. A pause. Then the bang of the knocker on the door.

"Jen! It's me, Matt."

I leaned against the sink, afraid to move.

Crash. The knocker again, slammed with force now.

"Jen. I know you're in there. Come on. We need to talk."

I didn't want to talk. I didn't want to see him. I crept across the kitchen and into the hall, feeling my way in the darkness. I made it to the bottom of the stairs, and took hold of the banister.

The clatter of the letter box rang out. His voice came again, clear now. I imagined him sitting or kneeling on the doorstep, his mouth against the metal, speaking into the darkness. I shrank into the wall.

"I know, Jen. I know how it looks. But let me in. I can explain."

My breathing blew through the silence of the hall. He seemed to sense me there.

"All I ever wanted was to take care of you. You and Gracie. Don't you see? I love you so much. Come on, give me a break. Did I ever hurt you? Or Gracie? I would never do that."

A pause. I held my breath, waiting.

"Don't do this. Let me in. We can sort this out. We can. We belong together. We're a family now."

He broke off. A strangled noise. A sob.

"I love you, Jen! For God's sake. Please. Give me a chance to explain."

The letter box clattered shut, then, a moment later, opened again, even wider. I sensed his eyes there, peering into the house, into the shadows, reaching for me.

"Come on, Jen. Open up. I know you're there." His voice was thick. "I'm begging you. Don't do this."

I turned and ran up the stairs, climbed into bed beside you, and drew the covers over us both, panting. I tightened my arms around you, your slight shoulders, your small body, pressed you to me and rocked.

You stirred, twisted onto your back, murmured: "Mummy?"

"Hush, my love. Mummy's here."

I buried my face in your hair. Your neck tasted salty.

From down below, footsteps crunched on the gravel as he retreated down the path. Then, again, silence. I sensed him out there in the dark night, his hands in his pockets, looking up at the house, at our bedroom window, keeping watch as he had so many times before.

I lay stiffly against you. My body shook the mattress. Your small, warm feet pedaled my leg as you made sure of me, even in your sleep.

I stroked your hair and managed to whisper: "It's all right, Gracie. It's all right."

CHAPTER 53

I woke early the next morning and lay, groping my way to consciousness, my eyes trying to focus on the blank spread of the ceiling.

As I hung, for a moment, between sleep and waking, life still seemed normal. Then the memory of the day before, of Matt and his mother and his unspeakable lies, came crashing in like a tidal wave, knocking the air from my chest. I felt sick. I lifted my head from the pillow, twisted to see you. You lay curled on your side, your breaths puffing through parted lips, deep in sleep.

I peered past you to the bedside clock. Already seven. I slid sideways out of bed as stealthily as I could, pulled my dressing gown from the back of the door. Your hair was flung out across the sheet and I bent to smell it, then to touch my lips to your forehead.

The kitchen floor gleamed with shafts of weak morning sunlight. The wine bottle, almost empty now, sat on the table with my dirty glass. I clicked on the kettle, reached for a mug, and turned back with it. Screamed.

Crash. The mug, slipping from my fingers, exploded like a grenade on the hard floor. Shards and splinters skimmed in all directions.

"Get out!" I didn't recognize my own voice. It was high. Scratched at the air. "Get the hell out. How did you—"

"Jen." He rose from the settee, there in the sitting room, arms out, hands extended as if he were calming a storm. "Please."

I put a hand out and grasped the edge of the sink.

"Any nearer, I'll call the police."

"Really?" He shook his head. "Don't be like that, Jen. Please. Hear me out."

I pulled the folds of my dressing gown more firmly round my body, tightened the cord.

He blinked, his eyes heavy and red-rimmed. "Let's talk, Jen. Work it out. Can't we do that?" His tone was wheedling. "Please, darling. I love you. What else can I say? We're good together."

I narrowed my eyes and looked past him to the sitting room windows. The curtain on the right hung crookedly and the lining billowed as a breeze stirred it.

"Forget about Richard. He and Ella—they aren't like us, Jen. They don't love deeply and forever. Not like we do."

Beyond, out in the street, a car passed. The noise was too loud, too clear. The window was open. He'd forced it, lifted the sash high enough to climb in.

"What do you want?"

The kettle burbled, shuddered on its stand as it began to boil.

"I just want to talk. That's all."

He came slowly toward me, his arms outstretched, his face pleading, crossing the threshold into the kitchen.

"Don't." I flinched.

"For heaven's sake." He stopped and stood there, running his hand through his hair. His skin was gray.

He must have sat down here all night. All the time I was holding you close upstairs, imagining I was keeping you safe, he was here, in our home. He could have come into the bedroom in the darkness. I started. Perhaps he had.

"I won't touch you, if you don't want me to. OK? Jen, please. Don't do this."

As he advanced farther into the kitchen, I took a step backward and bumped up against the worktop.

He shuddered. "This is ridiculous. All right, I've got some explaining to do. Hands up. I admit it. But I'm the same person, Jen. I'm no different." He hesitated, his face tense. "I love you so much. You know that. And deep down, you know you feel the same about me."

He pointed me to a chair. I sat on the far side of the table, putting a barrier between us. The kettle boiled and he took down mugs, made tea. His hands, usually so capable, shook as he poured the water onto the teabags. I thought about his mother and her teapot, her strainer and knitted tea cozy. I opened my mouth to say something about her and where he really lived, then, uncertain, closed it again.

We sat opposite each other. He hunched forward over his cup, his chin moistened by rising steam. I stared at him, taking in the curve of his cheek, his jaw. I was seized by a strange sense of nothingness, of floating unanchored between two worlds, between reality and illusion. I knew this man, knew him intimately. And yet I didn't know him at all. All the times. All the times we'd sat at this table, dined on food he'd cooked. Talked through his difficult cases, the small children struggling against infections, against diseases. It was all lies.

"A doctor." I couldn't stop myself. "Why did you say that?"

"I'm almost a doctor. All right, not a pediatrician, not at the hospital. I shouldn't have pretended. I just thought, well, would you have bothered with me if I'd told the truth."

"All that stuff about seeing us in the street, wanting to know if we were OK—"

"I did want to know. I was concerned."

"You followed me for weeks. Took photographs of me. Why? You didn't know anything about me."

"Of course I did. I heard what happened. What Ella did to you. Her mother and mine still talk." He spread his hands. "We're two of a kind, you and I. She hurt me, just like she hurt you. I admit, that's what it was about, in the beginning. I wanted to use you to get to her." He shrugged, smiled. "Then we fell in love. We couldn't help ourselves. I know you love me too, Jen. Don't fight it."

I stared at him. "Why didn't you tell me? Why didn't you say she was your ex? All that stuff about a mysterious ex who took your daughter from you."

He looked at me, his face calm now. "She did."

"Matt, I know what happened. She was stillborn, your baby. I'm sorry. That's awful. But you can't blame Ella for that." I paused, remembering. "You encouraged me to think she killed her own baby!"

He shrugged. "She did, in a way."

I thought of Catherine, her tiny eyes closed, lying in Ella's arms.

"How can you even say that?"

"You really want to know?"

I looked down into my cup and the tea swirling there. "Not really."

"She was reckless. Wild. I liked it when I met her. But then she had a baby to think of, our baby. I told her to calm down, to be careful. She just laughed in my face. I couldn't bear it. That poor little girl. She was my daughter and I couldn't protect her." He paused, ran his hand down his cheek. "Ella fell, you see. In Torcello. We had a fight about her going up that tower and she wouldn't listen. It was her fault. Her fault our baby died."

I blinked, thinking of the winding stone slope, the giggling up ahead as I climbed.

"I don't believe you."

He lifted his head, looked me in the eye. "That's up to you."

"Why did you take me there?"

"Why?" He looked incredulous. "I didn't want to. You wanted to go so badly. You pushed me into it. Remember? All that nonsense about Gracie's angel. I went for you, Jen. To show you how much you mean to me."

I lifted my tea. I didn't want to listen. I just wanted him to go. To leave us alone.

"And then she walked out on me, Jen. I told her how much I loved her. I said I'd take her back, despite what she did. But she wouldn't listen. I thought, for a long time, that she'd realize what we had and come back to me. I kept telling her I'd forgive her. We could start again. We were made for each other."

I shook my head. "That's what you said about us."

His voice rose. "I mean it, Jen. Ella doesn't matter to me anymore. We've got each other now. You and me and Gracie. We're bound together. You can't leave. We love each other too much."

He pushed back his chair and got to his feet, made to come round the table to embrace me, his eyes on my face.

"No, Matt..." I put my mug down on the table, sloshing tea in a dark ring round the base. "I'm sorry."

I got to my feet. Matt's eyes were brimming with tears and all I wanted was to go back upstairs, crawl into bed, and wrap my arms round you. Lie there, lost in your smell and the slow, steady rhythm of your breaths, until you woke.

I took a deep breath. "Please go."

He bit down on his lip. "Don't do this, Jen. *Please*. I love you."

I didn't answer. We both stood there, a few feet from each other, tense. When he spoke again, his tone was sneering.

"All that stuff about Gracie going to Heaven and meeting the dear departed. I mean, really?" He shook his head. I thought again how little I knew him. "I didn't argue. I kept my mouth shut. Did I tell you it was nonsense?"

"Maybe it isn't nonsense." I swallowed. "How do you know? None of us do." I looked past him, through the house to the shadows in the sitting room. "How could she know those things? About the accident. About Catherine." *And about my father*, I thought. The quiet man still taking care of the children as he always did in life.

He shrugged. "She heard things. She sensed them. She's bright. That's all."

I hesitated, watching him. "It was you, wasn't it? On the phone to Ella."

His eyes flicked away from mine, just long enough for me to know I was right. I thought of what you'd said. *Auntie Ella had shouted down the phone. Go away. Stop it. Leave me alone.* The fury and frustration of a woman whose ex simply wouldn't stop calling, wouldn't stop stalking her.

"It was you."

He didn't answer. And that night in the club when I'd come across them arguing so furiously. She hadn't followed us there at all. He'd gone looking for her.

"Go." I didn't want to hear any more. I wanted to be rid of him. "Go away. And don't come back. Ever. Don't phone. Don't follow me. If you do, I swear, I'll call the police."

"You don't mean that." A look of sudden panic crossed his face. "We belong together, Jen. We do. I'll make it up to you. Just give me a chance."

He reached for my hand and I snatched it away.

"Leave me alone." My legs shook. "Don't you understand? I don't want to see you again. I mean it. It's over."

He didn't move. He stood, wordless, staring at me. Something in his eyes seemed to fold and crumple and I saw the pain there but couldn't respond, couldn't speak. His breathing was short and hard. I stood very still, holding myself separate from him, willing him to recover enough to leave. From above, the drone of an airplane's engine swelled, then faded as it crossed the sky.

Finally, he seemed to regain control of himself. He pulled his eyes from mine and looked down. His voice became quiet: "So that's it."

When he looked up again, his expression had changed. Where before his eyes seemed desperate, pleading, now they seemed cold. "How very sad."

"I'm sorry," I stuttered, "but you need to go."

He stood for a moment, looking down, broader and stronger than me.

"Fine." His voice was too calm. "I need the bathroom, OK? Then I'll go."

I stood there in the silent kitchen, listening to his heavy, familiar movements round the house. Up the stairs. The thud of the bathroom door. Later, the rush of the cistern as the toilet flushed, the creak of the banister as he came down again. I didn't look up, didn't go through to the hall to watch him go, just listened to the bang of the front door as he left.

CHAPTER 54

The silence in the house became intense. My head ached. I made my way slowly up the stairs, my legs shaking, exhausted by him, by his strange, intense emotions. I wondered if you were still asleep. I wanted to crawl back into bed beside you and stay there, cuddled round your body, for a little longer.

The door to my bedroom stood open. Morning sunshine reached round the curtains and sent weak streaks of light down the carpet. I walked in, already unfastening my dressing gown, moving round the edge of the door toward the bed. Stopped.

The bedclothes were tossed back. A rumpled sheet. A pillow, twisted to the side. You were gone.

I turned and ran blindly next door to your room. Your own bed was empty too, the sheets neat, unused.

"Gracie? Gracie!"

I rushed back to my room and fell to my knees, scanned under the bed. Your bear, arms crooked, abandoned. Wildly now, I pulled open the doors to the wardrobe, pushed the clothes aside. They screamed along the rail.

"Gracie!" Panic suffocated me.

I hurtled to the bathroom, nowhere there to hide, then stumbled downstairs, crossed the hall in a second, and heaved at the front door. I ran into the street, my dressing gown flapping round my legs, my bare feet pricked by the gravel.

"Gracie!"

A man, passing. A steady, unhurried step. A middle-aged man in a sensible coat.

"Please. Help me!"

I ran to him, grabbed his arm. He stopped, looked down at my hand as if the sight of it on his sleeve worried him.

"Quick. He's taken her. Go after him."

"What?" He frowned. His eyes traveled over my naked feet, the dressing gown cord unraveling at my waist.

I clutched at him, clawing at his coat even as he pushed me away.

"Please." I started to sob, losing control. "My little girl."

My face was close to his, my breath sour with last night's wine. He grimaced, turned his head away.

He nodded past me to the house, the front door standing open. "Call the police if you need help."

CHAPTER 55

The policewoman was restless. She strode round the sitting room as I talked and looked things over, her eyes making professional judgments, of the windows, of the house, of me. Her radio kept spitting static and I strained to hear if there was news.

From the kitchen, the light slap of cupboard doors. The kettle rattled on its stand and boiled in a rush of steam. A few moments later, the young Asian officer came through with a cup of strong, sugary tea and set it in front of me. He gave me a meek smile.

"Forced entry?" The policewoman lifted back the curtain and studied the gaping sash. "No locks?"

I shook my head. Time had stopped. I was hoarse. Dizzy. They kept asking meaningless questions. Exactly how much had I had to drink last night? What exactly was my relationship with Matthew Aster? Was there anything else I could tell them about him? Anything at all, however trivial?

I could barely think. All I could say was: "Please. Hurry. Please find my daughter."

My eyes were sore from crying. My arms ached with emptiness. He'd taken you. My beautiful daughter. I'd given them photographs of you. The portraits last term, taken by the photographer at nursery. They didn't do you justice but they were clear. They'd reproduce well, the young man said, and he was trying to be kind, I could see, but the senior shot him a look. I thought about posters with your face pinned to noticeboards, stuck on trees: *Missing*. It set me crying all over again.

If I closed my eyes, I could almost feel you against me. Your small, hard body on my knee, your face against my shoulder, your warm breath on my neck.

"And this was, what time?"

I opened my eyes. Her words hung in the air.

"What?"

She spoke more slowly.

"At what time did he enter the property?"

I took a deep breath to stop myself from shouting at her. What did it matter?

"I don't know. Some time in the night. I came down at about seven and he was here, sitting right here."

Scratch, scratch of the young officer's stubby pencil.

"Are you aware of any missing items?"

My voice trembled, hit a higher note. "Just her, my daughter. I keep telling you. Why don't you find her?"

"There's no need to shout." She looked down at me without expression. "We're doing everything we can."

The young officer, glancing from her to me, said in a low voice: "I know you're upset. But just try to answer the questions. OK?"

I shook my head, feeling tears rise again.

He set down his notebook for a moment, lifted the mug of tea from the table, and put it into my hands.

The police officer's radio squawked. She raised it with her thumb and forefinger, talked into her lapel.

She spoke across me to the young officer. "Not at the property."

"What property?" I said.

She sat beside me, rested her hands on her thighs. "We sent a car to Mr. Aster's home. To the address you gave us. He isn't present but officers are interviewing his mother."

I thought of the dingy sitting room and of his mother, presiding over the teapot, dignified and endlessly polite. Of the officers, bristling with kit, perched on the old-fashioned suite, helping themselves from a plate of biscuits or buttered scones.

"So now what?"

"We've already extended the search. Believe me, we're doing all we can. We could have news any minute." She hesitated, her eyes on my face. "We've every reason to stay hopeful, at this stage."

She and the young officer exchanged glances and drifted through to the hall together. Furtive whispering. Another blast of radio static and a short, sharp exchange on the walkie-talkie.

Something tightened in my chest. I tried to relax my shoulders, panicked now, and focused on breathing. In, out, in, out. Slowly, the pressure eased. My arms, my legs hung like weights. The room tipped, shivered, then righted itself. Your books stood in a row against the edge of the mantelpiece. The shiny purple cover of *Beauty and the Beast* stuck up above smaller books. The spine, weathered, curled up at the bottom.

When they came back in, the senior officer asked: "Is there anyone who could come over? Anyone we can call to sit with you?"

I shook my head. "Not really."

"Any news at all, we'll let you know. OK?" She pointed to the windows. "I'll send someone to fix those."

As she left, the young man said gently: "They're trying to get hold of the family support team. I can stay until someone comes, if you like?"

"No." I got up. "I can't just sit here. I want to look for her too."

He looked worried. "Please don't go far. In case we need to get hold of you." He hesitated, then seemed to reach a decision, gave me a final nod, and turned to leave.

The front door opened and slammed shut. His heavy boots slapped down the path. The gate clanged as it closed.

I thought of the bed upstairs, its sheets still crumpled. The clock said ten past nine. Two hours ago, we both lay there, you and I, my body curled round you, keeping you safe from the world. Now you were gone.

I picked up my phone and dialed Matt's number for the twentieth time, my fingers trembling. Again, it clicked onto voicemail and I left another frantic message.

"Please, Matt. Bring her back. We can talk. But please don't hurt her."

I ran to get dressed, trying to think where Matt might take you and where you might run to hide if you managed to get away from him.

CHAPTER 56

The church café had just opened. The young woman was unloading metal trays of scones and croissants and Danish pastries into the glass-fronted cabinet. She didn't look up as I ran through the door.

"Is she here?"

She frowned. "Who?"

I scanned the café. Deserted.

"Gracie. My daughter." *What was the matter with her?* "You know. She's three. Nearly four. About this high."

She shrugged. "I've been in the back." She gestured to the fresh food. "Still setting up." She went back to fiddling with her pastries, straightening them in their baskets.

My heart pounded. I ran through to the church. The morning light filtered softly through the stained glass. I crossed to St. Michael's window and checked under the pews there, trying to think where a three-year-old might hide. Nothing. The Lady Chapel too was empty.

I stood beside the altar, looking back down the body of the church, breathing hard. I'd been driven by the sudden hope that she might be here, that she'd seek refuge here if she could. Now I was again at a loss, deflated by the silence, the emptiness. I didn't know where to go next. What to do. I checked my phone. Nothing.

The loss of you pressed down on my head and shoulders, a suffocating weight. I slid sideways into the nearest pew and leaned forward, rested my forehead against the worn wood.

I closed my eyes. I saw you again in the hospital, a frail, small figure, stabbed with wires. I remembered the commotion as machines sounded and nurses and doctors came rushing in. Richard smelled faintly of aftershave when I pressed against him, close in his arms. You were saved. I thanked God for it. Thanked Him for sending you back to me.

"Are you all right?"

A shift in the light. I looked up. The vicar, Angela, looked down on me, a cardboard file in her hand. Her face was creased with concern.

"Oh." Her expression altered as she saw who I was. "Jennifer."

She bent over me, put her hand on my shoulder. Her breath smelled of coffee.

"What is it? Do you want to talk?"

My thighs trembled on the wooden pew. I felt a stab of anguish, of fear, deep in my stomach. I needed so desperately to see you, to hold you. No one seemed to know how to help.

"It's Gracie." I put my hands to my face. "He's taken her. Matt. I don't know where she is." I started to shake, then to sob, managing to blurt out: "What if he hurts her?"

She slid in beside me on the pew, a warm, soft bulk of person.

"What do you mean, taken her? Should we call the police?"

"I have." I raised my wet, running face to look at her solemn one. "They're looking." I pointed to my phone. "They said they'd call me the minute they had news." I paused, trying to explain. "I just thought she might be here, you know. If she got away. She loves this church."

She nodded. "She does."

I gulped, tried to stop crying, to stop the shudder in my breath. I looked past the pew to the swimming patterns of light on the stone.

"She likes to play up there, under the windows." I could almost see you, sitting on a hassock with your knees drawn up, jumping and swinging on the end of a pew.

She reached out and put her hand on mine. "Wherever she is, Jennifer, she's in God's hands. That's what I believe. He's taking care of her."

I thought of Matt's eyes, so desperate and full of pain.

"But what if he hurts her?"

She sighed but didn't answer. We walked together back toward the café. The young girl was unpacking a bundle of newspapers and setting them out on one of the long, wooden tables.

My legs buckled and I sat heavily. My hands shook so much that I fumbled my phone, scrabbled on the floor to pick it up again, dropped it on the table. The sharp lines of the counter, of the tables, started to blur. I hung my head and stared unseeingly across the café. Please God. Bring her home. Please. I was too exhausted now even to cry.

A low buzz. On the table, my phone rang. I snatched it up.

His voice. But different. Desperate. "Jennifer..."

"Is she all right?"

He paused. I strained to listen to the noise in the background. The throb and rattle of traffic.

"You called the police, didn't you?"

"No." My voice was wild. "Where are you?"

"Don't lie to me." His breath juddered as if it were close to breaking. "They've been to my mother's house. Upsetting her. Why did you do that? What's she ever done to you?"

"Matt. Please."

Angela, listening, came to stand beside me and put her hand on my arm.

"Just bring her back. Please."

"What about me?" His voice rose in a wail. "I love you, Jen! You can't leave me! Don't you understand?"

I felt sick, took a deep breath. "Please. We can talk. Just tell me where you are."

"Come on your own. Promise? No police."

A few moments later, as I ran across the café to the door, Angela called after me: "Is she all right? Was that the police?"

I didn't stop to answer.

CHAPTER 57

It was cool by the river. A low breeze blew across the water and stung my cheeks. I walked quickly, shoulders hunched, arms folded, down the path through the park, toward the embankment, scanning always for him, for you, sick with dread.

The concrete path running alongside the bank was quiet. I stood at the rail, looking down at the river far below. The tide was in and the brown, swirling water was fast-flowing, carrying sticks and duck feathers and scraps of water-logged plastic.

Off to the left, beyond the park, buses and cars roared across the curved stone bridge that straddled the river. It was edged by ornate Victorian streetlights, shaped like lanterns, which gleamed in the sunlight. I thought of Venice and the wrought-iron lights there, which made pools across the darkening campo and glistened on the canal. Another time, another world.

On the far side of the river, a battered Land Rover was parked just above the slipway. A crewing car. Teams of rowers, hearty public-school boys with floppy hair and branded gear, carried two boats, upturned on their shoulders, from a boathouse to the water's edge. Their calls to one another, jovial and mocking, flew on the breeze. Jeremy and Roland and Sebastian.

Mallards and Canadian geese scrabbled away from the bank as the boys lowered their boats into the water, making sudden waves. They waded out into the shallows and clambered inside and their oars slapped the water.

A middle-aged woman in a headscarf and sensible shoes strode past me, her eyes too scanning the river, the boys and their boats. Her dog, a wiry terrier, ran back and forth, nosing in the bushes. The air between us was thick with the scent of blossom and rising sap.

You used to scoot here, up and down this path. We played hide-and-seek in those bushes. It was just there, at the far end of the path, close to the rampart of the bridge, that you crouched and looked down into the water and said you saw Catherine in the depths of the river, waving to you. Saying, when I found you: *I wasn't lost, Mummy, I was right here*. I swallowed hard, wiped my hands across my eyes.

I paced back and forth, restless and afraid, then stood with my back to the railings, leaning back against the flaking metal, waiting.

I recognized him from a distance, as soon as he came down from the bridge and turned into the park. He had you by the hand and you ran at his side, uneven and stumbling as you struggled to keep pace with him.

His strides were loose and long and his coat flapped round his knees and I sensed the strength in his body, the lean muscle I once found so attractive and which now only frightened me. His hair stuck out in clumps as if he'd raked through it with his fingers and his chin was dark with stubble.

I lifted my hand. He saw me but didn't respond. He steered you instead to the far end of the path, some distance from me.

You twisted and strained, held tight by the wrist, and shouted: "Mummy!"

When I started to walk toward you, he called: "Stay there!" Then, to you: "Be quiet, Gracie."

He pushed you down, sitting you on the edge of the low wall that ran beneath the railings. I waved at you, trying to make a game of it.

"Hello, my love. Be a good girl. Do what Uncle Matt tells you."

I was close enough now to see him properly. His eyes were red-rimmed and bright and he was agitated, shuffling his feet, brimming with anxious energy.

A blast of sound flew out from the river and he started, looked round.

He doesn't trust me, I thought. *He's afraid of what he's done, of the police.*

The current drew the schoolboys farther into the river and they rowed, backs bending, muscles straining, searching for a common rhythm. Their coach, a young man in a speedboat, shoulders hunched in his windcheater, made loops against the tide and shouted instruction through a megaphone.

Matt swung his eyes back to me. You sat at his feet, your head low between your knees. You looked unhappy but resigned, studying your shoes, the path, waiting for this strange adult drama to play itself out and for normal life to resume.

"Why did you have to spoil it?" Matt's voice shook. "Why? What's the matter with you?"

I took a quiet step toward you both. "I'm sorry. It was just a shock, that's all. Maybe you're right. We need to talk. Maybe we can work it out."

He shook his head. "You don't mean it. You don't care about me." His fingers made furrows through his hair. "After everything I did for you. I looked after you, didn't I? What more could I do? I did everything on your terms. Don't you see? For what? You only care about yourself."

I took another small step. "That's not true. I do care."

His face was pinched. "Don't you know what it cost, that trip to Venice? I don't earn a lot. But I didn't complain. I wanted to make you happy. That was all."

I nodded. "It was wonderful, Matt. We were happy, weren't we? It was special."

His face clouded. He seemed lost, vague, a different person from the calm, capable man I thought I knew.

"I thought you were special. But you're not, are you? You're just like her. You're all the same, in the end. You take and take and when there's nothing left, you walk away."

His words came more thickly now, as if he almost forgot where he was, that we were there with him. "I can't go on without you, Jen. Without you, what've I got left to live for?"

Blood throbbed in my ears. I took another step toward you, my eyes on your lowered head. You picked up a stub of stick and traced a pattern on the concrete.

"Maybe I was too hasty. Maybe we could give it another go. If you want to?"

He didn't seem aware that I was moving, closing the distance one slow step at a time.

I kept talking. "Do you want to do that? Give it another try?"

I was only a few meters from you now. If we caught him by surprise, if you realized what I was doing and suddenly ran, I might snatch you up, save you from him. My body ached with longing to hold you. It was so intense, I could almost feel you in my arms, your hard, slim body pressed into my chest, the sweet, fresh smell of your hair, your skin warm and soft against my face.

A sudden blast of static. We all jumped.

Out on the river, the coach screamed: "No, Justin! No!" A pair of mallards, startled by the noise, rose from the water, honking, and soared high through the air.

The megaphone split the quiet: "One, two! One, two!"

Matt came back to the present, as if from a dream.

"I loved you so much, Jen. I adored you. I really thought—" He saw now, I read it in his eyes, how close I'd edged toward you both, that I was steadying myself, choosing my moment, ready to pounce.

He reached down in a single strong movement, grabbed you round the waist, and hoisted you up, pinning you under his arm even as you struggled, kicking, beating feebly on his chest with your fists.

"Gracie!" I screamed, transfixed.

He stepped in a single, fluid movement onto the low wall, swung a leg over the railing, then climbed over altogether, balancing on the far edge of the narrow wall, one hand on the rail, holding himself in place, the other locked round your waist.

His eyes were on mine, bright with self-pity.

"All I ever wanted was a family. A family of my own. Was that so wrong? Was it?"

He leaned away from the railing, suspended over the rushing river below, holding my gaze as if it were the one thread that held him steady, held him to life.

"Matt. Please."

The sounds all around us, of the park, of the road, of the river, fell away to silence. The world held its breath, watched with me. He hung there, his eyes on mine, you clinging now in fear to his side, then with a sudden twist, he jumped, falling into nothingness, still clutching you.

Time stopped. You hung there, your eyes wide with shock. Your hair, caught by the rising breeze and shot through with sunshine, flew out from your head in a circle of perfect yellow. You were suspended there, for barely a second and forever. Then you fell, plummeting, and disappeared from sight.

I ran to the railing, clambered over, and jumped.

CHAPTER 58

A smack, so hard it seems to shatter my bones, to break me in pieces. The shock of cold. Water filling my mouth, my ears, my eyes. Splashing, closing over me. White sky, high above, blurred by a wash of brown. Light flying in shards and specks on the surface, disappearing. Bubbles bursting in my ears, then the slow, dense whoosh of underwater quiet.

My mouth, opening, drawing in liquid. Peat and mud and filth. My feet kicking out, frantic, trying to stand, finding nothing, slipping, falling through emptiness.

My head breaks the surface. Water in my throat, then both air and water. Eyes, blinking, water-logged, struggling to clear. Air noise: wind, birds, shouts. A blur of greenery high above, bright sun, the bank already drawing away, the current catching me, sweeping me, into the depths.

Ahead of me, you rise and fall, arms flailing, eyes panicked, your mouth too full of water to scream. The surface churns to foam. I throw myself forward through the current, my lungs bursting, arms pumping, straining for you, Gracie, my love, my life, seeing you swept on always by the water.

The tide draws us both into the narrowing, sucking channel of the bridge, funneling us together through one of the high Victorian arches. My fingers lock round your hair and I pull your head toward me, rest it on my chest, my hand cupping the curve of your jaw, willing you to stop struggling, to be still against me and let me hold you, keep you afloat, keep you here in this precious world with its sun-flecked water and rushing noise. I hold you steady in the current, my body flat under yours, bearing your weight as water washes over my face. My eyes close.

Sudden lightness. All at once, the weight of my body falls away and I soar, rising clear of the river's dirty, snatching water. Below, I see my own body, gently rising and falling, arms limp, legs splayed, with you, lying on your back on top of me, your own human life-raft, your panicked face white and turned to the sky.

Coach in his speedboat, the motor racing, bounces like a skimming stone across the surface toward us. His face is gray with shock. He reaches over the side, tipping the boat, gropes for your billowing clothes, your arm, and drags you up.

You hang there on the side, then flop, a caught fish, smack into the bottom of the boat. He, panting with exertion, pumps your arms, puts his mouth to your chill, dark lips in the kiss of life.

My body, inert now, moves rapidly away from him, lost in its own silent music, floating on downstream.

The boys watch from their boats. Chastened by the horror of it. Oars dangling. One, Jeremy or Roland perhaps, bends over the side and vomits noisily into the water and no one mocks him.

Far ahead, farther downstream, Matt drifts ahead of me, face down, unseeing and unseen. His hair streaks in tendrils from his skull. His coat, bloated now by mud and water, spreads round him. A stream of blood trails from the gash where his head, driven forwards by the current, crashed against the rising stone arch of the bridge. The blood divides into streaks and finally disperses.

Now I am soaring, seeing the boats, the bridge, the river all shrink as I draw away from them, propelled with a great whoosh of energy into a swirling tunnel of darkness and, even as I fly down it, I think: *you told me*. This is what you said and I didn't believe you, *why did I never believe you, my love, when all you ever told me was the truth?*

A pinprick of light at the end of the spinning vortex grows like an exploding sun and we seem, both of us, the light and I, to rush always toward each other.

I hear nothing but I feel myself soaked in laughter. In peace. A figure then, emerging as a silhouette from the brightness, steps forward, arms open to embrace me. My father. A smile on his face, those kind features I've almost forgotten, his eyes gentle, his hair jet-black as if he were again young.

And even as I sense him, another figure emerges, smaller and more distant and I fly forward to greet you, weeping with joy, my arms reaching for you, my lovely girl, hearing your giggling and seeing your smile, your eyes on my face. Gracie, my love. Thank God. Don't leave me. Don't ever leave me again.

And you cling to me, your arms warm and tight round my waist and your hair soft and sweet-smelling and your eyes, when you tip back your head to look up at me, more radiant with love than I have ever seen on this earth.

"I can only visit, Mummy," you say. "I've got to go back."

"Gracie." It's all I can say. "Please. Not yet."

But even as I try to speak, to cling on to you, your words are lost and you fall backward, away from me, out of the radiance and back into the darkness we call life.

EPILOGUE

Venice, eighteen years later

Something's changed. I sense it at once, as soon as you appear. You step with care up the worn stone steps from the *vaporetto* and emerge on the edge of the piazza, your leather travel bag in hand. You are always beautiful, my love, but today your eyes are preoccupied, thoughtful, and I watch you from a distance, wondering why.

We meet often here in Venice, always at this time of year. In April, the city is still lazy with pleasure, relieved to have emerged once more from the chill and fog of winter but not yet hardened by the summer heat and the invading tourists.

It is still early in the day and the air blowing into Piazza San Marco from the lagoon is fresh and salty. Waiters, crisp and self-important in formal dress, set out tables and metal chairs along its fringes. Shopkeepers clatter open their shutters. Street cleaners in green municipal coats sweep and sluice.

You walk slowly, your loose coat billowing, and send up swirling, wheeling arcs of pigeons. You are dwarfed by the

great basilica with its round arches and vast domes. Its gold
façade glints in weak sunlight. You pass the foot of the red-
brick campanile, which shoots an eternal arrow to Heaven.

A waiter pulls a chair for you as you approach the café
and his smile as you settle is part chivalrous, part flirta-
tious. You sit, your face lifted to the sun, looking back
across the vast grandeur of the piazza. You seem a little
lost. Your eyes stray to the waterfront where you've just
disembarked and your expression is wistful.

You're waiting for someone, my love. I know you too
well. Your thoughts are divided between me and this
unknown someone, and at once I am both hopeful and
afraid for you, as only a mother can be.

The waiter brings you a glass of ice-cold orange juice,
freshly squeezed, and a brioche. You love them. You
always did. No coffee though. That surprises me. You
seldom start with the day without it.

You are more radiant today, my love, than I think I
have ever seen you. Your skin glows. You are young and
happy and very lovely. The waiter sees it too. He hov-
ers, lingers too long when he returns to remove the empty
plate, smiles as he asks if there's anything else you'd like.

When he leaves, you put on your sunglasses and tilt
back your head, basking in the early sunshine. Waiting.

I am only here because you are thinking of me, of that
strange, intense time we shared in Venice, all those years
ago when you were a little girl. This place is special to
you because you know you always find me here and now, I
sense, you've brought someone else to share it.

I wait quietly with you, watching, grateful to be here
again, to be with you.

I miss you. Sometimes it seems as if that is all I am
now. An emotion. A depth of love for you that even death

can't destroy. If I exist at all, it's only in these moments. Moments when you think of me. When you stop and pause in the midst of all your busyness, your helter-skelter of a life, and remember me and at once, here I am, right here, with you. Do you feel me now?

Richard gave you my jewelry when he cleared the house and for a long time, when you were a teenager and brim-full of feeling, you wore it and I was glad to be so often with you.

No one else can ever be your mother. Not even death can take that from me. And although no one else could ever replace Catherine, Ella loved you. She cared for you as if you really were her own. I'm grateful to her and to Richard too. The three of you learned to be happy and found joy in each other as a family, despite all the suffering that went before. Perhaps Angela was right. Perhaps you were always in God's hands. Perhaps He is taking care of you. Perhaps His universe is, after all, unfolding as it should. I still don't know.

And there he is. A man strides quickly across the piazza, sending up clouds of scattered pigeons, hurrying as if he's late. A young man, perhaps three or four years older than you. He wears his hair long and his shirt and trousers need pressing but as he hurries across the stone flags toward you—as he catches sight of you there, languishing in the sun with your eyes closed—he smiles to himself and his eyes are so full of love that I forgive him the crumpled clothes and decide yes, this is a kind man, a good man, and clearly he is in love with you, as any sensible young man should be.

He creeps round the table and approaches you stealthily from behind, cups his hands over your sunglasses and when you jump, he says: "Guess who?"

And you laugh and say: "The waiter?"

"What waiter?"

"The handsome one who's been keeping me company all this time. Where were you? I've almost finished."

He pulls out a chair and sits beside you, leaning in to make his excuses, to kiss you and in the kiss everything is forgotten, everything is forgiven. I am still here with you, my love, but at a distance now. Which is exactly how it is supposed to be.

Later, when he finishes his coffee, he pulls back your chair and helps you to your feet with such care, such tenderness that my heart sings.

And then I see. Finally, I understand why you're so very lovely today. The soft swell is barely visible under your loose clothes but, as you walk, you touch a protective hand to your stomach and although it lasts only a moment, it's a gesture I recognize at once, from the time long ago that I was carrying you and so full of happiness I could barely contain it.

And that's when I realize that I have nothing to fear. I will not be erased by this man and your love for him. I will be remembered all over again, in your future child and your love for her and in the overwhelming joy she brings you, as powerful as the joy you gave me.

And you'll understand, finally, why I jumped without hesitation into the river that day and why, my love, you would too, to save your own daughter's life.

I don't know what happened to me when you were pulled alive from the river and I was not. I don't know what it meant. The flight into the light. The sense of peace and of finding my father.

I know what many people would say. And perhaps they're right. Perhaps it is just chemical. The fantasy of a desperate, fading mind as it fights to hold on to life. Perhaps I have now come to dust and exist nowhere but here, in your memory.

But today, as I follow the two of you across the piazza and into the cool of the basilica, into the gentle hush of this ancient, echoing building undulating with arches and domes, the sculptures and mosaics crafted by fingers that long ago ceased to move, where so many have worshipped who no longer have tongues to pray, I look into the dance of light across the stone flags and see the shadows shift and, just for a moment, I feel that all too familiar hope that something of us all is truly eternal, and that one day, when your time does come, you will fly, twisting and weightless, through a great swirling funnel of light and I will be waiting for you, my love, my own sweet child, my eyes radiant and my arms stretched wide in welcome.

A LETTER FROM
JILL CHILDS

I want to say a huge thank-you for choosing to read *Gracie's Secret*.

I started writing this book when one of my twin girls—she was three at the time—started asking me tough questions. *Will you die, Mummy? If you do, will you miss me? Will I ever see you again?*

I always try to tell the girls the truth but in this case, I struggled. Yes, I will die—hopefully not for a long time. And what will become of me afterward? Well, I'm really not sure. Not very reassuring answers for a small child.

But her questions also rekindled an idea I'd had years earlier. It was inspired by accounts of near-death experiences from young children. I found the stories fascinating. Sometimes children accurately described events taking place when they were clinically dead or described meeting people who'd long since died.

Was it possible they briefly visited another world, something like Heaven? Or did it all have a rational, medical explanation? I didn't know what to think. And I wondered how I'd cope if one of my children woke from a coma with an equally extraordinary tale to tell.

And, like many parents, I was caught off guard by how utterly overwhelming my love was for my children. Yes, I would run into a burning building if they were inside. Or lift a truck so they could crawl free. I just would. So what else might a besotted mother be willing to do to protect or save her child? It was out of all this that *Gracie's Secret* was born.

I hope you loved *Gracie's Secret*. If you did, I would be very grateful if you could write a review. I'd love to hear what you think and it makes such a difference in helping new readers discover my books for the first time.

I love hearing from my readers. You can get in touch on my Facebook page or on Twitter. Thank you!

All best wishes to you and yours,
Jill Childs

ACKNOWLEDGMENTS

Thank you to my wonderful editors, Kathryn Taussig and Amy Pierpont.

Thank you to my brilliant agent, Judith Murdoch: the best in the business.

And thank you, as always, to Nick and the rest of my family for all your love and support.

ABOUT THE AUTHOR

Jill Childs has always loved stories—real and imaginary. She's spent thirty years traveling the world as a journalist, living overseas and reporting wherever the news took her. She's now made her home in London with her husband and twin girls, who love stories as much as she does.

Although she's covered everything from earthquakes and floods to riots and wars, she's found some of the most extraordinary stories right here at home—in the secrets and lies she imagines behind closed doors on ordinary streets, just like yours.

You can learn more at:
Twitter @Author_Jill